Henstra, Sarah

We contain multitudes

WE CONTAIN
MULTITUDES

WE CONTAIN MULTITUDES

SARAH HENSTRA

LITTLE, BROWN AND COMPANY

New York Boston

Copyright © 2019 by Sarah Henstra

Cover art copyright © 2019 by Adams Carvalho
Cover design by Karina Granda
Cover copyright © 2019 by Hachette Book Group, Inc.

Little, Brown and Company
Hachette Book Group
1290 Avenue of the Americas, New York, NY 10104
Visit us at LBYR.com

Simultaneously published in 2019 by Penguin Random House in Canada
First Edition: May 2019

Little, Brown and Company is a division of Hachette Book Group, Inc.
The Little, Brown name and logo are trademarks of Hachette Book Group, Inc.

The publisher is not responsible for websites (or their content) that are not owned by the publisher.

Library of Congress Cataloging-in-Publication Data
Names: Henstra, Sarah, author.
Title: We contain multitudes / Sarah Henstra.
Description: First edition. | New York ; Boston : Little, Brown and Company, 2019. | Summary: As pen pals for a high school English assignment, poetry-loving sophomore Jonathan and popular athlete senior Adam explore their growing relationship through a series of letters.
Identifiers: LCCN 2018022802| ISBN 9780316524650 (hardcover) | ISBN 9780316524643 (ebook)
Subjects: | CYAC: Dating (Social customs)—Fiction. | Love—Fiction. | Gays—Fiction. | Poetry—Fiction. | High schools—Fiction. | Schools—Fiction. | Letters—Fiction.
Classification: LCC PZ7.1.H468 We 2019 | DDC [Fic]—dc23
LC record available at https://lccn.loc.gov/2018022802

ISBNs: 978-0-316-52465-0 (hardcover), 978-0-316-52464-3 (ebook)

Printed in the United States of America

LSC-C

10 9 8 7 6 5 4 3 2 1

Do I contradict myself?

Very well then I contradict myself,

(I am large, I contain multitudes.)

—Walt Whitman, "Song of Myself"

Thursday, August 27, 2015

Dear Little JO,*

I guess when you read this letter you'll be sitting right here looking at what I'm looking at. The front of Ms. Khang's English classroom with the old-fashioned blackboard and the posters of famous book covers and the *Thought of the Day* and this new thing, this big wooden box painted in bright colors. I mean you don't know me because I just drew your name randomly. And if you're in tenth grade this will be your first course with Ms. Khang, which means you don't know her as a teacher yet either. Pretty weird getting a letter from a total stranger I bet. Or how about getting a letter period, in this day and age.

Khang stands up there taking as much time as possible telling us what this box is for. She's turning it around and around to show off her paint job, tilting it forward to show the two slots in the top, pointing out the separate combination lock for each lid. All that buildup. After a while we're all expecting doves to fly out of it or something. And then poor Khang looks all disappointed when *we're* disappointed that it turns out to be only a mailbox. Which is the whole problem with buildup. Well you'll see it for yourself pretty soon I guess.

On the board it says *Introduce Yourself.* So my name is Adam Kurlansky and this is Twelfth Grade Applied English. One of the courses I flunked last year, which now I'm regretting because this

1

assignment is not something I'm all that interested in. A letter every week for the entire semester. *JO stands for Jerkoff in case you were wondering. I'm sticking it here in the middle of the letter instead of at the top because Khang wants us to hold up the paper to show her before we put it in the envelope. To prove that we filled the minimum one page, since she's not actually planning on reading our letters herself. If she asks me I guess I'll just say JO is short for your name, Jonathan.

Don't take it the wrong way. I figure it's fair game to call you a little jerkoff even though I don't know you personally because I was one too, as a sophomore. Only most likely not as little. I was already pretty close to my full height by then: six foot three.

I mean I see you all in the halls with your faces turning red whenever I catch you staring at me. You're like these arcade gophers popping in and out of holes. People know who I am because of being a bunch of credits behind and not graduating and having to come crawling back for the so-called victory lap. Or not because of that. More likely because of football I guess. Because they decided to let me keep playing football.

Sincerely,
Adam Kurlansky

Dear Kurl,

May I call you Kurl? From what I've overheard in the halls and absorbed from the general atmosphere of this school, the nickname "Kurl" is used nearly universally in addressing or referring to you, so I assume you're content enough with it. You don't know me, of course, but I do know a bit about you by reputation if nothing else. When my older sister, Shayna, started ninth grade, she tore the photos of the football and basketball teams out of the *Lincoln Herald* and put them up in her room. Then she set out to memorize all the players' names, not because she was a particular fan of those sports but because she surmised—correctly, I believe—that members of the football and basketball teams would be the key tastemakers in the Abraham Lincoln High School social scene, and back then she was still interested in keeping abreast of that scene. This was prior to Shayna becoming best friends with Bronwyn Otulah-Tierney and entering her Age of Skepticism, as our father, Lyle, calls it.

We haven't discussed it in so many words at home, but I would say that my sister has moved further in the last year or so, to what I'd call an Age of Nihilism. Sleeping all day, staying out late, greasy hair, plummeting grades, glowering. I wonder if this state of existence rings a bell for you, Kurl, if you're repeating courses this year? Did you have an Age of Nihilism? What comes after it?

Anyhow. I have a very clear memory of these team pictures. I was twelve years old and would assist Shayna by quizzing her on the players' names, so I would probably still be able to greet many of those boys by name if I met them in the hall—but of course most of them have graduated by now. You were one of the younger players at the time; I suppose you would have been a sophomore, one of the little jerkoffs you mention in your letter.

I remember your picture in particular because you were one of only two boys who played on both the football and basketball teams. *Adam Kurlansky*, the photo's caption read, but Shayna referred to you as *Kurl*. Hearing my sister say it—there was a kind of reverence in her voice, or at least a deep respect—I immediately sensed the power that a good nickname conferred upon its bearer. I've been "Jojo" to Shayna and Lyle on and off since I was a baby, but that was obviously not going to suffice in the context of high school.

I began testing out possible new nicknames for myself. I asked my father to call me "Kirk" from that day forward. Lyle was really generous about it, but after attempting it for a day or two he said it was too strange for him because Hopkirk is his last name, too. When Shayna caught wind of my nickname quest, she informed me that it doesn't work that way, that one never, *ever* gives oneself a nickname, that one has to simply be admired and beloved enough for a nickname to magically and spontaneously be granted by one's peers. And even back then—even in seventh grade—I knew I would never be cool enough to warrant a nickname. So Jonathan it is, or JO, I suppose. (A confession: I saw your *Dear Little JO* and, for approximately five seconds before

4

noticing your asterisk and dropping my eyes to the middle of the letter, I did imagine it might be a pet name for Jonathan. Nonsensical, of course. Why would you give a nickname to someone you have never even met?)

I just asked Ms. Khang if I could finish this letter at home and deposit it in her mailbox first thing tomorrow morning. She said that although I'm always welcome to write additional and/or supplementary letters in my spare time, I have to turn this one in now to avoid the "perils of lost or reconsidered correspondence," as she put it. She smiled in a secretive way when she said it, so I suspect she was quoting from one of her favorite eighteenth-century novels. My apologies for the abrupt ending, Kurl.

From Ms. Khang's list of *Acceptable Sign-offs* on the blackboard I will choose the one that resonates most closely with my personal philosophy—something I will have to explain in a future letter.

Yours truly,
Jonathan "Kirk" Hopkirk (I know, I just can't quite pull it off, can I?)

Wednesday, September 2

Dear Little JO,

I had to laugh when I read your letter. Is this the way you actually talk? Or is it a special style you use for writing? A style of long sentences and lots of commas.

I guess I didn't really answer any of the *About Me* questions on the board last time. I should warn you up front about myself. I mean I wrote enough last time but not really any of the right things. And then just now after I read your letter, for about ten minutes I was just sitting here. The rain coming down the window reminded me of this one week last month in summer training. I'm going to guess that you do not play football. I mean judging from your letter, all that stuff about nicknames and personal philosophy, whatever that is. I probably would have heard of your name at least if you did play football. I know most of the junior team by name.

So they do this summer training for the senior team, like a boot camp. And this one week it wouldn't quit raining. I remember my shoulder pads got this sad basement smell to them, and my cleats croaked. I mean they literally croaked like frogs every step I took. And no matter what we tried, every play Coach Samuels called ended up in a pile of mud-coated slippery bodies.

Last year in this class the assignment was that we were supposed to keep a journal. Except Khang called it a Book of Days, like medieval virgins kept under their pillows or something. And I knew how much of our grade it was worth et cetera. But whenever she gave us time to write I would sit here remembering stuff like this rainy football week. I'd end up staring out the window the whole class and somehow the entire school year passed like that. I am not planning on letting that happen again but I guess I'm saying don't get your hopes up.

sincerely,
Adam Kurlansky

Dear Kurl,

Ms. Khang suggested that we write on the theme of heroism today, and specifically "whether you would identify someone in your life as a hero, and why."

I understand the large hearts of heroes, Walt Whitman writes, *The courage of present times and all times.* Do you know the poet Walt Whitman, Kurl? Perhaps not: I don't think Whitman is anywhere on the curriculum at Lincoln High.

Anyhow, when I think of heroism as large-heartedness, I can't help but think of Lyle Hopkirk. It's not that any father wouldn't have stepped up to the role of single parent after the sudden death of his spouse. My mother, Raphael, was riding her bicycle and got hit by a taxi when I was only five. Lyle turned down a possible record deal in LA and took a full-time teaching position at the music school so that Shayna and I wouldn't have to face any more upheaval.

But the truly heroic part, in my opinion, is that he never became moody or resentful about it, or took on any tortured-artist airs. He underwent a period of grief, of course, but I only know this because there are no photographs of Raphael in our house, and when I once asked him why, he confessed that "back when they were too hard to look at," he had gotten rid of them—a rash action which he now regrets. My father has an upbeat personality by nature, and he simply made sure to let that natural buoyancy be the reigning principle for our family life. I think Lyle gets everything he needs from music, the way I get it from poetry. You should see him the day after his bluegrass band, the Decent Fellows, plays its regular gig at Rosa's Room. He practically floats through the house, loose and relaxed and dreamy.

My father's personal motto is *Be real and be true.* Since Lyle is my hero, I've been trying to make his motto my own. And this involves being forthright about myself, in particular. So prepare yourself for full disclosure on the subject of Jonathan Hopkirk. You'd never pick me out of a crowd, Kurl. I am short for my age and fine-boned. I have sandy brown hair that sticks out from my head in whichever direction is least fashionable no matter how much Hard Hold Paste I may attempt to work through it in the morning.

My passions are live music, especially folk and bluegrass, and poetry, as I've already mentioned—especially the work of Walt Whitman. Have you ever come across Walt's seminal poem "Song of Myself"? I would be tempted to claim that poem as my personal manifesto, but it is altogether too complicated, too magnificent, for such a claim. Like Walt, I am an ardent believer in

> *...going in for my chances, spending for vast returns,*
> *Adorning myself to bestow myself on the first that will*
>   *take me,*
> *Not asking the sky to come down to my good will,*
> *Scattering it freely forever.*

A beautiful sentiment, isn't it, Kurl? Risky and beautiful. And, in the spirit of being real and true, I would like to divulge something Walt never could admit to directly, in his day, for fear of recriminations: I'm gay. My sexuality has never been something I've tried to hide.

Does being "out" make for a thornier social life? Quite possibly. The unfortunate reality of homophobia is already announcing itself to me two weeks into the new school year. There are certain members of my cohort—certain little JOs, Kurl, in your parlance—whom I hoped might have matured over the summer and thereby lost interest in me and whatever vague and intangible threat I seem to represent to them. Instead the interest seems keener than ever. But hiding and lying takes considerable energy, too.

Lyle, in any case, is strongly queer-positive and always wholly supportive of me. It's another aspect of his heroism, I suppose.

The bell has just rung, Kurl, and my hand is cramped from writing nonstop for fifty minutes straight.

Yours truly,
Jonathan Hopkirk

PS: I'm enclosing Part 14 of "Song of Myself" in case the quotation above didn't make any sense on its own. Sorry about the woolen fuzz along the creases. I've been carrying it in my trousers pocket for the back-to-school transition, but I've more or less memorized this section of the poem at this point, so I'm happy to pass it on.

Dear Little JO,

I'd never pick you out of a crowd? I mean are you sure?

So the day after Khang hands around that second batch of sophomore letters to us I'm walking down the hall as usual. There's a cluster of the usual little JOs. All laughing, especially the girls, and watching a couple of guys kick a book back and forth to each other across the floor. Pages flying everywhere. And there's this one particular little JO even smaller than the others running back and forth after the book, going, Very funny, okay, joke's over, come on guys, give it back. This high sort of squeaky voice.

This little JO is dressed up in some kind of costume, it looks like. A white shirt with a high collar buttoned all the way up, and suspenders crossed at the back. I mean he looks like a character in a historical novel. A chimney sweep or something. I'm thinking maybe he's in the school play, auditioning maybe, only I don't think they do auditions until after Christmas.

So this small guy keeps reaching down for the book one second before it's kicked away. At one point his hand gets nailed pretty hard by one of the little JOs' shoes but he doesn't even pause, just shakes out his fingers and sort of scrambles across the hall to try to intercept the book again. This continues—and I have to say it's pretty painful to watch—until Mr. Carlsen, the Business and Tech teacher, steps into the circle and picks up the book, takes a quick look at the spine and goes, *Major British Poets.* Young people, I fear for your generation, I really do.

Of course all the little JOs are laughing their asses off. Except for that littlest one. His face is all flushed and he's out of breath. He goes up to Mr. Carlsen and sort of scrapes his hair off his forehead and sticks his fists on his hips. Like after everything that's been happening, now he's finally found the one thing worth getting upset about. He goes, Actually, sir, I would argue that poetry has real relevance to our generation if you can learn to take the poet on his own terms.

I mean it's not exactly rocket science to figure out which one of the little JOs in this scenario is Jonathan Hopkirk.

And I have to say your big confession about being gay is also not as much of a shocker as you probably thought. I figured that one out right around the line *May I call you Kurl?* Not to mention *My passions are live music and poetry.* I hate to break it to you but normal high school students don't have *passions.* They don't have mottoes and personal philosophies. They don't have manifestos written by historical gay poets.

You getting harassed like that in the hall? It's probably not only about you being gay. From where I sit I would say you're getting shoved around not for being queer as in *homosexual* but for being queer as in *weird.* I mean weird kids do have this aura to them. It's like a smell almost. They're stuck somewhere in their heads, in some kind of a bubble. People can't really help themselves: They see a bubble, they want to pop it.

sincerely,
Adam Kurlansky

Dear Kurl,

Drama! Scandal! Intrigue! Mystery! Guess whom I read about in the *Lincoln Herald* this morning? Front-page news:

Kurl Walks! Wolvies Up 16 at ¾ Home Opener, Fullback Adam Kurlansky Quits Team, Costs Game

I suppose it testifies to my near-total social isolation and my alienation from the culture of the school that I didn't hear about this event until reading it in the *Herald*. I'm certain it officially makes me the last person at Lincoln to receive the news. The fact that my sister's friend Bronwyn wrote the story adds irony to my ignorance, since she and Shayna undoubtedly spent half of last night talking about it and I still didn't catch on. I haven't yet mentioned to them that Adam Kurlansky is my assigned pen pal, I suppose because at some level we seem an unlikely match.

Permit me to quote from the news story:

"Coach Samuels told the *Herald* he is focused on keeping things positive, helping the Wolverines pull together to fill the gap left by Kurlansky. 'I'm concerned, sure,' he admitted. 'But Kurl is a good kid, a fighter, a real lion. I'm sure he'll turn it around in time to contribute this season.' Kurlansky himself declined to comment on Friday night's walkout. When we asked

13

him whether we can expect him back on the field this year, his reply was simply, 'I doubt it.' "

I hope you won't hold it against Bron for writing the piece. Perhaps, like me, you feel it edges into the sphere of celebrity gossip. Bronwyn Otulah-Tierney can be, at times, overzealous. She is very focused on building her portfolio for her applications to the best journalism schools in the country.

I reread your most recent letter last night, Kurl, and I'd like to clarify one point: I never meant to imply that I get bullied only because of my sexual orientation, or even that it's in any way mysterious to me why I get singled out. Above all it was not my intention to complain about being mistreated. Maybe I am *queer as in weird*, as you theorize so eloquently. But my weirdness is merely a natural by-product of having my sights set on something beyond high school, namely poetry.

Kurl, can you truly blame me for wanting to focus on something other than my immediate surroundings? Be honest: If you could, wouldn't you want to immerse yourself in something bigger than the squalid little torments of adolescence? Wouldn't you want to transcend the mind-numbing boredom of, say, tenth-grade Business and Technology class? Mr. Carlsen stands up there in front of us in his Gap cords, rocking back and forth on the balls of his feet and rhapsodizing about Excel budgets and search engine optimization, and the only reason I can refrain from running out and lighting myself on fire is that my mind is elsewhere. Call it an aura; call it a bubble. I understand how it incites others to malice and torment. It drives even Shayna and Lyle crazy when they talk to me and I don't seem to hear their voices.

I was rereading Walt Whitman's book *Leaves of Grass* last night, and I copied out these stanzas for you (enclosed). They capture the spirit of heroism I was trying to describe. Whitman is talking here about lending his spirit to humanity in general, but *You shall not go down! Hang your whole weight upon me* sums up my father's steady, positive strength and his devotion to me and Shayna.

Yours truly,
Jonathan Hopkirk

Dear Little JO,

I guess I can tell you about heroes. Sacrifice et cetera. My dad died falling off a roof when I was ten. My uncle Viktor held up the business alone for a few years but it nearly went bankrupt. So my brother Sylvan quit his job and went to work for him full-time. He was twenty or twenty-one by then and halfway through his electrician's training, but he just dropped everything. You should see his shitty apartment. I mean I'm pretty sure all his savings went into Kurlansky Roofing and they're not exactly making a killing. He has never said a word about any of this to me.

The thing about heroes is they make you look at yourself. Your brother is a hero, people will say to me. Meaning my middle brother Mark actually, not Sylvan. Meaning Afghanistan. They'll say it to me because they want to remind me. Also because according to Sylvan Mark always shrugs them off when they say stuff like that to him. No such thing as the world becoming a better place, he'll tell them.

Mark's earned it for sure. He was deployed just after his eighteenth birthday. I mean he was a few months younger than I am now. Even Uncle Vik shuts right up when Mark's around.

I don't know about those poems you keep sending me. That last one especially. *I dilate you with tremendous breath* or whatever? I don't know if Walt Whitman is really who you want to

16

model yourself after. I have to say he comes across as sort of a douche. I could do without all the poems.

The thing about heroes is that they ask without asking: What about you? What are *you* waiting for?

I would have to tell them I'm actually waiting for nothing.

sincerely,
Adam Kurlansky

Dear Kurl,

Will you permit me a random observation on the group of little JOs who've taken to habitually hassling me (I call them, collectively, the butcherboys)? It's difficult for me to focus on any other letter-writing topic when, just before class, my satchel was co-opted by the butcherboys and flung onto the roof of the school.

You may or may not have noticed a certain little JO named Christopher Dowell in the group. Now, *there's* a young man who, you can be sure, will never earn himself a cool nickname. In my experience, it's always the one in the group whose own position is most precarious, the one who walks the thin, thin line between insider and outcast—you can count on it, it'll be him who hits the hardest, who laughs the loudest. The other butcherboys don't particularly care whether I live or die, but this one, this Dowell—he's the one who really hates me. Because Dowell knows, and he knows I know, that he's a lot closer to being like me than his so-called friends are.

I was sorry to read about your father passing away. I hadn't realized we'd both lost a parent; in an oblique, circumstantial way, this gives us something in common.

You sounded somewhat depressed in your last letter. I hope

18

you're not regretting your decision to stop playing football? I am going to assume, Kurl, that if you want to share with me your reasons for quitting the football team in such a dramatic and precipitous manner, you will. I'm curious, of course. But as I sat there earlier today in Math, rereading Bron's *Herald* story under my desk, I suddenly thought about what it must be like for you, at school and maybe at home, too, being continually judged for your actions and asked to explain yourself to everyone.

Please don't feel any obligation to explain anything to me. My point is quite the opposite: I want to invite you to feel free to use the space of these letters to talk about things that actually interest you, to muse about the topics that dominate your thoughts when you're alone. We might as well take advantage of the fact that we don't owe each other anything, that no one else is ever going to read what we're writing, that it's just me and you and whatever we feel like saying.

Let me be the first to enact this advice. Here is what I'm currently thinking: If you've concluded that Walt Whitman is, in your words, a *douche*, then you've failed to properly appreciate the extent to which he threw himself, body and soul, into the workaday life of nineteenth-century New York City. I'm enclosing a few photocopied pages of "Song of Myself." Have a look at the sheer variety of the types of people and activities he describes. The fishing boats, the funeral, the washerwomen, the beehives, the church choir—all on one page of the poem. Maybe you can give me your interpretation of it, and then in my next letter I'll share with you what I think it means. We'll both be wrong and right.

Poetry's like that, Kurl: slippery and coy. It means different things to different readers. You shouldn't feel embarrassed if it makes you nervous. You're not alone in that reaction. Look at Mr. Carlsen. He'd rather see *Major British Poets* being kicked down the hallway than read, let alone discussed, studied, cherished.

Yours truly,
Jonathan Hopkirk

Dear Little JO,

This is a bonus letter for you since we're actually supposed to be researching our topic for a PSA slide show in Khang's class. Public service announcement. The captivating sort of stuff you get to do in Twelfth Grade Applied English.

In case you're dying of curiosity though, my PSA is on Explosive Emergency Situations. I've been reading quite a lot about the Taliban, al-Qaeda, and ISIL in Afghanistan since my brother Mark came back. He doesn't talk about it but there's a lot online. Since the US withdrawal, all three of these groups are getting involved in infighting and jostling for power. During Mark's deployment, though, I think it was mostly the Taliban.

So there's this dog walker who walks his dogs past my bus stop in the morning. He has a skin graft stitched down over a missing eye and a sideways scar from his nose to his ear area. The ear is also missing. It's a combat injury for sure. He's about the same age as my brother but I haven't asked. I mean what if they knew each other over there but hated each other? What if this guy is upset because Mark didn't get hurt nearly as bad as him? You never know with veterans.

What made me think of this dog-walking veteran after reading your letter is that he attracts comments from people. People see that he isn't paying attention. That he's talking to himself or

21

whatever. I'm not saying you do that, but he's got that aura I was talking about. He's in that bubble. So people say things to each other about him, for kicks. You can see them laughing at him. I don't know. It's not respectful considering his sacrifice but that's how people are.

From what I can tell the basic difference between suicide bombers and US military personnel is that the suicide bombers would prefer to die and the US soldiers would prefer not to. Now that the US troops are mostly drawn down, the Taliban is focusing on political and civilian targets. You can make yourself a list of Taliban strategies just by reading the news. An example of a Taliban strategy is: Drive a car bomb into a loaded bus. This just happened recently in Kabul.

Another Taliban strategy: Enter an elementary school in Logar and open fire. That's the province where Mark was deployed, at least at the start. I don't know where they sent him after the first year.

It's sort of ironic I've been reading about all this insurgency stuff because when we were younger Mark always used to turn the news off. He'd switch Mom's radio in the kitchen from her news station to Top 40. Adam, he'd say, let's not be the type of people who believe everything we hear on the news.

None of this will make it into my PSA assignment. I'm just writing it down because you said to write what I'm thinking about. I mean you're sort of right. People keep asking me about the football team and what my problem is and when I'm coming back. Meanwhile what I'm thinking about is a Taliban strategy: Knock out the streetlights at a specific intersection. When the political motorcade stops there, send three suicide bombers diving under the police trucks.

I'm not saying this is the sort of thing I really want to be thinking about all the time. It just happens to be on my mind. It makes me think football and school and my uncle et cetera aren't worth worrying about all that much.

sincerely,
AK

PS: I think your sister and her friend Bronwyn are both in Math with me this year. Bron was in Physics with me last year too. I mean she's hard to forget with the fact that she always asks the teachers about stuff like their *hidden bias* and *unspoken assumptions*.

Dear Kurl,

Instead of writing about my "primary influences" as Ms. Khang suggests, I'd like to take this opportunity to answer the question you asked me yesterday at lunch. "Why aren't you sitting at the gay table?" you said, and you pointed at a table way across the room, beside the composting/recycling sorting station, where a heavily pierced eleventh grader was making out with her Goth girlfriend. Two or three freshmen were also over there, hunched miserably over laptop screens. It was hard to say whether they knew it was the gay table or not. Shayna and Bron call it the Gable, and its eradication is one of Bron's pet causes. She points to the existence of the Gable as an example of social apartheid, the formalization of hierarchy, and the perpetuation of power imbalances. I'm sure you didn't intend your suggestion that I go sit at the Gable as an insult or a slur of any kind, Kurl, even if it does unfortunately stand out in my mind now, in retrospect, as the first and only sentence spoken aloud between the two of us. Your tone was exasperated in a way I recognized from many of my conversations with Shayna on this same general topic. An elder-sibling impatience.

My difficulties, before your appearance in the cafeteria, had resulted from simple mathematics. There were more of the butcher-boys than there were seats left at my table. Naturally I was in the middle of taking my first sip of milk when I got the classic hip-to-shoulder nudge from behind. It was Christopher Dowell who made first contact, and my milk spilled all over my vintage poplin shirt. "Move, fudge-packer," Liam VanSyke ordered me. "This is our table."

I attempted the Stonewall Maneuver, named after the great gay-rights moment in American history but in reality nothing more than behaving as if one is a wall made of stone. I stared down at my tray, unwrapped my tuna wrap, bit into said tuna wrap, and commenced chewing.

"You deaf?" Maya Keeler picked up what was left of my milk and poured it over the tuna wrap. Maya is the blond girl who isn't more than an inch or so taller than me. I can't fathom why, but it appears that she may currently be romantically involved with Dowell. In any case, Maya seems to have emerged, in these first few weeks of sophomore year, as the butcherboys' mastermind, the brains behind the whole operation. She's the one, for instance, who engineered the poetry-anthology soccer game you witnessed a couple of weeks ago. Just before Dowell knocked the book from my hand, it was Maya's voice behind me saying, "There, check it. Right there."

But let us return to the scene at hand. Phase two of the Jonathan Hopkirk Defensive Plan: Look for Rescue. I took a quick, surreptitious scan of the cafeteria for a lunchroom monitor, but of course the butcherboys had already done that before they moved in on me. No one wants a detention, let alone a mandatory anti-bullying essay assignment. Even I am not worth that hassle.

The last drops of milk were shaken out over my hair. The other kids at my table were now looking decidedly uncomfortable. Two senior girls zipped up their backpacks and vacated, leaving more than enough space for the butcherboys, but we'd moved past mere logistics now and were well into the principle of the thing.

Dowell reached down and "tased" my ribs with his fingers so hard that I winced sideways and almost toppled off my chair. "Pay attention, faggot," he said.

Pardon the cliché, but at that moment I really did heave an inward sigh of relief. Phase three—Hope They Hang Themselves with Their Own Rope—was a triumphant success. Believe it or not, *faggot* is a word I don't hear all that often. The F-word has become so strongly associated with homophobia and gay bashing that it's almost magical in its ability to attract public disapproval.

Dowell had overstepped. The other butcherboys leaned away and shuffled back slightly, putting a tiny amount of space between themselves and Dowell and me, isolating us, glancing around for reactions. A couple of nearby kids had turned to watch.

"C'mon, asswipe, get up," Liam said, but I could hear it in his voice; he was embarrassed, almost apologetic. "We need your seat."

I swear, Kurl, me continuing to sit there with my sodden sandwich wasn't just mulishness. I was preoccupied with a whole array of anxious thoughts: about how everyone was watching, about how I'd forgotten to set my alarm that morning and had to run out without breakfast, and how I'd spent all my money on this tuna wrap which was now a soggy mess, and how now I'd be shaky and stupid with low blood sugar for all my afternoon classes.

Anyhow, I finally looked up, and my eye met Dowell's, and he reached over and grabbed me by the scruff of my neck and hauled me up out of the chair and cocked his fist and—well, you know the rest, Kurl, because that's the precise moment you intervened.

My deus ex machina. It's as though you appeared out of nowhere. You stepped right up to Dowell and me, and he immediately let go of my collar. Your face was utterly expressionless. I had noticed that about you already, watching you pass in the halls or sitting out on the steps behind the gym: You have this way of keeping your face perfectly still and serene no matter what's going on around you.

Last Thursday, for instance, I watched a couple of junior girls approach you in the parking lot. They'd been whispering and giggling about you—I could see that even from halfway across the lawn, so I'm sure you saw it from where you were standing beside the driver's-side door of your car.

You had a vicious new bruise on your cheekbone from some fight or another. I've heard the rumors about your fighting habit, of course. People are saying it was fighting that got you booted off the football team. I even overheard someone say you punched the coach.

Anyhow, when the girls finally worked up the nerve to approach you and started to chat you up, I wasn't sure whether you would grin and flirt back or drive them off with a snarl. But you chose Option C, Kurl: Perfect Neutrality. You lifted your chin in a polite "hey" gesture and put a hand to your cheek and dropped it again—I guessed correctly about their opening line; they must have asked you about the bruise—but your expression stayed blank and you turned back to your car so soon that the girls practically wilted and slumped away.

That's more or less how events proceeded in the cafeteria, too, isn't it? You didn't shake a fist, didn't say, "Get lost, punks," or whatever a person would typically say to disperse a group of butcherboys—you didn't even sneer. You didn't have to. That fading bruise on your face makes you look downright menacing. "Will fight anyone, for any reason," it proclaims.

You gazed down upon Dowell for less than three seconds before he caved. He barely paused to snatch his bag of chips and his bottle of Dr Pepper off the table before turning tail and scuttling away. They'd all disappeared by the time I got my heartbeat back under control, and I collapsed into my chair at the now-empty table.

You picked up my milk-flooded tray and stood looking at me. For about one millisecond there was the tiniest flicker of something troubled across your face—I don't know, I've thought it over quite a bit and I can't puzzle out what it might have been. Maybe you were considering whether to ram the tray down my throat. You said, "Why aren't you sitting at the gay table?" And then you turned and stalked off.

My answer? I am squarely with Bron on this one, Kurl. The Gable is Discrimination 101. Designating a specific area of a supposedly common space for a minority group, even unofficially, implies that the rest of the space is off-limits for that group. But in the interests of being forthright, I do know what you meant. You meant, "Why are you putting yourself in the path of these monsters, and if you've found yourself in that path accidentally, why are you staying here?" Answer? Choose one of the following: A. Stupidity. B. Stubbornness. C. Fatalism. D. Masochism. E. All of the Above.

Yours truly,
Jonathan Hopkirk

Dear Little JO,

You're kind of a nosy little bugger aren't you? Watching my face in the parking lot et cetera. How about you quit stalking me and spying on me around school. And I think I was pretty clear when I said no more poems. Do you really believe you're the guy Walt is writing about? Do you think you've figured out the *disdain and calmness of martyrs* like he says? Do you think getting pushed around in the caf by a bunch of little jerkoffs makes you *understand the large hearts of heroes?*

I mean come on. Even the fact that you call them the *butcherboys* turns the whole thing into something more poetic and romantic than it is. Where did you come up with that name for them anyway? It doesn't even make sense given the fact that half of them are girls. The thing about you, Jo, is that you seem to be sort of fooling yourself a lot of the time.

My brother Mark started in the Reserves when I was twelve years old. I guess he would've been seventeen at the time. Sometime a few months in, he told me about this one recruit at Camp Ripley who got caught giving a blowjob to a UPS delivery guy. Before his hearing the guy shot himself with his assault rifle. I remember Mark saying, At least he did the honorable thing. At the time it made me think of old-fashioned knights, samurai or something. The honorable thing. I mean when you think about it like that I guess you don't have it so bad at Lincoln, Jo.

sincerely,
AK

Dear Little JO,

I felt pretty bad about that last letter so I'm writing you another one during my free period. I mean it doesn't matter if we put extra letters in Khang's box. It's not like she's going to take marks off for doing that.

In Math I sit pretty close to Bron. We got to talking and at some point I told her about Khang's assignment and that I'm writing to you. She thought it was hilarious. She goes, I bet you're getting more than one page a week from him. And I bet he's making you write more than one page a week too.

I said she seems to know you pretty well for being the kid brother of her friend. She said she and Shayna let you tag along with them everywhere since you don't have friends your own age. I mean I was already aware you don't have friends from seeing you at school alone all the time. But Bron sort of calls it like she sees it, doesn't she? She says things that don't sound harsh at the time but look harsh when you write them down. As I'm sure you've noticed, I'm mostly alone at school too. Alone everywhere actually.

I don't know why I told Bron about our letters. I guess I was looking for a second opinion about you and the way you stand out so much. And how you do it on purpose, it seems. Wearing all those costumes et cetera. Drawing fire, is how I think of it. How you draw fire.

Writing that makes me think of something I read for the PSA assignment. In an explosion you will naturally want to hold your breath. Don't though. The blast wave will overpressurize the air and burst your lungs like balloons. Most explosion victims die from bleeding lungs not shrapnel.

So I asked Bron why you wear those clothes. Today it was that shirt with the little red flowers and that greenish-brownish blazer. Tweed or something. Like you're about to go hunting in Wales or someplace. Or that bow tie the other day with the swirly blue-and-yellow pattern. I mean I see those outfits on you and I nearly break into a sweat thinking about your safety. A walking target.

She goes, Hasn't he introduced you to his idol Walt Whitman yet?

I had to laugh. Yeah, me and Walt are already on friendly terms, I said.

Bron goes, It's cosplay.

I ask her what that is, and she explains that you're a hardcore Whitman fanboy, so you dress like him. Bron's exact words: *hard-core fanboy.*

Is that a thing? I ask her. Like, is there a club or something?

Nope, there's just Jonathan, she says.

Do you remember that dog walker I mentioned? I've been paying a bit more attention to him lately. This morning the dogs were sort of pulling him along the sidewalk, and he goes, They are scenting the death of the natural world. Those were his exact words. I mean it almost sounded like poetry, like some of that poetry you've been sending me. Or maybe he actually said *sensing*, not *scenting*. Sensing the death of the natural world.

So apparently what you're supposed to do in an explosion is reduce your lateral profile. This means lie on your side and put your arm over your exposed eye.

I guess the dog walker didn't have time to follow these instructions. When I talk to him he has to turn his head all the way around to the other side so he can see me with his one eye and hear me with his one ear.

sincerely,
AK

Dear Kurl,

This is an extra letter, as I don't have English again until Monday. I hope you don't mind receiving two letters this week. It'll just be a quick note, really—Lyle's picking me up for a dentist appointment at 3:30 p.m., so I've just ducked into Ms. Khang's classroom momentarily after school.

I want to explain why it looked like I was crying at lunch today at the bike racks, when you approached Bron, Shayna, and me. The moment was somewhat awkward all around, wasn't it?

You didn't technically approach us—it's more accurate to say that you were just passing by us on your way to the bus stop. I suppose it must have been a surprise, looking over and discovering me with tears leaking down my face and both girls laughing unabashedly at me.

"What's the matter?" you asked. "What happened to him?"

"Whoa!" Bron said. "What happened to *you*?" That black eye, Kurl! I'm sure all three of us were equally taken aback at the sight, but naturally it was Bron who didn't hesitate to inquire.

"Nothing. A fight," you retorted, and you veered off across the driveway before any of us could say anything more. I looked for you this afternoon, to apologize for our nosiness and to see if you were okay, but you didn't come back to school after lunch.

Anyhow. Please know that you're welcome to tell me about

all this fighting if you care to (I can't help but observe its frequency: that bruise on your cheekbone, today a black eye), but in the spirit of our "write about whatever you want" agreement, I won't press the issue.

Meanwhile, though, I'd like to explain the phenomenon of my tears. My sister had just shown us an old postcard she found in one of Lyle's books at home, in his *Encyclopedia of Band Names*. The postcard pictured a dive bar downtown called the Ace—do you know that place upstairs from the Skyline Diner, that diagonal sign with the sleazy-looking neon arrow pointing up the stairs? Anyhow, Shayna thought it might be our mother Raphael's handwriting on the back of the card. Two short sentences: *I must have impressed Axel anyways. He said the gig is mine if I want it.* No address, no salutation.

Bron said she thought it must be an ironic postcard, printed as a joke by the bar, because there was no way the Ace would have been a bona fide tourist destination even back then.

Shayna said she was totally missing the point. "It must have been a solo gig, right? Not a Decent Fellows thing," she said. "Mom must have had a side thing going."

I badly wished to inspect the postcard more closely, but Shayna snatched it out of my hand and stuffed it in the inside pocket of her jean jacket. It was the snatching and stuffing that must have led to the tears on my face when you happened to pass by us. Something about this precious artifact from the past being handled so roughly. As I may have mentioned, there aren't any photographs of Raphael Vogel in the Hopkirk house, so any evidence of my mother's existence on this earth is freighted with extra emotional significance.

The truth, Kurl, is that I tend to cry quite easily. It's a physical reflex I can't seem to control, and I cry not only in reaction to sadness but to almost any emotional experience, including atypical ones like surprise and embarrassment. *Cry* is actually too strong a word for it. It's more like involuntary leakage of a few tears, which I hardly notice and can try to hide with a surreptitious sweep of my fingertips. Naturally, though, it tends to throw more fuel on the fire when it comes to bullying and public-mockery scenarios.

Yours truly,
Jonathan Hopkirk

PS: I've found myself wondering, these last few days, how your brother got injured in Afghanistan. Don't feel you have to disclose it, if you don't care to.

Dear Little JO,

All right. Here's a quick note back to you. It's not a secret or anything. Mark's hip bone got shattered on a rock when he was thrown from the back of a truck. He'd been over there a little more than eighteen months. Apparently he was standing in the truck bed with everyone else, and they came around a corner and there was a goat in the road. So of course the driver slammed on the brakes and swerved.

Mark was the only one who fell out. His rifle slid down an embankment and he lost it. He also broke his wrist. The bad luck was that the hospital in Fallujah was so under-resourced that he had to wait ages for surgery. Way too long. Then an insurgent attack on the base filled up the whole hospital, so in the end he got sent to Germany for the surgery. All that waiting apparently made the damage worse.

Sincerely,
AK

Dear Kurl,

Have you ever been to Basement Records? Shayna and I practically grew up there. As kids we would loiter in the store on Saturday afternoons while we waited for Lyle to finish teaching his
classes at the music school upstairs.

Today Bron and Shayna were there with me because Bron
has undertaken a project on her blog she's calling "Life Notes."
She finds a fan of a particular record, interviews them about
the role the record has played in their life and its influence, and
then turns the interview into a song-by-song mini-biography
(accompanied, of course, by the playlist). I'm enchanted by the
notion that one could conceive of a project like this and just go
out there without further ado and execute it. If it were me, I'd
get utterly hung up about which record to post first. I'd be par-
alyzed with the implications of every choice: What tone would
I be setting for the blog, what sort of readers might gravitate
toward title x versus title y, what is the color scheme of the
album's cover art and will it clash with the blog template I'm
currently employing? I'm exaggerating here for effect, Kurl, but
only a little.

Anyhow. The three of us were spread out across the store,
flipping through albums in various categories. Bron had already

found Etta James's *Tell Mama* for the post she was writing about her maternal aunt, Constance Otulah, so she was back in the P-for-Prince subsection of R & B. Shayna was over in Metal, and she and Bron were chatting across the aisles, reminiscing about some party last spring at which everyone had spontaneously gathered around and started dancing to "You Shook Me All Night Long." I'd been absorbed in the liner notes of an early Flatt & Scruggs record, only eavesdropping with half an ear.

They were a couple of minutes further along in the conversation when I snapped to attention: "He sounded like some kind of wild animal in a trap!" Bron was saying. "I swear to God, the hair on my arms stood straight up."

"Is this Kurl?" I asked. "Are you talking about Kurl?"

Shayna rolled her eyes; I'd told her about our English assignment. "Jojo is some kind of Adam Kurlansky anthropologist, now that he's getting letters from him."

"I heard," Bron said. "You do know that guy would swat you like a gnat if you ever tried to talk to him in real life, right?"

"What happened at the party, though?" I said.

Then Bron recounted how the members of the football team had bent a wire coat hanger into the letter *W* for *Wolverines* and heated it up on the stove and burned it into each other's skin. When they came around to you, Kurl, you sat down in the kitchen chair like everyone before you. The others had taken off their shirts or jeans to accept the brand somewhere hidden, but you told them you wanted it right on your bicep. When they brought the hot wire near your arm you kept flinching away, and when they tried to hold you steady for it, according to Bron, you "suddenly went nuclear."

Everyone thought it was funny, at first, and they jeered and piled on and held you down on the kitchen floor. Strongest guy on the team scared of a little pain, Kurl dishes it out but he can't take it—that sort of thing. But you really went crazy, Bron said. Shayna chimed in at this point and said that you broke the quarterback's nose. Dented the door of the stainless-steel dishwasher. Burned somebody's face when you shoved the brand away. For a while it became a real brawl, and by the time you got free you were pretty banged up, and some of the Wolvies were quite upset. You just sort of disappeared from the party after that.

"You know, that's why he got kicked off the team," Shayna said.

"He wasn't kicked off," I said. It bothers me that people at school seem to be embracing this new version of the story so wholeheartedly. "He quit. Bron, you wrote the article. You said he quit."

"Well, it was never a hundred percent clear. The coach wouldn't say, when I asked him, and they certainly haven't been begging him to come back."

Shayna shook her head and waved an AC/DC record at us. "That party was the beginning of the end," she opined. "Refusing the brand made him an outsider. He could never win back their trust."

I said, "I really don't think that's how it went."

"I'm just telling you what Rachel told me," Shayna said. "She said things weren't the same after that night."

"You mean with Kurl and Teresa?" Bron asked. "Rachel said they broke up because of that party?"

"Wait, who's Rachel?" I said.

"She said that was the beginning of the end, yeah."

"Well, Rachel is full of crap. Teresa's grades were slipping, that's all. Her parents were worried about her Princeton acceptance."

"Who are these people?" I said. "Are we still talking about Kurl?"

"Rachel is Teresa's cousin," my sister said. "You know Teresa Lau, Kurl's girlfriend from last year?"

No, I did not know. I didn't know you had a girlfriend, Kurl, or had had a girlfriend, at one point. Alienated from all the common knowledge of Lincoln High, as usual.

"They broke up," Bron told me, but I'd already gathered that much.

"She was such a snob," Shayna said.

"Because she wanted to go to college?" Bron said. College is currently a slight point of contention between Bron and Shayna. Bron is already starting to study for her SATs, and this behavior is unacceptably nerdy to Shayna. She works in little jabs whenever she can about Bron being "so bougie" and "so extra" and "such a tryhard."

"Was Kurl..." I wasn't sure what I wanted to ask them. "Did it bother him?"

Bron shrugged. "Teresa goes to Princeton now, Jojo. She wasn't really Kurl's type."

"She was a snob," Shayna repeated, catching my eye and grimacing meaningfully in Bron's direction. Given the dramatic drop in Shayna's grades last year, she will likely not be going to Princeton next year, either.

41

Yours truly,
Jonathan Hopkirk

PS: It's Sunday evening now. I wrote this letter in bits and pieces over the whole weekend. Reading back over it just now, I'm noticing how the tone has changed, and the pacing: It's much less breathless and rushed, isn't it, when one isn't trying to cram everything in into forty-five or fifty minutes? Here at home I have the time to sit at my desk with a cup of hot chocolate or a bowl of cereal and stare out over our street, piecing together the details of the day in a way that makes sense. It's easier to write what I'm thinking about if I actually have time to think.

Dear Little JO,

I guess technically it's your turn to write. But I feel like writing a letter more than I feel like starting my ecology report on amphibians. And it's not like we can't cross over once in a while. Khang doesn't seem too fussy about how many letters I write, now that it's obvious I'm actually sticking with the assignment.

We did a roof today down in Bloomington. All day there were dozens of turkey buzzards in the sky. I asked Sylvan what he thought they were after and he said maybe a deer.

I chose amphibians for this ecology report because once in the forest I found an animal I couldn't believe was even real. A tiny lizard red as a fire truck. I was maybe nine or ten. It skittered across my palm and dug its way under the leaves and was gone. The fastest living thing I'd ever held. I remember looking it up afterward and it wasn't actually a lizard but a newt. A Red Eft. The librarian told me the Red Eft doesn't live in Minnesota. She showed me a map at the back of the book with its habitat range. It must have come down from Canada, she said, around the whole north shore of Lake Superior.

Turns out mostly this newt never leaves the water. It goes straight from larval stage to aquatic adult, which is olive-yellow, speckled, with a flattened tail. But sometimes for unknown reasons it takes a detour. It grows lungs. Turns red. Goes to the woods and spends one to three years as a Red Eft before it returns to its pond or river and transforms back into a water creature. Red Efts are bolder than other salamanders. They hang out aboveground and gather in groups. They don't even mind the sun. Probably it helps that the red skin is toxic to predators.

I don't know why I'm giving you all these details. Chances are not good that you'll ever spot a Red Eft in this part of the country. But I guess if you ever do you'll know how chancy and amazing a thing it is.

Sincerely,
AK

Dear Little Jo,

I meant to write before that if you ever get a chance you should watch a turkey buzzard fly. From the ground you can't see its ugly face or its naked scalp. You don't care about its filthy diet. It climbs the wind and tilts itself across the clouds. I mean it gets far enough away and what it is is magnificent.

I'm aware that I keep coming back to these topics that have nothing to do with anything. These letters I'm writing are starting to feel like one long ongoing letter in my head. I should tell Jo about that time I saw the Red Eft, I'll think, or, I forgot to tell Jo that these birds actually look magnificent in the sky.

And then I'll read one of your letters and think, People have no idea what I'm like. I mean the gap between what people see and what's actually in my head sort of shocks me when I read your letters. I guess everyone has this gap. It's just that they don't come face-to-face with it very often. It's a shock to hear that people are still talking about stuff that happened last year.

That party. My breakup with Teresa. I mean it wasn't even a breakup. Not in the way you hear about breakups, where there's arguing and someone or both people are heartbroken afterward and going around saying things about each other to their friends. Bron was probably right. Teresa's parents were really serious about her grades. They probably didn't like that I was failing my classes.

45

That's not what Teresa told me though. She said it was because they didn't like me fighting. She said her mother thought I needed counseling and unless I would go talk to this psychotherapist her mother knew through work, Teresa wasn't allowed to date me anymore. I felt bad about it for a while. You probably wouldn't remember Teresa but she was a calm, gentle person. She looked great in blue. I mean she knew she looked great in blue, so when she wanted to dress up she wouldn't wear makeup or do anything special to her hair. She would just wear something blue. That's what she was like. Sort of low-key like that compared with other girls.

The whole thing happened because once after school we were watching TV at her place and her dad came home from work early and asked what happened to my face. I never would have gone over that day with my face bashed in if I thought her dad might come home from work so early and see me.

Sincerely,
AK

Tuesday, October 6

Dear Kurl,

I owe you an apology, I believe. While I was reading your last letter, I found myself becoming desperately sorry for recounting that gossipy conversation we had about you in Basement Records. It must have been agitating in the extreme for you to read about how these personal experiences of yours have stayed in the gossip archive after all these months. It must have been painful to read. To your immense credit, you didn't express any anger about it, just a mild surprise. My letter must have also made Bron and Shayna and me look like shallow and even vindictive people, which we are not—or at least, I'd really like to believe we are not.

I questioned myself about why I laid out the conversation for you like that, with so much effort to remember Bron's and Shayna's exact words and so little consideration for how it might feel for you to read those words. The truth is, Kurl, that I burn with curiosity about you but am too cowardly to ask you questions about yourself directly. My motivation in relating that record-store gossipfest was one hundred percent selfish: I wanted to know which version of the story you would tell if I provoked you into telling it. And I confess I was gratified to read what you wrote about Teresa, your perspective on her and the reasons for your breakup. But what a roundabout, dishonest way to seek the information! In the future, Kurl, if something piques my curiosity, I solemnly swear to ask you about it rather than try to trick you into writing about it.

And on this same subject, you asked if I mind that you "keep coming back to these topics that have nothing to do with anything." No, I don't mind. Quite the opposite: I want more, please.

I looked up the Red Eft last night—not the science, but the mythology. Did you know it's also called the Fire Salamander? It was once believed to be unharmed by burning. Apparently Fire Salamanders were seen after Pompeii, after Hiroshima, walking around in the flames. Sometimes they glowed so brightly they made people blind. I'm not sure why, Kurl, but reading these marvelous facts about your creature made me suddenly so happy that I laughed aloud. You can ask Shayna. My bedroom door was ajar, and my sister heard me laughing and asked what was so funny. I didn't tell her, because somehow it felt like a secret—like I'd discovered some kind of arcane, secret knowledge—and this made me even happier.

Yours truly,
Jonathan Hopkirk

PS: I don't know if you pay attention to these things, but they're running a talent contest at school called Lincoln Idol, and Shayna's audition tape got picked for the live competition. Somehow she has talked me into serving as her backup band. Even accounting for familial bias, it's my opinion that Shayna Hopkirk is seriously talented. She'd like nothing more than to quit school and join the Decent Fellows, and it's a point of increasing friction between her and Lyle that he hasn't let her sing with the band in the last couple of years, though she was pulled up onstage for cute little duets and solos frequently enough when she was younger.

Anyhow. The show is tomorrow at 6 p.m., if you want to sit in the back row looking stony-faced and not clap for us, Kurl. I believe you have English in the morning, so I'll be sure to put this letter in the box first thing. You've been dropping by Ms. Khang's room to check for mail even when you don't have English class, haven't you? So have I. When we're writing letters off schedule like this, I can never be sure when a new one will show up. It gives me something to look forward to at school besides being tossed around by the butcherboys.

Dear Little Jo,

I had to help with a roof after school yesterday. All the rain the last couple of weeks has put us behind schedule. By the time we wrapped up it was almost seven, so I figured I'd probably missed the talent thing at school.

But Sylvan got it into his head that I had to attend this particular extracurricular event. I tried saying, Never mind, it's no big deal, but he started telling me how he's been worried about me since football dried up.

You're all bunched up under your skin, he said.

What's that supposed to mean, I said.

You're like a dog in a cage, he said, biting your own fur and bashing your head against the bars.

Okay, okay, I'll go, I said, just to get him to stop with the dog comparison.

So I guess I did exactly what you predicted, Jo. Snuck into the back row of the auditorium. I took a seat next to a man with partly gray, shaggy hair and a black cowboy shirt. One of the many dads in the crowd, right? Could have been anybody.

A couple minutes later, after this group of rappers finishes up onstage, it's intermission, and the guy next to me turns and offers me his hand and says, Hi there, I'm Lyle.

Of course it's Lyle. Now that the lights are on this guy looks exactly like you, Jo. The cowboy shirt is unbuttoned and under it he's wearing this T-shirt that says GOT GRASS? with the word *grass* in blue letters. No way I would have worked out that little inside joke if you hadn't mentioned in one of your letters that it's bluegrass music your dad plays.

He's offering me his hand but my hands are still filthy from shingling. Tar-black nails and dried blood all across my knuckles. I sort of show Lyle my hands to apologize for not shaking his, and of course he asks me what I've been up to. So I tell him about Kurlansky Roofing, and before I know it he's taking down the number because apparently your roof has needed reshingling for about a decade.

On the other side of your dad is this guy Cody, who Lyle tells me plays bass in their band. Cody says he used to work for a roofing company as a teenager too. He flexes his bicep and says, You'll be thankful for that job later in life.

You know how when you're in an audience and you talk to the stranger next to you, and then for the whole rest of the show it's like you're sort of watching it together? I mean it's not like you say anything more to the person or even glance over at each other much. But somehow it feels like you're sharing your reactions with each other. That's pretty much how it was for your dad and me. Some of the kids in our school are really bad. It's not even lack of talent so much as lack of judgment. Trying to tap-dance to a Beyoncé song is never going to be a good idea no matter who's doing it. And that thing with the yoga and the yodeling. That was one of the times Lyle and I sort of looked sideways at each other. He did this whole elaborate coughing maneuver into his fist to cover up his laughter. You could probably hear him from backstage, Jo.

51

Shayna's voice isn't at all how I imagined. I guess I expected some airy, folky sound. You know those songs with the cutesy chorus and the verses with too many lyrics crammed in? Instead Shayna sounds like a sixty-year-old chain-smoker. And I'm saying that in a good way.

Watching you two onstage Lyle can't even help himself. He leans over and goes, Those are my kids up there. Grinning like a maniac with fatherly pride.

Shayna is a good singer but I have to say the real shocker was you. I mean you never said anything about playing the mandolin. Okay yes, I had to ask Lyle what the thing was. I'd never seen one before.

You said you were Shayna's backup band but you didn't say you were going to sing. And you didn't say you were so good at it. Your voice is the opposite of Shayna's. Higher than hers, for one. It made me realize I've never really heard you talk, even. It's weird to know so much about the way a person thinks without ever having heard their voice. When you sang it was this high, pure kind of sound. I don't know. It felt like I recognized you and didn't recognize you at the same time.

Then the judges did their thing. One of them compared your sound to Donny and Marie Osmond and Lyle said, You've got to be kidding me. He was laughing but actually looking sort of irritated about it.

Cody said, She should be in the band, man.

Don't tell her that, Lyle said, or I'll have her down my throat about it twenty-four-seven.

Exact same sound as Rapha, Cody said. That could have been Rapha up there.

Lyle didn't answer, and Cody sort of ducked his head and

gave Lyle a quick little pat on the shoulder as if to say sorry. I guess Rapha must be Raphael, a.k.a. your mom?

I asked whether you and Shayna took voice lessons et cetera. Lyle said it was never really necessary. You could tell he was trying not to brag, not to talk about you too much, but he couldn't help himself. While the next kids were performing he leaned in and told me how you, Jo, quit talking for almost a year when you first started school. They had you tested and everything, Lyle said, but then he discovered that you really liked to sing, and it was as if you somehow didn't realize that song lyrics were words. So Lyle would sing with you all the time. Not just real songs but made-up stuff, songs about How was your day? and What shall we have for dinner? so that you would communicate with him that way. Even Shayna got in on the action apparently. The year our life became a musical, Lyle called it.

I think I dozed off for a few of the remaining acts. Three hours on a roof and no time for supper will do that to you. Sorry I didn't stick around afterward to congratulate you in person. When I heard the vote-with-your-phone system was glitching out and they would have to recount, I said a quick goodbye to Lyle and Cody and took off.

This morning I heard that somebody else won. I hope you're not taking it personally, Jo. You and Shayna weren't flashy enough is all. You should be proud because I know your Hopkirk motto is *Be real and be true*. On the way home last night I remembered that and I thought, That's how they sounded up there. Real and true.

sincerely,
AK

Dear Kurl,

After school yesterday you pulled up to the bus stop and unrolled your window. "Where's your bike?" you called.

It caught me off guard. "Nowhere," I said.

"What?" you said.

"I'll tell you later," I said, and I felt my face get hot, so I turned away and scurried into the bus shelter, behind the map. I apologize for my extreme awkwardness-bordering-on-rudeness. But you and I don't, technically, "tell" each other things, do we? We write them, but it would have been even more bizarre for me to say "I'll write you all about it later." And anyway, truth be told, I didn't want to tell you about my bike. Its name was Nelly, a.k.a. the Fagmobile (so christened by the butcherboys the first time they saw me locking it at school). Suffice it to say that Nelly has met with a violent, homophobic death and now lies, hopefully finally at peace, in her watery grave. Drew Saarinen, whose brother Michael hangs out with Dowell, told me in Civics that they dumped Nelly in Cherry Valley. I went down there yesterday to fish her out, but she's in the spillwater portion of the creek, half sunk in the mud and dead leaves, and those six feet of water appeared bone-shatteringly cold. I couldn't tell from the embankment, but I imagine the butcherboys probably slashed the tires and cut the brake cables before they dumped the bike, anyhow.

Enough! On to a pleasanter topic: Today the blackboard invites us to *Describe your Inner Sanctum*. A portion of the class began sniggering when Ms. Khang wrote this on the board, because they'd somehow managed to read the word as *scrotum*. There were a lot of jokes—"Mine is wrinkly and has my balls in it"—that sort of thing. Thanks all the same, Alex Federsholm, but there's a mental image with which I really didn't need to be saddled.

My Inner Sanctum is my bedroom, because it houses my two most prized possessions. The first is my record player, a 1970s made-in-Holland Philips that Lyle had refurbished for me for Christmas when I was thirteen. I have a few favorite artists, of course, but Lyle's vinyl collection is so massive that I feel as though cultivating too intense a loyalty to certain records would be premature at my age. When I get home from school, the first thing I do after taking off my shoes and backpack is head directly upstairs to my room, close the door, put on a record, and climb into my tent.

The tent is the second reason my room is my sanctuary. Instead of a bed, I sleep on a double mattress on the floor of an old army tent. Another of Lyle's youthful castoffs, this heavy canvas-and-aluminum structure was his and my mother's Inner Sanctum back when his band was too poor for motels, and they'd pull into whatever highway rest stop was closest to their next gig and pitch the tent on the grass. Lyle set the old beast up for me a few years ago when I was going through a period of insomnia for some reason or another, and it hasn't come down since.

Yours truly,
Jonathan Hopkirk

Friday, October 9

Dear Little Jo,

Somehow it's not the biggest shocker that you sleep in a tent. It gave me a laugh picturing you curled up in there with your flashlight and your poetry books or whatever.

At one point my bedroom was decorated with all kinds of football stuff. But once I was off the team I took everything down and trashed it. I figured, no point dwelling on it.

So it's bare walls, faded green carpet, an old piece-of-crap computer, a bed too short for my legs. Not exactly an Inner Sanctum. Except for this one thing I sort of like because it's so ugly. It's a quilt my mom and her mom, my babcia, made for her hope chest. She had a hope chest, like an actual chest made out of wood to hold her wedding stuff. Dishes and towels and silver spoons, that sort of thing. Anyway this chest came with my parents when they immigrated, and this quilt is put together from pieces of things that got too worn out or full of holes to use for anything else.

There's something about this idea I like. Things getting used till they're not useful anymore, and then cut up into pieces and put together into something useful again. I mean it is a horrifically ugly quilt. There are orange and pink and brown bits, and the bits that were probably white originally are all various shades of beige. I like it exactly for its ugliness though. I like how my mom, and my babcia before her, and so on, back a bunch of generations, must have been thinking one hundred percent about warmth and bed coverage and not looks.

sincerely,
AK

Dear Kurl,

A quick note between classes, because I forgot to ask you to please not mention anything about Nelly (my bicycle) to Shayna. Lyle bought me that bike brand-new for my birthday, and Shayna spent her own money on a seat upgrade for me after the first one was stolen a month later. Honestly, I just don't have the heart to tell my family that their effort and hard-earned money was wasted.

Also, I keep forgetting to answer your question about the word *butcherboys*. It's Walt's term, of course. One of the American "roughs" he observes as he goes about his day is the butcher boy. When I first came across it last year, something about the description reminded me of Dowell—the dullness, the meatiness, the fists. I don't think I told you, but Dowell and I used to be friends when we were younger.

Anyhow, I paged through "Song of Myself" after you first asked, but I didn't find the reference to the butcher boy, and I only just remembered your question now. I'll find it eventually on one of my rereads.

Yours truly,
Jonathan Hopkirk

Dear Little Jo,

I get this one nightmare every couple months. Whenever it happens I know I'm not going to be able to sleep again the rest of the night. We're doing a roof, and the rule on a roof is always lean forward, but in this dream I stand up and instead of leaning forward I lean back. The others all give me these looks like, *Now you're in for it.* My whole body clenches up trying to correct it, trying to lean forward again. I mean my guts are like a fist, they've clenched so tight. But of course nothing works. My arms start to wheel around and my feet pedal air and I fall. You know that thing about dreams where they say that you always wake up right before you hit the ground? Not me. I hit the ground and my head bursts open. I mean I can feel hot liquid pouring over my skull and out of my ears. I feel each of my ribs stab through my chest. Lungs deflating. Leg bones pleated like accordions. Then, only after all that, do I wake up. My stomach muscles ache the whole day after one of those roof dreams, like I've done a thousand sit-ups the night before.

So now it's 2:30 a.m. and I'm supposed to be ready at 5 a.m. to leave with Uncle Viktor in the truck. That'll be about two hours total sleep tonight.

To be honest, Jo, I sort of hate roofing. Not just my uncle power-tripping on me all day long either. I hate everything about that job. I hate the grit of the shingles and the stench of tar. I hate the pounding of our hammers all day going in and out of sync so that it can never become rhythm, only noise. In summer I hate the way the heat beats down but also gets absorbed by the tarpaper and boils up from underneath. Burned shoulders, burned knees, burned hands. Drinking water all day but still feeling thirsty. In spring and fall I hate the cold wind that whips across the housetops from all directions at once.

I'm glad my dad isn't around to hear me saying this. I mean I doubt he was crazy about the job either, but I don't remember him ever complaining.

I was just picturing you asleep inside your army tent. Your Inner Sanctum. I have to say it made me feel a bit better, that mental picture. Thank you for giving me all those details about the records you listen to et cetera. It's actually making me smile right now, sitting on the rug on my bedroom floor.

I guess maybe what I have is an Outer Sanctum instead of an Inner one. It's this stretch near my house along the railway tracks. Mark and I used to go there a lot as kids, before they fenced it off and put up all those NO TRESPASSING signs. We used to ride our bikes down the middle of the tracks, between the rails. Mark got so he could ride right on the rail, but I never got the hang of it.

He made this sort of sled out of plywood that we could pull along the tracks. We would pile rocks or branches and slide it along the rails. Once we found an armchair in the ditch and put that on the sled, and he would let me sit in it and pull me along. For some reason it was the biggest thrill.

They've fenced it all off now so you can't go right up to the tracks except through this one area where the chain link is rolled back. Recently they put in an asphalt path for bicycles and dog walkers et cetera. But it's still fairly wild down there. Grasshoppers everywhere. Unmowed grass, that kind Walt Whitman says sounds like *So many uttering tongues* in the wind. And I don't know. A feeling of being on the edge of things. A dividing line between the city and wherever those trains are heading.

Sincerely,
AK

Dear Kurl,

Well, I can say this much for the Kurlanskys: Your family certainly knows its way around a roof. Two men were tarping the front steps and shrubs when I left for school yesterday, and by the time I got home you were nearly halfway across with the new shingles already. I figured you must have been part of the crew when I didn't see you at school. My apologies in advance for lecturing you, Kurl, but I hope you don't make a habit of cutting school for work. It's not very conducive to passing your courses and graduating.

Anyhow. When I walked up the driveway after school, you waved down at me and I waved back. Bron and Shayna were lying on the living room floor doing homework—or, more accurately, Bron was writing something on her laptop that might or might not have been homework, and Shayna was paging through a back issue of *Rolling Stone*. I went up to my room, but the hammering overhead was more intrusive on the second floor, which explained why the girls had taken over the living room.

I kept thinking about how you confessed you hate roofing, Kurl, all that noise. I could hear it exactly as you'd described it, the hammers beating out of sync, someone barking orders—I assumed this was Uncle Viktor—and lower, quieter voices murmuring that I assumed were yours and Sylvan's. It wasn't too hot a day, but I thought about making lemonade, maybe bringing a tray with glasses and a pitcher out to the bottom of the ladder. But we don't have a pitcher, and I don't know precisely how to make lemonade. More to the point, I couldn't think of a more blatantly gay thing to do for a bunch of roofers. I try to recognize and not succumb to my internalized homophobia, as Bron would put it, but there are times when it simply freezes me in my tracks and I just give up. After trying to read in my tent for ten or fifteen minutes without success, I went back downstairs and joined Bron and Shayna.

It started to rain just after Lyle got home with Cody Walsh, the Decent Fellows' bassist. You Kurlanskys had quite a difficult time tarping the roof—the wind had kicked up along with the rain, and there was lots of shouting and swearing and scraping of ladders along the siding—and then Lyle invited you all in for a beer.

Your brother Sylvan is like a shrink-wrapped version of you: several inches shorter, narrower across the shoulders, less muscle mass overall. Wiry and deeply tanned. Your uncle Viktor is yet another variation: broad like you but meatier, almost squat-looking, with slightly sloped shoulders and round belly. But you all have the same strong brow, broad cheekbones, straight nose, severe mouth. It made me wonder about your middle brother, Mark. Does he manifest all those same Kurlansky genes?

"Sit down, sit down," Lyle said. So you stopped protesting about your wet clothes and dirty hands and sat, Viktor on a dining chair, Sylvan on the sofa next to Cody and Lyle, you on the floor with the girls and me. I tried not to stare but kept thinking of what you told me Sylvan had said about you being "bunched up under your skin." You sat in an approximately cross-legged position, but as though your quad muscles couldn't quite conform to it, so that actually, only your ankles were crossed in their wool work socks, your knees in their soiled denim pointing diagonally to the ceiling and your forearms pinning them in place.

I'm afraid that after the few initial, polite exchanges—how long have you been roofing, what do you think of the new "lifetime" roofing products, what does Lyle do for a living, what sort of music does the band play—you Kurlanskys didn't have much opportunity to participate in the conversation. You and I were probably the most conspicuously silent, Kurl. *Conspicuously* is the wrong word, since no one else noticed. Perhaps even you didn't notice how silent we were. It just occurred to me now, writing this, that we're both the youngest members of our families. Something in common.

Anyhow, with two of the Decent Fellows in the room, I suppose it was inevitable that bluegrass would be the topic of conversation. At Sylvan's request, Lyle demonstrated a basic bluegrass forward roll on the banjo.

Bron then told us, "One of the sustaining myths of bluegrass music is that it's an exclusively white tradition."

"That's not a myth," Cody said. "Bluegrass was white hillbilly music right from the start. Black music was jazz, gospel, and blues. Two totally different things."

"Before the Civil War," Bron said, "poor black and poor white people shared most of the same spaces and activities, including their music. The banjo is an African instrument, originally, right, Lyle?"

"Sure," said Lyle, always affable. "But the banjo didn't invent bluegrass. Bill Monroe did, and he was white."

"Bill Monroe is part of the myth," Bron insisted. "He took

all his riffs and picking patterns from the people playing around him when he was growing up. In his biography he makes it crystal clear he didn't invent anything. He just absorbed, and copied, and then got recorded and popularized and canonized as the father of the whole genre."

"Really, we're *all* a bunch of rednecks," Lyle joked.

"Maybe you are," Shayna said, disloyally. "Maybe you've raised Jojo and me to be rednecks, too, Lyle."

"I was just using the Decent Fellows as an example," Bron said. "Your band is certainly not the exception, when it comes to the erasure of black history."

"I'm not a redneck, I don't think," I said. I was wearing my robin's-egg blue velvet bow tie and my suede vest, so I knew this would get a laugh.

So I suppose I did contribute one point to the discussion, Kurl. And so did you, now that I'm thinking of it. The pizza arrived, and we passed around the paper napkins and lifted the gooey slices onto our laps. Your brother helped himself to the Meat Lovers' Supreme, but when you leaned forward to take a slice, your uncle Viktor said, "No, we'll wait to eat at home. Your mother is cooking."

I suppose Lyle could see you were starving. "One piece won't ruin his appetite, right?"

"No, that's okay, I'm okay," you said, and sat back, twisting your napkin and stuffing it into your back pocket. You hadn't touched your cola, either. There was a moment of silence, and chewing, and then Uncle Viktor stood up and said you had better be going.

"How about an official dinner invitation, then, for tomorrow?" Lyle said. "Whatever time you finish the roof. We'll do Tex-Mex or something."

He and your uncle shook hands, and then you and Sylvan shook his hand and Cody's hand, too, and it was "Nice to meet you" and "See you tomorrow" all around.

Sylvan mentioned that you weren't needed for the rest of the job and you'd be at school today, so maybe I'll see you at some point this afternoon—but I hope you'll come by tonight for dinner as well?

Yours truly,
Jonathan Hopkirk

Dear Little Jo,

Khang just told us she's through with offering suggested themes to use in our letters. Not that you and I have been using them lately anyway. Khang said that as we must know by now, all writing shares something of yourself. So share away, she said.

Memories though. A memory can't be shared even when you write about it. Words won't transfer a memory anywhere or help you reabsorb it. It just sits there, the memory. Pooled up under your skin like a bruise.

For example, I remember there was this bird down by the tracks that hated Mark and me. All black except for a flash of red on each wing. It would come diving out of the trees and flap right into our faces. It left a scratch once under the hair on Mark's forehead. Its chirp sounded like stones smacking together.

You're right that you and I didn't say anything last night over pizza. Once or twice we looked at each other. I thought maybe you were a bit uncomfortable with us there, but maybe that was just in my head. I guess if you don't talk you can't really tell.

Give the people what they want, Uncle Viktor says. If they want the cheap shingles, give them the cheap shingles. Cheap shingles is how he underbids AA Roofing, who stole a lot of Kurlansky customers after my father passed. Don't worry, Jo. We used good quality materials on your roof. The thing about

Uncle Viktor is that it's better just to keep your head down and do what he says and let him think what he thinks. Most of the time I remember and catch myself in time. Like with the pizza at your house. It might seem like a dumb thing. Why can't I have a slice of pizza? It might be a dumb or embarrassing thing but it's a little thing. Definitely not worth turning into a big thing.

Mark thought it was hilarious the way this bird kept attacking him but to be honest it creeped me out, how interested it seemed in hurting us. It reminds me of how in ancient wars they would smear crows with tallow, light them on fire, and free them to fly over the enemy walls. You could burn down a whole fort with these firebirds. A whole town.

I found a bird guide in the library and looked up this murderous bird's name. Surprise surprise: Red-winged Blackbird.

I spent a lot of time at your house yesterday trying not to stare at everything. I've never been inside a house like yours before. There is no decoration anywhere that I could see. No drapes, just bare windows. No pictures on the walls or things sitting around on shelves. None of those extra pillows to decorate the sofa. The kitchen has no cabinets, just open shelves with dishes stacked and some mismatched sections of drawers with a plywood countertop.

The thing about your house is there's nothing just for looking at. It's all for using. There's that massive stereo with all those separate parts: turntable and receiver and CD player and huge speakers. Even a cassette deck. There are all those stacked wooden crates full of records and books and cassettes. And I mean there must be at least ten different musical instruments in your living room. Some I didn't even recognize, like that long wavy one with the little hearts carved into it and that rectangular one with the big silver circle under the strings.

On our way out the door Sylvan asked Lyle about this clock-like object made of brass and wood on the wall. A barometer, Lyle said. My son dragged it home from somewhere. He's a fan of the obscure and the obsolete, aren't you, Jojo?

There were two words on the face of your barometer: *regen* and *mooi*. When I got home I looked them up. They're Dutch words that mean *rain* and *fair*. Apparently what a barometer does is measure changes in air pressure and tell you whether it'll rain soon. Useful as well as beautiful, see?

I'll see you tonight, Jo. Thank you for specifically inviting me.

sincerely,
AK

Dear Kurl,

Your uncle Viktor strikes me as a difficult man to please some-times. He seemed pleased enough with the meal (Lyle makes a decent enchilada, doesn't he?) and the drink (you have to admit that breaking the vodka out of the freezer even before we sat down to the table seemed another stroke of brilliance on Lyle's part. My father is a genius at anticipating needs).

My sister had to be fetched down for dinner. Lyle had called up the stairs three times, but she hadn't responded. I found her humped under her blankets like a badger, dead asleep. From what I could tell she'd been in there all day. I knew she wasn't at school, anyway.

"I'm not hungry," Shayna mumbled, when I was finally able to rouse her.

"We have company," I said. "The Kurlanskys, remember?"

She came downstairs fifteen minutes later wearing a pajama top and a pair of overalls, rubbing her eyes like a toddler, her hair a comical tangle.

Viktor was in the midst of addressing Lyle, adult to adult. He was complaining about you, Kurl. "You would not believe how much trouble it is to get this lazy son of a bitch to lift a finger. The biggest and dumbest of them all, and he thinks he's too good for a day's work."

70

"Adam's in school, Uncle Vik," Sylvan said. He sounded somewhat weary, like he'd had this argument with your uncle about a thousand times before.

"But why? Why is he in school?" Viktor said. "He has no reason to be in school. He doesn't even have football anymore. All that big muscle for no reason."

Shayna looked around the table with sudden interest. She asked, as an obvious-bordering-on-sarcastic change of topic: "So have any of you guys ever been to this bar downtown called the Ace?"

You Kurlanskys shook your heads.

"It's this awesome music venue nobody knows about. Lyle, didn't the Decent Fellows used to play there a million years ago?"

"Nope."

Everyone looked at Lyle, who picked up a leaf of cilantro from his plate and shredded it into smaller pieces over his pork *al pastor*.

"There's a picture of Mom on the wall, over the bar," Shayna said.

And I suddenly recalled that the Ace was pictured on the postcard Shayna showed Bron and me at school, the one with what she thought was Raphael's handwriting on the back.

Lyle stared at her. "What were *you* doing there? You're underage."

Shayna rolled her eyes.

"These kids," said Viktor. Again he appealed to Lyle, as if the two of them were out at some pub together, commiserating about their good-for-nothing children, and we children weren't all sitting there listening. He pointed again at you, Kurl. "You know this one can lift two bundles of shingles with one arm. Like

71

Popeye!" A nasty laugh. "He is costing us money every day he isn't up there with his family. His own brother, his own father."

"You're not my father," you said.

This produced a decidedly awkward silence. The rest of us stared politely down at our plates. It occurred to me that the vodka bottle next to Viktor's glass was nearly empty, though Lyle and Sylvan had only had one shot each. I couldn't remember whether the bottle had been completely full when it came out of the freezer, but I think it was close.

Why am I recounting this whole scene detail by detail? Why have I just written all this out, pausing to remember as accurately as possible the vocabulary each person used, the precise tone of voice, the glances exchanged among the others sitting at the table? You were there, after all. You don't need me to reconstruct the scene for you.

Perhaps I'm retelling it in order to understand something in it, something about its emotional undercurrents. Obviously Shayna is trying to get under Lyle's skin by flouting her breaking of rules like that in front of company. But that's nothing new. Or rather, I suppose it's new in that it's more dramatic, more in-your-face. Your family dynamic is more mysterious to me, of course, because I haven't observed it often. Kurl, I honestly don't know how to describe what I was feeling as your uncle talked about you like that. I kept trying to read the expression on your face—but as I've observed before, your expression is always perfectly, immaculately serene.

Yours truly,
Jonathan Hopkirk

Dear Little Jo,

So I found the part you were talking about in Walt's book, about the butcherboys. It goes,

> The butcher-boy puts off his killing-clothes, or sharpens
>   his knife at the stall in the market,
> I loiter enjoying his repartee and his shuffle and
>   breakdown.

I wasn't actually looking for it specifically. It just jumped out at me, and it was exactly like you said—right away I pictured that little jerkoff Dowell. It's the way he walks I think. The way he shuffles along with his head down and his shoulders hunched.

Meanwhile there's you. This morning I saw those gray felt things you were wearing over your shoes. They reminded me of baffles, these things you use on a roof along with insulation to stop heat transfer. So I thought about how all your Walt outfits operate kind of like baffles for you. A way of stopping school from leaking in and stopping you from leaking out. I looked up those shoe covers, so now I'm aware that what they're actually called is *spats*.

I guess I never really explained about my uncle, did I? He married my mom three years after my dad died. I was thirteen.

Sylvan had had his own place for a while by then, and Mark left for the army that spring right after graduation, so it was just her and me left with Uncle Viktor.

Shuffle and breakdown. Somehow it's really hard to picture Walt the poet just hanging around the slaughterhouse listening to the butcherboy talk. I wonder how he gets away with it. I mean he never gets beat up or anything, does he? Nobody says, Why don't you put down the goddamn poetry notebook and quit staring at us? I don't know. Somehow Walt is immune to all these people. He just gets to enjoy everybody and everything in the world.

sincerely,
AK

Dear Kurl,

My wardrobe is mostly composed of thrift shop garbage, in case it's not obvious. I shoulder right in there beside the old ladies at the Goodwill, looking for bargains. However, I do attempt to bolster the overall quality and style of my outfits with a few one-of-a-kind vintage pieces procured for me by Mr. Ragman.

Do you know his store, way out on Lake Street? It's probably never been on your radar. The owner actually goes by the surname Ragman; I've seen him sign an invoice. His first name is Mischa or perhaps Michel, but I've always called him Mr. Ragman. He has slicked-back hair and a fat belly, and he wears a black shirt with a vest and gold rings on every finger like a movie mobster. He's in his late sixties now, and I am terrified that he'll decide to retire before I'm old enough to drive to auctions and estate sales, or wealthy enough to buy antique clothing at market prices.

I can't afford much of what Mr. Ragman sells. Most of his stock is women's designer clothes, labels like Gucci and Prada. But Mr. Ragman has my measurements on file and will put things aside for me whenever they have a moth hole or two, or frayed cuffs, or anything else that will slow a sale.

Shabby, some of it. But even the shabbiest of these items will still outshine the quality of anything you can buy in a store at the mall.

Yours truly,
Jonathan Hopkirk

Dear Little Jo,

Sylvan was supposed to have finished the chimney cap on your roof yesterday, but it was *regen* not *mooi*. Now they've moved on to a job across town so he asked me to come by after school and take care of it.

Shayna answered your door and said, Lyle's not home but whatever, go ahead. It was a five-minute job that turned into forty minutes thanks to Shayna and Bron throwing cookies up to the roof for me and stealing my ladder and pointing out to me all of Lyle's pot plants hidden among the tall weeds in your backyard. I guess it's party time at the Hopkirk house when Lyle has an out-of-town gig.

They asked me to stay for supper. They asked if I wanted a Coke. They asked if I was a pad thai fan, because Bron was making her vegan pad thai and they defied me to miss the meat. Bron's words: I defy you to miss the meat.

I said, I don't care about meat as much as people think.

I didn't think about how weird it would sound until it came out. Bron started laughing, saying, What does that even mean? So I had to explain that people always assume I must be this strict carnivore because I'm so tall. And because it's a football cliché. Steak and eggs for breakfast et cetera.

I didn't ask them about you, Jo. It seemed weird to ask I

guess. But I pictured you upstairs lying in your tent. I don't know why I thought you would be in your tent at that time of day, but I did. At one point I went upstairs to use the bathroom but your bedroom door was closed.

So Bron is in the kitchen cooking her pad thai. Shayna's telling us all these stories from school. At first I sit in the living room with her, but Bron is not really happy being in the kitchen by herself. She keeps popping out to say, What? Who said that? No way. That's not how I heard it. Et cetera. She's spending more time in the kitchen doorway dropping bits of green onion on the rug than she is actually cooking.

Finally I go stand in the kitchen doorway so the three of us can talk back and forth and Bron can stop abandoning the stove. She's making big piles of carrots and cabbage and ginger. Everything cut into tiny slivers. I mean I actually like to cook, so I was watching how she did it.

Bron has these amazing ideas, but she isn't the best on the follow-through is she? She fries up the onion and ginger okay. She puts the rest of the vegetables into the pan but then leaves them just sitting in there. We're out in the living room talking to Shayna, and I can tell Bron is not even thinking about the food anymore. She is describing how a tanker car on a train will explode if it derails. Apparently they want to route these oil tanker cars right through downtown Minneapolis, so Bron is planning to write an article about how dangerous it is.

But I mean I can smell the carrots starting to scorch. So I go back to the kitchen and stir it all around. I find a lid in the cupboard and add a bit of water to the pan and cover it.

Bron follows me and goes, Oh, awesome, thanks, but she's

still not really paying attention. You should see the way they buried the public safety and risk statistics in their report, she says.

Listen, listen to this. Shayna, listen, your voice says.

It's you, Jo. You've come tearing downstairs right past the kitchen without noticing me standing in there. You're sitting next to Shayna on the couch with your mandolin. You're barefoot. Still in your starchy, high-collar shirt from school, but it is unbuttoned and hanging off one of your shoulders.

You don't look up to see us in the kitchen doorway, and Shayna lifts her finger to her mouth and grins, so I stay quiet.

What is that song you sang? I had never heard it before. I've been listening to bluegrass but it didn't sound like bluegrass. Some kind of Renaissance song maybe. Some ballad. The song itself didn't even matter once you started to sing though. The whole point was your voice.

Bron is standing there beside me in the doorway with a package of tofu in her hands. I mean none of us even moves after you start to sing. We barely breathe.

You sit right at the edge of the couch with one bare foot reaching forward for balance, tapping the beat. Your collarbone sticks out when you strum. When you sing you lean forward with your eyes closed and your head tilted up to the ceiling. It's like you are listening to some other person singing inside you.

And it sounds like another person too. Or it's not a person at all—maybe more like a creature. An animal. Your voice has broken, is breaking. I mean I guess that's what you are demonstrating to Shayna. What did she call it afterward? The ravages of puberty.

You are singing in this new voice of yours. A crazed split-note tenor crawling up the scale like a creature outrunning death. Like a wild creature's death song. I guess it was something about the contrast. Such a civilized, old-fashioned love song sung in a savage voice like that, and watching your throat make such a sound. I mean it made the hair stand up on my arms and my scalp prickle. I felt Bron shiver beside me.

You sang these words: *And still I hope someday that you and I will be as one.* And meanwhile your voice somehow sang the opposite: that there was pretty much no hope of any reunion or happy ending. It must have been the contrast that was so beautiful and creepy.

Afterward Shayna reached over and put her hand over your mouth even though you'd already finished the song. Goddamn, Jonathan Hopkirk, she said.

You laughed and tossed your mandolin onto the sofa cushions and butted your head into her side. You heard that, you said. You heard it, right? Did you hear that voice? That was *me*!

Bron tucked the package of tofu under her arm and started applauding to signal that we were standing there.

I turned fast and ducked back into the kitchen. I don't know. I needed a minute to get my face in order. I mean it's one thing to write letters. It's another thing to be invited by your dad for dinner. But it's a different thing to show up by surprise. To watch you doing something private. Or something not quite public, anyhow.

Sure enough when I came back into the living room you were hiding behind the sofa, down between the sofa and the front window.

Hi, Kurl, you said, but you sounded strangled.

Hi, I said. Shayna and Bron were killing themselves laughing.

I came over and looked behind the sofa but you held up your hands to shield your face.

Oh, don't cry, Jojo, Shayna said. Come on out. We love your totally fucked-up voice, don't we, guys?

We love it, Bron said.

We do, I said. We love it.

So you came out. You had buttoned up your shirt, but your hair had rubbed along the back of the sofa or something because it was sticking out everywhere.

Saying not to cry makes him cry, Bron explained. It's like Pavlov and his dogs.

Something's burning, I told her.

The peanut sauce! Bron gave a shriek and ran to the kitchen.

It's not real crying, you said. I just wasn't expecting you.

I know, I said. I'm sorry.

I was asleep before, you said.

I figured, I said. Your Inner Sanctum.

His what? Shayna asked, but neither of us told her.

You smiled, still sort of teary.

I don't know exactly what to say about Bron's pad thai. The noodles were all stuck together. It tasted like ketchup, basically. I ate three helpings because I was shaky with hunger by then. I volunteered to cook next time. I make an excellent schnitzel, I said. I thought schnitzel was a normal food that everyone knows about, but I guess it isn't. It had the three of you rolling around laughing.

After we ate, we all took turns arm wrestling. When it was you against me, Shayna put her hands over ours to pull in your direction. I'll save you, Jojo! she said.

Don't call me that, you said. And don't help. I've got this.

You stood up and leaned your weight into it. Oh my God, you said, it's like felling a tree.

Strong oaks from tiny acorns grow, I said, and again you all thought it was the most hilarious thing you'd ever heard. I don't know where I even got it from.

Ancient Kurlansky wisdom! Bron said, and maybe she was right.

I'm aware I'm doing the same thing you did in that letter after Lyle had us to dinner. I'm writing a blow-by-blow of everything everybody said. Every little joke and look and movement. I mean you were there in the room too, so you hardly need me to do this. But I get why you wanted to do it. It all feels like it goes by pretty fast, like I could miss something happening unless I take some extra time and write about it afterward.

We got you to sing some more. Bron requested "Imagine" and it was like the apocalypse.

It hurts, Bron said, and I mean that literally. Physically. She said, It makes my tits ache.

I have to say I understood exactly what she meant. The sound of your voice pressed on my chest like my ribs had shrunk. My throat felt like I'd been screaming.

One thing I was noticing was that every time Bron or Shayna called you Jojo, you said, Don't call me that. But a few minutes later they would do it again.

So just before I left, I asked you: Do you mind it when I call you Jo?

That depends, you said. Does it still mean Jerkoff?

No! I laughed. I swear I'd forgotten all about that since the first few letters. I said, It's just that I've come to think of you as Jo.

Well, then it's okay, you said.

Okay, I said.

Okay, you said again.

sincerely,
AK

Dear Little Jo,

I was just reading some old letters here at 3 a.m. in my room. You asked if Mark has the Kurlansky genes. He doesn't. He's about Sylvan's height only narrower. Angular. He has my mom's pale skin and brown eyes. Girls go crazy for Mark because of his soulful expression. Or that's how he explained it to me, back when he started getting all these texts from girls and I wanted to know why.

In Afghanistan once Mark watched a man die of a snakebite. He told Sylvan how they tried to make him lie still. Stay calm. But the guy kept jumping around in a panic. Sylvan didn't know what kind of snake it was. He said a viper maybe.

I mean Mark never talks to me about Afghanistan. He will tell this stuff to Sylvan when Sylvan goes to the Texas Border, the bar where Mark works as manager. Then Sylvan will tell me when we're on a roof without Uncle Vik.

Mark used to be a vegetarian. A vegetarian in a houseful of animal killers, is how he put it. I learned to cook by watching Mark, because he started cooking back when he was thirteen or fourteen. He got stacks of vegetarian cookbooks out of the library to find new stuff to try. Mark introduced our household to the concept of seasonings. Fresh oregano in the veggie lasagna. Cumin and coriander in the Marrakech stew.

I loved the way Mark would unthinkingly wipe his hands on

84

his T-shirt the whole time he cooked. Fingers flicking front and back along his ribs before he opened the fridge or turned the page in the cookbook.

Adam, he said, let's not be the type of people who think about cleaning up the whole time we're making a mess.

It's actually the cobra, not the viper, with the deadliest venom in Afghanistan. A neurotoxin. I looked it up: It would have been either an Oxus cobra or an Indian cobra. The US military had to buy vials of cobra antivenin from Iran. The problem is your heart, Sylvan explained to me. The faster your heart is beating the faster the venom gets to it.

What woke me up tonight wasn't a nightmare for a change. It was missing Mark. I woke up feeling sick with missing him.

I mean he didn't die over there or anything. He returned intact, is how they describe it. The screws in his hip, the way he limps, is nothing compared with most vets discharged for medical reasons. Of course I missed him the whole time he was over there. But I don't know. Somehow I miss him more since he got back. It's like five years ago when Mark was deployed, I promised myself that when he returned everything would be just like when we were kids. Hikes and wrestling and pancakes and target practice and joking around all the time. I wasn't aware that I even made such a ridiculous promise to myself, let alone that I believed it.

Now that he's back it's obvious. It's so obvious you would think I'd just get over it. Instead missing Mark sometimes wakes me up at night like a hole punched in my skin and all my insides escaping.

sincerely,
AK

Dear Kurl,

You weren't at school today, which of course meant there was no letter from you in Ms. Khang's box, either. Maybe you were doing a roof, but it was raining this morning, so it seems unlikely. I'm a little worried you might be sick or something, because of what happened on Saturday.

I went down to Cherry Valley Saturday morning to make another, more serious bicycle recovery attempt, but the water level had risen and Nelly had sunk even deeper under the rotting leaves and silt at the creek bottom. Even if I'd had the courage to strip down and plunge in, I doubt I'd be strong enough to lift the bike out.

From that discouraging venture I joined Bron at an SAT information session at the community center, which was about as entertaining as it sounds, and then we ate pho and watched *American Sniper* at the Riverview. My objective was simply to stay away from the house while it filled up with Decent Fellows, since their regular rehearsal space wasn't available.

We got home around 9 p.m., and Lyle mentioned that you had dropped by, Kurl. You were on a run, you'd told him, and had found yourself nearby. He said you hung around to listen to a couple of songs but wouldn't even sit down. He said you seemed keyed up: "Twitchy, or spooked or something."

He asked you if you'd be into smoking a bowl, and when you said no thanks, he packed the bong anyhow and smoked a bit himself, just in case you changed your mind, which eventually, he said, you did.

"Did it help?" I asked.

"Of course it helped, Jojo," he said. "It always helps."

My father is something of an evangelist when it comes to this particular drug (which, as I'm sure you've noticed, he and the other Decent Fellows all refer to as *green*). He adores the fact that it's being legalized in a number of states and can't stand how long it's taking in Minnesota.

Of course, by the time you retrieve this letter from Ms. Khang's box, you'll be back at school, meaning you'll have recovered from whatever was, or still is, ailing you—but I have to admit it's unsettling not knowing, as I write this, whether you're okay. Will I hear from you tomorrow, or the next day, or the next? This is one of those occasions when a simple phone call would be infinitely more reassuring.

Yours truly,
Jo

Dear Little Jo,

Just a quick note to say sorry if I had you worried there. I probably shouldn't have gone for that run on Saturday in the first place. I had a sore back and the run made it worse. So much worse that I stayed in bed Sunday and yesterday. It's fine now though.

Sincerely,
AK

Dear Kurl,

Three letters from you in the box this morning! And one of them appears as long as a novella! If the disadvantage to a letter-writing relationship is an occasional period of suspense, then the upside is this joyful abundance when it commences again. I'm taking these missives home to read at my leisure, Kurl. As for yesterday's short note, I'm so sorry to hear that your back was bothering you. Yet another reason to reduce your time hunched over on rooftops, regardless of your uncle's opinions on the matter.

Yours truly,
Jo

Dear Kurl,

Saturday night, schnitzel night! You arrived at our house tonight laden with shopping bags, embarrassed, apologizing for not asking ahead of time, saying you'd planned to cook at home but your uncle Viktor wasn't feeling well, and your mom had decided to go visit your aunt Agata at the nursing home. I asked you whether it'd be okay if there were extra people for dinner. Bron, you probably expected—she is a fairly good bet for dinner on weekends—but Rich, the Decent Fellows' guitarist, and his wife, Trudie, were over tonight, too.

Bron and I helped you unload the groceries and find the right skillet. Rich, Trudie, and Lyle sat in the living room, chanting, "Wienerschnitzel, Wienerschnitzel, Wienerschnitzel," which I can only assume was some jingle from the 1980s. They'd all hit the green pretty hard by that point.

You'd brought some tools from home, including a knife sharpener. You took our biggest knife from the drawer and dragged it through the metal discs. I had just read your letter about how you learned to cook from your brother Mark, so I watched you with new fascination and respect for your skills.

"Technically," you told Bron and me, "it's not called Wiener schnitzel unless it's made with veal and comes from this officially designated area of Germany."

"You mean Austria," Bron said. "*Wien* is Vienna."

"Nope, I mean Germany," you said. You unwrapped a stack of pork chops and peeled the top one off, slapped it onto the cutting board, sliced it horizontally in half, and opened it like a greeting card. "It's a tourist thing in Vienna now, but the dish didn't come from there. They think it was imported from Italy, originally."

"Wait. Did you *research* this meal?" Bron asked.

"He researches everything," I said. "Ask him about salamanders."

Bron loved this. She latched right on to it: "Tell me about salamanders, Kurl. I'm dying to hear about salamanders!"

You'd produced a small, spiked metal hammer from your grocery bag and started pounding the pork chop to make it even thinner. The noise brought Shayna into the kitchen. "It's dead, man, it's already dead," she shouted, and grabbed your forearm and pretended she was trying to wrestle a weapon from your hand. You relinquished the hammer, and she took a turn with it. "Look, I'm beating your meat," she joked.

I was worried I'd embarrassed you with that comment about the salamanders. I hadn't meant to bring up a subject from your letters like that. It completely violates the principle of freely writing about whatever topic you're thinking about, doesn't it, if the recipient of the letter is going to turn around and hold up the topic for social mockery? The whole time the meal was cooking, I was racking my brain for a way to apologize.

And then during dinner, Bron had to go and bring up the subject again. "Kurl, I'm begging you," she said. "Please tell us one fun fact about amphibians."

You didn't seem particularly offended by it, though. You

simply grinned, chewed your mouthful of schnitzel, swallowed, and said, "The word *amphibian* comes from Greek. What it means, or used to mean, is living a double life."

Bron put down her fork and stared at you. "Adam Kurlansky, that is the most profound thing I've heard all day."

You shrugged. "It's just facts."

I know you dislike it when I scrutinize you too much, Kurl. But at the risk of being called a *nosy little bugger* again, can I simply state that you're a good deal more handsome than I suspect you quite realize? You have a broad, Slavic face and a wide, smooth brow. Deep-set eyes. Small ears lying flat to your head. All of these in themselves could be considered neutral-to-positive attributes. There's a pleasing angularity to your cheekbone and jaw that contrasts with the softness of your mouth.

"A generous mouth," they say in novels. However, at school very few people would describe your mouth as "generous," because you keep it in a straight line. Similarly, your brow is locked into a slight crease. Eyelids slightly lowered. Jaw slightly clenched. I've observed these tiny efforts on your part to hold your face still because I've been laboring for months now to decode your expressionless expression, Kurl. It falls midway between I-don't-care and don't-mess-with-me. The moment you become distracted, it all changes, though. When you were cooking your schnitzel, for example—your face was completely different than I've ever seen it at school. And I saw the change again when we sat down to eat and everyone was exclaiming over the food.

"This is incredible, Adam," Trudie said. She held up a forkful of schnitzel to show the layers between the breading. "What all's in it?"

You said lemon peel, sardines, capers, and dill. Half the secret, you told us, was keeping the other dishes (in this case, the salad with sweet vinaigrette, the noodles in cream sauce) gentle in flavor so they don't distract from the schnitzel. We all spent a minute or so quietly savoring the food, which really was amazing.

And your face, Kurl, as we discussed the food! You can't possibly be unaware of how hard we were all working, the whole evening, to see this change come over your face. Not just Shayna and Bron and me—even Lyle makes more jokes when you're around, trots out all his most reliably crowd-pleasing stories for you. We're all bending over backward to get you to crack a smile, because when you smile it feels like the sun coming out.

You will point out, of course, that everyone does this. Everyone wears a different face at school. And you'll point out that the extent to which I have trouble switching faces explains much about how I get treated at school. You'll be right on both counts. But somehow with you the change is more extreme, like two different people. I wonder, Kurl, when you look in the mirror, do you ever get to see the unguarded face? Because I wish you could. It's a wonder to behold.

"Will you come with us to Paisley Park? *Please?*" Bron asked you at the table. Paisley Park After Dark—the thrice-yearly dance party advertised only twenty-four hours before the doors open and only to Prince's most devout acolytes, a.k.a. his Facebook followers.

"Don't come if you have to work early tomorrow," Lyle warned. "It'll be a late night."

"We're taking the day off, sort of," you said. You told us that your uncle had been paid today for a couple of roofs, so he wouldn't be in any shape to work tomorrow.

"It's a done deal, then," Trudie said. "You're coming with us tonight."

I've got to stop writing and get dressed for Paisley Park now. You're downstairs watching TV with Rich, Trudie, and Lyle while Shayna and Bron are choosing what to wear.

I just realized something. When you first arrived at our house and said you weren't cooking at home because your uncle wasn't feeling well, I guess what you must have meant was he wasn't feeling sober. Have I got that right? If so, I'm really glad that tonight you had us to cook for, instead.

Yours truly,
Jo

Dear Little Jo,

You came downstairs last, so you didn't see the reaction the girls got. Bron in bare shoulders and shiny gold overalls and glitter in her curls. Shayna in that little skirt and all that eye makeup. I mean your sister looked like a completely different person. I guess I'm used to seeing her in sweatpants and baggy T-shirts. She comes into the living room and goes, Hey, does anyone here know a guy named Axel?

Dead silence. The adults all shoot each other these tense little glances.

Shayna put her fists on her hips and goes, Oh come on. You all know him, don't you? So who is he?

I mean she's not talking to me of course. I only recognized the guy's name because of that postcard you told me about, the one she showed you and Bron at school that time.

Rich and Trudie are both looking at Lyle. Waiting for him to decide what to say. He's pretty red in the face. He stares down at his jacket clutched in his hands like Shayna is the sun, too bright to look at straight on.

Finally Trudie goes, I don't think your dad really wants to talk about Axel, honey.

And Rich goes, You're freaking us out a little bit, here, Shay—how much you look like your mom in that outfit.

95

Rich! Trudie whispers at him.

Right then you came downstairs, last of everyone. A woolen suit and a bow tie. I asked you what you'd been doing that whole time.

Writing, you said, and you handed me a letter right in front of everybody.

I admit I was embarrassed by it. I shoved the envelope in my pocket pretty fast. How are you going to dance in that costume? I said, and Shayna said, Oh my God, yes, tell him he can't wear that.

So we all spent some time bugging you about it: Jojo, you're overdoing it again. Back in the 1920s or whenever your clothes were sewn, we're pretty sure they didn't have dance clubs. Maybe we should go find a speakeasy or a jazz hall. Et cetera.

We parked in overflow and walked forever in that freezing wind and waited forever in that line. I started having second thoughts. I mean I'm not one for crowds and standing around. Or concerts in general. I never stay up late either. It was only just after 11 p.m. and I was already tired. Shayna had said she heard Prince plays till sunup sometimes. So I'm standing there in the line thinking sunup isn't until eight this time of year. There's no way I'll make it.

I tell you all that I'm not feeling that great, and maybe I'll see if I can catch a train. That's when Bron starts making her speech. I don't understand how she does it. It's like a superpower. She starts off only talking to us, our little group. Then she realizes other people are listening, so she turns and raises her voice and makes the whole crowd her audience.

This is our chocolate factory right here, she says. We've each got a golden ticket in our pocket. This here is our Disneyland. Our Neverland, our Nirvana. We are the chosen ones. Prince is our religion, and Paisley Park is our Mecca. And if Prince is our religion and Paisley Park is our Mecca, then this right here is our pilgrimage, people! Tonight we are lowly pilgrims!

We are the young of this earth, she's saying. This, right here, is our revolution! I mean it's not even making sense after a while. But even the security guys at the door are grinning and nodding along to what she's saying: This is our time, and this is our music, and we gonna dance, muthafuckas!

Don't go, you said, but I was already staying. I mean who could go after a speech like that? And it was as if Prince heard Bron's speech too. Maybe he did. It's possible, if there are as many cameras in that place as Rich said. Anyway the doors finally opened and the line went fast.

What Prince did is he thought up a magical place and wrote a song about it. Before you and the girls came downstairs Lyle played us the song called "Paisley Park." When Prince was rich and famous enough he built the song into an actual place. I guess Elvis did that first with Graceland, but I don't know if he hosted dance parties there.

Now that I'm thinking about it, Prince sort of reminds me of you, Jo. I don't know. Obviously it's not the stilettos and spandex or his little wire glasses. But there's something. How he created himself maybe. How he invented a world to live inside.

There was this one moment toward the end (which luckily was 4 a.m., not 8 a.m.) when he was doing one of those endless guitar solos. Just tearing it up all across the front of the platform. I mean you could tell he had completely lost track of his band and even what song he was playing.

We were standing right in front of him, and Bron was screaming how much she loved him. Shayna yanked my arm out of its socket, saying, Oh my God, look at him, just look at him. Prince went down on one knee in front of us like he was telling us a story with his guitar.

Watching him it suddenly hit me how rare and amazing it was to be able to see something being made out of nothing. Up close like that. It reminded me how it felt watching you sing when you didn't know I was in the room. Halfway between dirty and holy. I don't know. But I suddenly found myself smiling like an idiot and looking all around the room and thinking, Anything, *anything* is possible in this life. This moment is everything. Right now.

I mean you must have felt it too, because when I looked over at you there were tears on your face.

So I guess I get it now. I get why the Decent Fellows and the girls and you and everyone else at Paisley Park believes this man is a god. It's because when he's onstage Prince believes he is a god. He *is* a god onstage, maybe. I mean I'm willing to say that.

sincerely,
AK

Dear Kurl,

You're right that watching Prince up close like that, with that degree of intimacy and intensity, is an experience only the tiniest percentage of his fans will ever get to share. Now that a few days have passed, I can appreciate that it was a memorable experience. I have to admit, though, that I found the whole night somewhat deflating.

I felt more and more self-conscious as the event wore on. When Prince slow-danced with one of his singers onstage—Shayna and Bron would know her name, the taller one—the lights came way down, and he told us, "Look away. Ain't nothing to see up here." And there we were in the dark for two or three minutes, with nothing to see and nothing to hold on to. You and the girls and Lyle had drifted away from me, so I just stood there feeling too small for the room.

Finally the lights came up a little, and Prince announced, "This here's your prom, children. Couple up now, couple up."

I don't think you noticed, because you were speaking to Bron and the others, but someone had been chatting with me in the line outside. He came over and asked me to dance. Rogan, his name was.

God save us, I thought, it really is like the prom. Except that

Rogan was older than high school, more like in his midtwenties. Too old for me, technically. But I said yes anyway.

While we slow-danced Rogan complimented the suit that the rest of you had thought so ridiculous for Paisley Park. He said my clothes reminded him of *Under the Cherry Moon*, so we talked about that movie, how we both thought Prince was expressing a great deal of sorrow on that whole album despite the bubbly, retro vibe. Rogan said, "I'm utterly enamored of this place."

I told him I wasn't sure I'd ever heard anyone use the word *enamored* out loud, in a sentence, before. He asked if that worked in his favor or against him, and I said, "In. Definitely in."

So I was dancing with Rogan, and I was finally starting to feel a little happier—a little less bored and irritable, at least, flattered that someone in the room was interested enough in my existence to seek me out, to find a reason to touch me and talk to me—when I caught sight of you, Kurl.

You'd paired up with Shayna, and over her shoulder from eight, maybe ten, feet away you were staring directly at me and Rogan. I can hardly recollect your expression without shuddering, let alone try to describe it in writing. Your face was perfectly smooth and neutral as usual, but tensed, taut, as though it took everything in your power to keep it that way. There was something around your eyes, something locked down and pissed off and shadowy.

I half expected to see your fists clenched for attack, but your hands were resting open and relaxed on Shayna's hips. When you noticed I was staring back at you, you dropped your gaze immediately, and the next time I looked over, Shayna was talking in your ear and you'd lowered your forehead to her shoulder to hear what she was saying.

Kurl, if you will recall, I informed you that I was gay in one of my earliest letters to you. You know that I have never tried to hide who I am. If you have a problem with my sexuality, I need you to be honest with me and admit it. Because if seeing me on a dance floor in a man's arms is enough to generate that intensity of disgust and hatred in you, and you aren't willing to deal with it openly and directly, then I'm afraid you and I are going to have a longer-term, larger-scale problem on our hands. There's no point in you denying it, either. As I've mentioned before, I've become somewhat of a self-taught expert at reading your face.

I am fighting an impulse here to tell you about my sexual history. I feel the need to make excuses, to exonerate myself, to impress upon you the fact of my relative innocence. In terms of physical experience, I've had very little: a couple of dare-based, fumbling grope sessions and one *affaire du coeur* at music camp that dragged itself out halfway through the summer. Painfully heavy on the overwrought text messages, painfully light on the actual physical contact. In fact, that middle-school melodrama is the reason I no longer carry a cell phone.

It makes me furious at myself to divulge any of this to you, Kurl. I know it's my own sense of shame and humiliation prompting me to do it. Probably it's my internalized homophobia as well. But how else am I supposed to feel? What else am I supposed to say? How else am I supposed to defend myself against being regarded as if I were something stuck to the bottom of your shoe?

Yours truly,
Jo

Dear Little Jo,

This is my third letter. I tore the other two up because it took me a while to calm down. I really regretted that one letter I sent you early on when I was angry, that one when I called you a *nosy little bugger*. I wrote you another letter right away to try to make up for it, remember? And you never forgot the insult either. You mentioned it just two letters ago: *At the risk of being called a nosy little bugger again*, you said.

At least now I know why you wouldn't talk to me at school these last two days. Not that we talk much anyway. It's more like Bron and Shayna talking and us standing around with them getting the occasional comment in. But these last two days at school you barely even looked at me. I was wondering what was going on.

Let's get one thing straight though. You are not a mind reader. You don't know anything about what I was thinking on that dance floor at Paisley Park. I mean I apologize if I looked at you strangely for a second. Or whatever the expression on my face was.

But it was not because I have *a problem with your sexuality*. Your words. If I had a problem with your sexuality don't you think it would have come up by now? You make it sound like I've been hiding these terrible gay-bashing thoughts and you caught them right there on my face. You are not a mind reader. You don't know what's in other people's heads. You have no reason to jump to conclusions like that. No right, in fact.

You and Lyle both. It's ironic really, because I figure Lyle jumped to conclusions right about the exact moment in time that you did.

Did you even notice how Lyle sort of cornered me after I danced with Shayna? He takes me by the arm and goes, Just because my daughter is dressed like that doesn't mean she wants that kind of attention from you, Adam.

I tell him I don't know what he's talking about. So then he starts going on and on about how teenaged girls will test out their sex appeal on boys by dressing up, sometimes, and it makes them vulnerable to sexual attention they're not ready for.

And the whole time he's lecturing me he's looking me up and down with this look on his face I've never seen before. I can't even describe it.

How about I take your approach, Jo, and tell you how it made me feel. It made me feel like Lyle Hopkirk was looking straight past my face into some secret place in my head that even I didn't know existed. Someplace ugly.

I don't even know what I said in answer. I shoved my hands into my pockets and mumbled something like, Yeah, no, of course, I would never.

But the thing about Lyle is that he's no mind reader either. He had no idea what was in my head while I was dancing with

Shayna. So how about both of you stop acting like you have everybody figured out, because you don't.

sincerely,
AK

PS: I only asked your sister to dance because that college guy asked you. I mean it seemed like the thing to do. He was already touching your hair and fixing your bow tie for you when I asked Shayna. You were already laughing. I mean let's at least get the facts straight.

Dear Kurl,

A confession: I am fairly certain it's my fault that Lyle chided you for dancing with Shayna. He wasn't attempting to read *your* mind so much as acting on notions I'd recently put into *his* mind. I owe you a double apology, Kurl, both for accusing you of homophobia and for inadvertently setting you up for trouble with my father.

It was when Bron and Shayna and I were upstairs getting ready for Paisley Park, after the schnitzel dinner and just before I sat down to write you that letter. You were downstairs with the others, and I was lolling on Shayna's bed while they tried on clothes. I was trying to figure out how much Shayna likes you, telling her I thought she should go for it, teasing her about how obvious it was to everyone that you two are crushing on each other.

It was incredibly immature of me, I'm aware. Classic annoying little brother behavior.

"He's not my type. He barely talks," Shayna said, and I jeered at that, because isn't that the classic defense a girl will offer when she's so extremely attracted to a boy that it's disconcerting to her? *I adore him as a person, but he's not my type.*

"He reads a lot, you know," I said. "And he's an excellent writer."

"Like I said, not my type," she said.

"He really likes you, Shayna. I'm just saying you should give him a chance."

"Who likes Shayna?" Lyle was suddenly standing in the bedroom doorway.

"Adam Kurlansky," I said.

"To be clear," Bron said, "we're working with little evidence and lots of speculation, here."

"Is that why you're dressed like that?" Lyle asked Shayna.

"Like what?"

"Inappropriately," Lyle said, gesturing to her short skirt. "I want you to change before we leave."

"Uh, I don't think so," Shayna retorted. "And anyway Jojo's just *jealous*. It's pathetic. You're *pathetic*, Jonathan Hopkirk!" And she shoved past Lyle, stomped down the hall, and slammed the bathroom door.

And so I was exiled to my room, where I had plenty of time to contemplate the events of the evening and write them up for you. And, well, you witnessed firsthand how ineffectual my father's effort to censor Shayna's wardrobe choices proved to be. She's never put any effort into her clothes or makeup before this, so Lyle may simply be trying to come to terms with the transformation.

Another confession (be real and be true, Jonathan, be real and be true): My sister was correct about me. I am jealous. I'm envious of the easy options all the rest of you enjoy. To date someone or not to date someone? Does she like him? Does he like her? You can try out whatever you like and change your minds at any time. Everyone is available to everyone else. Me? I might be permitted to admire someone from afar, to harbor a yearning in secret, but to act on it would cost me everything.

Anyhow. I am truly sorry, Kurl, for the mess I created for you at Paisley Park.

Yours truly,
Jo

Dear Little Jo,

There's no school tomorrow so you probably won't pick up this letter until Monday. Remember that PSA I had to write on what to do in an explosion? I mean it's not only the Taliban. Look at that marathon that got bombed. In an explosion what you do is get under a table or desk until things stop falling. If you can't get out from the rubble you wait. Use a flashlight or whistle to signal for help. Or tap on a pipe. You have to avoid shouting as it will dehydrate you and make you inhale dust. You breathe through your shirt. You avoid windows, mirrors, glass-fronted cabinets, elevators, electrical outlets, gas lines, kitchens.

Sylvan told me that Mark said suicide bombers were something you had to not take personally in Afghanistan.

I asked Sylvan, How is that even possible?

He said that according to Mark it's easier over there because you don't have to make any choices. All the choices are made for you. Back home is harder.

I asked Sylvan if that's what Mark had said. Back home is harder. Were those his exact words?

Sylvan said maybe it's time I asked Mark some of these questions myself.

I mean you might be following the procedure exactly. You might be hiding under the right furniture and signaling with your flashlight and not be taking the bomb personally at all. But there's a specific thing that happens to your internal organs when you're exposed to a bomb. The tissues of your organs vibrate and spray cells in every direction, like dust from a beaten rug. *Like dust from a beaten rug.* I remember reading that exact phrase. All the inmost personal parts of your body rattled and bruised.

sincerely,
AK

Dear Kurl,

You probably don't remember much. In fact, it's possible you don't remember anything at all.

I couldn't quite believe you had been driving in that condition. I consider it a miracle that you made it safely all the way to our house and managed to park, albeit more on the lawn than the driveway, before passing out. Maybe you passed out long before arriving, and the car drove itself to our house; as far as I'm concerned that would hardly have been more miraculous.

Some years we stay home on Halloween and hand out candy, but this time Shayna and Lyle and Cody Walsh and I had spent the evening at the Fright Night Movie Marathon at the rep cinema. I'd endured *The Shining* and *The Blair Witch Project* with them but had begged off *Saw*, the late-late show, and Cody drove me home. When it comes to horror movies, my father and sister are insatiable and omnivorous. I can't keep up, even physically: My eyes start to sting, staring at the screen for that long.

So it was me who found you in our driveway with your forehead resting on the steering wheel. Headlights on, driver's-side door ajar, radio set to AM and reporting the weather, the whole car reeking like a distillery.

I said your name and jostled you a bit. Your head rolled along the wheel, but you couldn't even straighten up.

And then you said, "I have to go."

"What?" I said.

"This is my mom's car," you said, slurring. "She leaves for work at five. I have to go." And you turned the key and started the engine.

I stayed wedged in the open car door. "You're drunk, Kurl. No way you're driving like this."

You lifted your head and looked at me. "Hi, Jo," you said. One of your eyes was swollen shut, the bruising spread all the way to your cheekbone. Your lip was split, oozing.

"What happened?" I asked. "Did you get in a fight?"

"Of course I got in a fight." You smiled at me, which only brought fresh blood to your lip.

"Come inside," I said. "Let's get some ice. I'll call Lyle."

But hearing my father's name must have spooked you, because you straightened up and put the car in reverse.

"Wait! Kurl, wait." I didn't know what to do. The car was rolling. I'd already been forced to take a couple of quick steps sideways so the door wouldn't sweep me off my feet. "Stop the car and move over. I'll drive," I said.

Immediately you slid into the passenger seat and curled up with your cheek against the headrest, as though me taking the wheel was what you'd been planning all along.

"Put your seat belt on."

You groped around for the buckle, all obedience.

As you must be aware, I am several months away from being eligible to apply for my regular driver's license. I'm fairly sure my learner's permit doesn't allow me to drive with a heavily inebriated eighteen-year-old for a copilot, either. Luckily, Lyle has made a point of putting me behind the wheel for practice whenever we have occasion to take the car outside Minneapolis, so I'm already a decent driver, even at night. Also luckily, I had recently studied the map, curious about the location of your Outer Sanctum, so when you mumbled your address I knew approximately how to find your street.

You were so quiet that I suspected you'd passed out again; I wasn't sure, because I was utterly absorbed in the task of not committing any traffic infractions. I turned onto your street, but I was worried that someone might look out your front window, so I parked the car at the curb a few houses down from your address.

Your face was turned away, to the window, and you didn't respond when I said your name, so I got out and walked around to your side of the car and opened the passenger door. I was relieved to find you bleary but conscious, at least, awake and looking up and blinking at me with your one good eye. Your face was like meat.

"Maybe I should have driven you directly to the hospital," I said.

"Come here, Jo," you said.

You were asking for assistance, I thought, so I leaned in and unbuckled your seat belt for you. You grabbed my arm and swung one foot to the ground, and I braced to take your weight.

Instead of trying to stand up, though, you took my wrist and waggled my hand back and forth. "Hi," you said, as though we'd just now happened to run into each other, and I was waving at you.

"Hi." I laughed despite my worry.

You lifted my wrist with your fingers around it like a bracelet. "Fine-boned," you commented.

Kurl, there are all kinds of reasons for you to have done what you did next. You were still deeply in shock from the fight, from your injuries. Or it was simple curiosity. Or you thought I was someone else. You thought I was Shayna, maybe—you'd driven half-unconscious to her house, after all.

You moved your hand to my waist, to my belt, and gave the end of it a little tug.

Then you brought your other hand up and undid the buckle.

"Hey." I straightened up, but you held on.

"Dear little Jo," you said. Your voice was low and soft, and you frowned at my zipper in great concentration. Suddenly you seemed less drunk.

All that scrutiny, not to mention your hands so close, had the predictable effect. More than the predictable effect: I felt like I'd been plugged into a socket. Trying to hide it was futile, and anyhow you were splayed halfway out of your seat, and you weren't trying to hide anything, either.

You undid me. I gasped at your touch, and I think I must have swayed or lurched, because you brought your thigh in hard against mine to steady me.

The truth, the whole truth, Kurl: After the first five seconds I didn't much care why you were doing it. Your hands were callused. It didn't hurt, exactly, but there was a kind of rough pressure that seemed somehow to spread from your hands and build up everywhere under my skin, as though my whole body was scraping against itself from the inside like sandpaper. My breath came fast and I felt scratchiness in my throat, too, as though words were lodged there and would either choke me or come pouring out into the street. I was pinned between pain and the perfect, stunning opposite of pain. I held on to your shoulder with one hand and your head with the other, and I could feel my own pulse in my fingertips as though I was transferring my hectic heartbeat directly into your ear, your hair, your spine.

I heard a high, whiny little moan and realized it was me. I didn't recognize the sound, didn't recognize my own voice. For a second I thought to myself, about myself, Who *is* this? Who could this person possibly be? and at the discovery of this entirely new person, I could feel myself smiling, utterly delighted, right in the middle of everything.

You weren't looking at me, Kurl. I hadn't noticed it until that exact moment—in my defense I was somewhat distracted. I guess I assumed you were focused on what your hands were doing, and you were, of course. But you were also avoiding my eyes, a fact that became clearer to me when you glanced up and caught me smiling, and in response you raised one hand up, to my face, and pressed it gently over my eyes.

"Don't watch this," you said. "Don't look at me."

I pulled away from you. I turned aside and—clumsy, trying to go fast—zipped my fly and buckled my belt and tucked in my shirt. My hands felt like somebody else's hands.

You reached out and jammed your finger through one of my belt loops, catching me and twisting me back around to face you. "Wait, wait," you were saying, attempting to hold me there and free your other foot to get out of the car. "Jo, Jo, wait a sec, hang on."

But I was shivering, going numb. The whole time, Kurl—for those two or three minutes, or however long it was, not long—I had been so wholly *right there*, suspended there between your two hands like a creature hardly human. I have never been so present in and aware of my own body as in those few minutes. I was right there—but you didn't want me there. You wanted to do

114

what you were doing in private, without me there to witness you. Or perhaps you wanted neither of us to be there. You wanted it not to be happening at all.

Either way, by that point I was entirely in agreement with you. I was so ashamed of myself! I wrenched my hips away, and you yelped—I'm afraid I may have sprained your finger trapped in my belt loop. If you found it damaged this morning, then I apologize, and you should be aware that that one injury wasn't a result of your earlier fight. I left you in the passenger seat and I sprinted off down your street, kept jogging back the way I'd driven until I got to the plaza at the corner, where I flagged a taxi.

It's possible you don't remember anything. Trust me, I have considered the possibility that the wiser course of action would be for me to say nothing. But I reminded myself I began this correspondence with you on the principle of honesty.

You undid me. That's all I'm trying to report in this letter. You undid me, Kurl, in more ways than one.

Yours truly,
Jo

Dear Kurl,

I know better than to read anything into an expression on your face, after Paisley Park. But your utter refusal to look at me at all, when we passed each other in the hall this morning—the lightning-fast cutting away of your glance and the hastening of your step, your face with your eye a little less swollen but a darker purple now, that nasty scab on your lip—was worse than any so-called withering look you could have shot me. I couldn't breathe. My ribs shrank into my lungs. Tears came, of course, and I had to scurry to Math and hide my face in my textbook until I regained my composure.

Consent. I've been thinking all day about the rules of consent, about how a person can't give consent to anything sexual if they are incapacitated by alcohol or drugs. Where does Saturday night fall on the consent spectrum for you, Kurl?

At lunch I found Bron and Shayna in their usual dining spot by the kiln in the art room. Neither of them is even taking an art class this year, but they like the vibe, and apparently Rhoda—they use Ms. Deane's first name, Rhoda—doesn't mind if they hang out in her room. You should check it out sometime, Kurl. With all those windows, it's one of the brightest rooms in the school.

Anyhow. Bron was eating rice-and-broccoli salad from a

Tupperware container, and Shayna was eating a bag of potato chips and poking her thumb into a lump of clay on the art table.

I dragged a third stool from the neighboring table, sat down, and took my sandwich out of my backpack. "If a girl is drunk," I said, "and she initiates sex with a sober boy, what should the boy do?"

Bron swallowed her mouthful. "What happened?"

I had to apologize for the overdramatic opener. "I mean a straight boy," I said. "This is a hypothetical scenario."

Bron and Shayna exchanged a look, and then Bron frowned and put down her fork. "If the boy is Kurl, tell him it's disgusting."

"It's not Kurl!" I said.

"He's not even technically a boy anymore; he's eighteen," Bron said. "Tell him he should be setting an example."

"It's not Kurl." My face was red, I knew. "Why would you assume it's Kurl?"

"Because you don't know any other boys," Shayna said.

"I do so," I lied, and then realized the lie was unconvincing and tried another one: "I overheard people talking in Math class, all right?"

"It's a gray area, legally speaking, if she initiates and she's clearly saying 'yes, yes, yes' the whole time," Bron said. "But think about it. Would you want to have sex with someone who probably won't remember it? Who can probably barely feel it, even?"

"Anyone who'd want that, you'd have to seriously question his motives," Shayna said.

"Would you rather go over to a friend's house and hang out and have a great time together," Bron said, "or go break into his house when he's not home and hang out there all by yourself?"

"Or go break in when he's sleeping"—a giggle bubbled

117

under Shayna's voice—"and, like, prop him up on the sofa, so you can pretend you're hanging out."

"Okay, I get it," I said.

"And the next day you say to him, 'Wasn't that awesome?'" Bron said.

"And your friend is like, 'What are you even talking about?'" Shayna said.

I snapped the lid on my sandwich container and put it back in my bag.

"Where are you going?" Bron said.

"Come on, Jojo, don't be like that," Shayna said.

"It's okay. I just remembered I'm supposed to talk to Ms. Khang." More lies, but they hadn't offered me the reassurance I'd been seeking. On the contrary, I felt guiltier than ever. It was you I needed to talk to, Kurl, but I looked for you everywhere and didn't find you. I think you must have left school at noon and not come back.

Yours truly,
Jo

Dear Kurl,

In English this afternoon, for the first time since the start of term except when you hurt your back that time, there was no letter waiting for me from you. I hadn't realized you'd never missed a single letter before this, until Ms. Khang crouched beside my desk and asked me if I thought you were okay.

"Adam seemed pretty tuned out in class this morning," she said. "Stared out the window and just shook his head when I tried to speak to him. Given the bruising on his face, I was worried."

Oh, Kurl, if this is a case of me having written too much, then I gladly, enthusiastically, wholeheartedly take it back. Burn my letter about the other night. Let's agree that I never wrote it. Let's agree that I never told you anything, that you don't remember anything, that there *isn't* anything. Honestly, you know me well enough by now to know how I can exaggerate. You know I can make drama from dryer lint.

Just, please, write me back. Write anything, I don't mind— write fake letters, write grocery lists, write *Blah blah blah*, over and over, to fill the page. Write *Little Jerkoff Little Jerkoff Little Jerkoff.*

Just, please, don't fail English class on my account. I couldn't handle being responsible for that.

Yours truly,
Jo

119

Thursday, November 5

Dear Little Jo,

Your bike is parked at the racks on the north side of the school. I taped the key for the new lock under the seat for you. I meant to do this a while ago but it took me forever to figure out where Cherry Valley actually is. Do you know it isn't officially called Cherry Valley at all? Officially it's just a part of the Mississippi River Gorge. They only call it Cherry Valley because girls supposedly lose their virginity if they go there. Am I the only person who doesn't get these jokes? I mean I don't think I am. I think everybody just calls it Cherry Valley without realizing it isn't the real name.

Sylvan was the one who told me, in the end. He thought it was hilarious when I borrowed his phone to look up Cherry Valley on the map and couldn't find it.

This is just a quick note. I wanted to get Nelly back to you ages ago but I'm doing it now at least.

Sincerely,
AK

Dear Kurl,

Thank you, thank you, thank you! Kurl, I can only imagine what it must have taken to recover my bike from that horrible cesspit of a creek. What I like most about having Nelly back: These mornings that aren't quite frosty but smell like frost, when I put on my woolen gloves with the extra mitten-flap to pull over the fingertips and my faded red silk paisley scarf with the fringe that flaps behind me like a flag when I coast downhill. If I time it correctly, for part of my ride I can join the fleet of commuters heading downtown to work—those dedicated cyclists who don't quit merely because the temperature has begun to plummet. I love the briefcases strapped to the racks, the saddlebags with umbrellas sticking out. I love those little ankle clips holding the trouser cuffs safe from the chain. The chorus of bells, the arm signals, the "on your left," the censorious glares at cars that cut too close on right turns.

Cycling is one of those experiences that, for me, points to life beyond high school. I may have to park Nelly a few blocks away and walk onto school property, so as not to lure the bike bashers back for a repeat performance, but at least I am regularly reminded again that freedom is waiting, less than three short years away.

That's all I'm going to write for today. I've decided I need to impose austerity measures upon myself so as not to drive you away entirely. It wouldn't be fair to Bron and Shayna, for one thing. They've grown almost as fond of you as I have, Kurl.

Yours truly,
Jo

Dear Kurl,

No letter from you again today. Shayna and Bron have been asking after you all week—whom did you fight with this time, why are you so grumpy to them in Math class, when are you coming over to cook for us again—and I confess, I snapped at them the last time they asked. "As if I'd know," I said. "It has never been me Kurl talks to."

Which, sadly, is the truth. I've been reading back over some of your letters and realizing how little you've actually shared, how careful you've always been to keep yourself to yourself.

I suspect this is the way you conduct yourself on all fronts, Kurl. Take football, for instance, the way you quit the team so abruptly. By keeping utterly silent about your reasons, you made certain that if you wanted to slip away, nobody could reel you back, because there was nothing to grab onto.

But in any case I wouldn't want to "reel you back"! Even though writing letters to me evolved beyond the minimum requirements for Ms. Khang's class, I'd never want you to keep writing them purely out of a sense of obligation. That would be awful. That would be worse than this silence.

Yours truly,
Jo

Dear Kurl,

Ms. Khang now has me writing letters to Abigail Cuttler. Do you know Abigail Cuttler? I am not allowed to call her Abby, for starters. *I've always gone by Abigail, and frankly, I prefer it,* she explained in her first letter to me. Abigail's original pen pal, Emily Visser, disappeared after her mother was transferred to Germany three weeks ago.

All of this to say that I'm writing to you today on my own time, and I'm doing it in my own defense: I don't believe it's quite fair of you to be angry with me for having my backpack ripped off my shoulder by the butcherboys in the hall this afternoon. In fact, it seems to me you were engaged in a bit of victim blaming.

If I made any mistake at all, it was failing to see them approach. Between classes I'm usually as alert as any prey animal, head swiveling to scan the perimeter, ears twitching for predatory footfalls.

This time, alas, they managed to sneak up on me. I hardly had time to register anything but the pain of my arm being wrenched by the strap before you were there, snatching the bag back from Dowell and shoving it hard into my arms.

"I'm sorry," I said.

"Don't apologize," you said. "Jesus! What's the matter with you?"

"Right. Sorry," I said. Honestly, I didn't mean to be so dense. I was still rubbing my sore arm, still not quite caught up on what was happening.

"It's like you do it on purpose," you said, and turned and stalked off.

Kurl, I know you weren't angry with me specifically for having my backpack snatched. You were angry at having to rescue me from the butcherboys again. I understand how frustrating it must be to feel obliged to step in, especially when you've decided to distance yourself from me in general. And I don't want you to think I'm not grateful for the help today, and for your rescue of Nelly, too, from Cherry Valley.

Do I do it on purpose, though? Do *what*, on purpose, exactly? You're not going to write me back in answer to this question, so I'll have to speculate on my own:

Drawing fire is how you described it once, in reference to my wardrobe. Remember that? You'd noticed that the outfits I put together with Mr. Ragman's help are basically Walt Whitman costumes. You called me a *walking target*. And yes, you're absolutely correct that these clothes draw fire from the butcherboys and contribute to a general impression of my eccentricity or cluelessness from which I undeniably suffer the consequences at school.

But "doing it on purpose"—if indeed I can map this accusation at least partially onto my wardrobe—isn't merely about dressing like my poetic role model. Even more than that, it's about continually reminding myself how short the present moment is, what a temporary torment I'm suffering at the hands of the butcherboys. These clothes of mine have lived longer than any of us, after all. The blazer you noticed in one of your letters is called Loaghtan tweed from the Isle of Man. It probably came to the US packed in some mill baron's trunk on a steamer in the 1910s.

I do it on purpose, because I want to be mindful of the decades and centuries behind us of people making beautiful things designed to last. I want to walk down the hallways of Lincoln High with one part of me in the eternal, the timeless, and the other part of me slipping so fast through the here and now that nobody can pin me down, not even the butcherboys.

Yours truly,
Jo

Dear Little Jo,

Speaking of Walt Whitman. It's pretty ironic that Khang assigns me an alternate writing exercise instead of the letters I'm not writing, and what it ends up being is a Walt Whitman essay. I mean she assigned a poem of my choice but I ended up writing about "Song of Myself."

I wasn't even planning on writing the assignment at all. I've been working every day after school. We're up there for a couple hours after dark every night trying to cram in extra roofs before it gets too cold. But then I came home the other night and just sat down and wrote the essay anyhow, all in one go.

So today Khang asks to speak to me after class. I'm thinking, Now what? Because she's spoken to me a few times after class already: about my black eye and about not writing you letters and about the alternative assignment.

It turns out Khang is all worked up about this essay I wrote. She's whispering almost. Standing on tiptoe to get closer to my ear, like it's a secret and she's worried people outside in the hall might overhear us.

Adam, I'm in complete shock, she says. She tells me my essay is insightful and elegantly worded. She says she hadn't had the slightest idea that there was an intellectual and an artist hiding under all that brawn. I mean I'm quoting Khang's words here.

All that brawn. She wants to know where I got such a mature and nuanced appreciation for Whitman's poetics.

I'm backed pretty much right up against the blackboard at this point. It's like Khang is somebody's poodle sniffing at my crotch and I'm trying to be polite about it, saying, Wow, ha, that's a friendly dog you got there, but what I really want to do is kick it in the ribs. I mean this woman really doesn't grasp the concept of personal space.

Finally Khang stops talking altogether and just looks at me. And it dawns on me that she's waiting for me to say something. She really does want to know where I got all that crap about Walt. So I start worrying that what Khang really thinks is that I stole that essay or paid someone to write it for me. Specifically you, Jo. I mean I'm sure in English class you never shut up about your buddy Walt and his metaphors for the American nation-building spirit et cetera. Khang probably figures that I've been exploiting our letter-writing relationship. Forcing you at knifepoint to do my essays for me or something.

I don't think she really thought this. Looking back on it now, I'm aware I was just being paranoid. But at the time I was standing there sort of panicking with guilt and shame about it. Trying to think of some sort of excuse.

Finally my mouth opens and what comes out is, I guess I'm kind of a Walt Whitman fan. Yes, I said that. Kind of a Walt Whitman fan. I said it out loud, to a teacher.

I didn't even stop there though. I told her about Mark going to Afghanistan and about how I found out that Walt worked in that Civil War hospital.

Khang said yes, she could sense I had a deep personal connection with the material. Her words: *a deep personal connection.*

Then suddenly she changes the subject. She starts talking about how she wants to nominate me for this special college program she knows about, up in Duluth. A teacher nominates a student, Khang says, and if you get admitted they'll pay for the whole thing. And they consider things besides your grades and SAT scores.

What things, I ask her.

The whole picture, Adam, she says. They do a holistic assessment of your potential. They're interested in students like you, who might otherwise slip through the cracks. Students who would be the first member of their families to attend college.

Bridge to Education is the name of the program. It's at the University of Minnesota up there in Duluth. Khang says she'll print off the information packet for me for next class.

Now that I'm thinking it over, it was stupid. Writing that essay about Walt's poem was a stupid thing to do. I mean it was a total fluke. I only did it because I couldn't think of anything else to write. And I only did a good job on it because of all the things I've heard you say about Walt. Now Khang is expecting something I'll never be able to deliver.

This program is all the way up in Duluth. And college in general—I can already hear my uncle Viktor laughing at that one. I can hear everyone laughing actually.

Sincerely,
AK

Dear Kurl,

I, for one, am not laughing. I, for one, am delighted that Ms. Khang has finally recognized what was obvious to me from your very first letters: You're a talented writer, Kurl. I suspect the compliment doesn't mean very much coming from a wannabe poet like me, and piggybacking on a teacher's praise, no less.

But take, for example, the vivid detail with which you portrayed your after-class conversation with Ms. Khang. The comparison to a poodle sniffing at your crotch made me laugh aloud. Poor Ms. Khang! She hasn't read your letters, Kurl, so it must have come out of nowhere for her. She must have been utterly gobsmacked to read your essay. She must have wondered if she was hallucinating it, if she was dreaming it. No wonder she couldn't contain herself.

You're wrong about one thing, though: Ms. Khang doesn't know the first thing about *my* literary tastes and aptitudes. Kurl, you must have noticed by now that in person, I am not particularly verbally inclined. To date I have never once opened my mouth in English class except to say "here" when she was handing out our first batch of letters from your class and wanted to know who Jonathan Hopkirk was. I don't speak in any of my classes, in fact. I fear that my letters have given you a wildly inaccurate picture of my student persona.

All of which makes me realize once more that your letters

have given me a warped portrait of you, too, Kurl. A person can never really know another person, I suppose. Not all the way through.

Yours truly,
Jo

PS: Before you break off your correspondence with me again, would you please do me one favor? Would you tell me which part of Whitman's poem you wrote about, and what you said about it?

Dear Little Jo,

I wrote about grass actually. Probably the most straightforward part in Walt's whole *Leaves of Grass* book is where he talks about the actual grass. Except the more I read it the less straightforward it seemed to me.

I mean he starts it off simply enough, describing how a child grabs a handful of grass and asks him, *What is the grass?* And Walt gives a bunch of possible answers. Just sort of trying them out.

At one point he goes, *I guess it must be the flag of my disposition, out of hopeful green stuff woven.* What he means is it's a symbol of his personality.

I didn't put this in my essay but if grass is the flag of anyone's disposition it would be yours, Jo. Not a tidy mowed lawn either. I think Walt is picturing that kind of long grass on the riverbanks. When the wind comes along it churns and sways so that it looks like another river running alongside the real one.

What I wrote in the essay was about grass growing from the mouths of corpses. *The beautiful uncut hair of graves*, Walt calls it. This is the part of the poem that got me thinking about Mark in Afghanistan. When you take the train up to the mall, you pass the VA hospital and on the other side is the military cemetery.

Watch the cemetery when the train goes past and you notice two things: One, it goes on forever. All those matching white crosses. All those dead. I mean Mark must ride that train and think, How did I ever not die over there? Why all of them and not me? Two, the rows of crosses with their grass aisles between sort of sweep past your eyes when the train passes. They look like the spokes of a giant wheel laid on its side and turning fast. Thousands of bodies under the grass and turning back into grass.

Walt Whitman worked in a veterans' hospital and he saw all kinds of death. But somehow in this poem he looks at the cemetery grass and sees it as a good thing, a good sign. *The smallest sprout shows there is really no death*, he says. I mean he's more or less talking about the circle of life. But I pointed out how hopeful Walt is about death. He goes, *To die is different from what anyone supposed, and luckier.*

For him to say things like that when war was all around him, and people were blinded or shell-shocked or their legs were blown off. I don't know. In my essay I wrote that Walt's kind of positive attitude seems ridiculous and dangerous. But it also seems like a revolution. I mean living with that kind of hope? That would change everything.

sincerely,
AK

Dear Kurl,

After school today Bron pulled up to the bike racks in her parents'
Escalade. She doesn't drive it to school very often, as it draws a lot
of unsolicited attention, so I knew there must be a special plan.

"Put Nelly in the back," she ordered me.

And then the car's back door swung open, and you stepped out.

"Oh, hi, Kurl," I said. I felt everything at once: surprise,
relief, embarrassment, joy.

"Hi." You lifted Nelly into the back as though she was made
of drinking straws, and you rolled your eyes when you saw that
tears had sprung to my eyes.

"It's not crying," I said.

"Sure," you said. But you smiled.

"It's Sagittarius season," Shayna announced when we'd
climbed into the back seat. "We're going to show Kurl Detritus.
Can you believe he's never been there? He's going to nerd out so
hard over all the old kitchen crap they have."

Sagittarius season means Bron has to buy birthday gifts for
most of the Otulah-Tierney clan. Her mother, her grandmother,
her sister Zorah, and her twin brothers, Izzy (Isaiah) and Ezra,
all have birthdays in December.

Lyle's birthday is December 5, and then there's Christmas

134

just around the corner, so for the last couple of years Shayna and I have teamed up with Bron and tackled all of our collective shopping at once.

We stopped in at Basement Records but didn't stay long, as none of the Otulah-Tierneys except Bron has a turntable, and Lyle already has every record in existence. Then it was onward to Detritus, which opened a few years ago on a street with nothing but a nail salon, a Mexican grocer, and a bunch of empty storefronts. Nobody thought it would survive, let alone become such a draw that a whole series of similar vintage stores would pop up in the same few blocks.

I watched for your reaction, Kurl, as we entered the store. I wanted to see Detritus through your eyes. You stood still as the girls fanned out, Shayna disappearing behind a row of library ladders tethered to a heating duct, Bron exploring the drawers of an apothecary cabinet.

You turned a slow circle on the spot, taking in the crumbling plaster cornices, the fireplace mantels, the factory carts. You sneezed. You said, "Historical stuff. I should have guessed. Right up your alley, Jo."

It was the first time I'd heard you say my name aloud since you stopped writing to me. I am not pointing this out to complain about it but to explain my reaction, which was to flee to the back of the store with the girls so you wouldn't see me tear up again. It's not crying, but it can certainly make me look pathetic, especially to someone who's only recently resumed contact with me.

It was a successful visit for Bron. Within ten minutes we'd found and paid for a velvet-backed oval mirror for Bron's grandma, a brass swing-arm wall sconce for Zorah, and oversized tin letters *I* and *E* from a theater marquee for the twins.

"Ready to go?" Bron said.

135

"Not exactly," you said. I wasn't surprised, Kurl. I'd kept half an eye on you as we roved around the store, and you'd stayed in one small area, methodically surveying only about four square feet's worth of merchandise. You were still examining the first item you'd picked up: a small portable lantern with a red glass shield that spelled out the product name in raised lettering: LITTLE WIZARD.

"Those things run on kerosene," Bron informed you. "They're totally unsafe."

Obediently, you put the lantern back on its shelf.

"Did you want to keep looking?" she said. But it was clear from her body language that Bronwyn was on a mission, and Bron on a mission means no dillydallying, no waffling, no lingering—three activities that more or less define my entire existence. She'd decided that our next stop was the mall.

You said that, actually, you had to head home and would take the bus, since the mall is the opposite direction from your house. I decided to head home, too, since the mall is the opposite of what I consider a pleasant retail experience.

I don't know how I managed to forget about Nelly. The Escalade was turning the corner at the end of the street before I realized my bike was still in the back. Mine would be a different bus but the same stop as yours, on the other side of the park.

The park was more beautiful than I remember ever seeing it before: Two-thirds of the leaves on the ground and the remaining one-third fluttering in the cool wind like party decorations. Some of the maples were uniformly orange except for a fiery red crown. You pointed out a section of grass hemmed in by fallen logs where they hadn't mowed, and then we were talking about your Whitman essay. I told you I always thought of my mom when I read Walt's lines about grass being *the beautiful uncut hair of graves*, and you asked me what she'd looked like.

"Like Shayna," I said, "apparently. Everyone says Shayna takes after her. But I don't remember her very clearly."

"I didn't even think of my dad's grave," you said. "The whole time I was writing the essay, I didn't think of him."

"He's not in the military cemetery?" I said.

"No," you said. "He's in Faribault, where my grandparents used to live. I guess they bought a big family plot or something."

We spent a minute walking in silence, shushing along in the fallen leaves with our feet.

"I sort of dig old pain under new pain," you said.

I asked you what you meant by that.

"I don't know. I almost never think of my dad."

"You think of Afghanistan, instead," I guessed.

"Yeah, or whatever crap is going on with my uncle," you said. "Whatever's newer, it sort of buries the older stuff."

I thought about that. Did I bury old pain under new pain? I liked to think I didn't. I liked to think I didn't bury anything but dealt with it, worked it out. "Maybe it's an adaptive strategy," I said. "Maybe if you laid out all the separate pieces of suffering, it would all hurt at once, and it'd be paralyzing. Crippling."

You looked at me. "It's really hard for me to picture you *not* talking in class," you said.

"Public speaking is not one of my skills," I said.

"So what are your skills? Other than mandolin and singing?"

I considered. "I'm fast."

"Like, running?" you said.

"Yes, running," I said. "You underestimate me because I'm wearing vintage two-tone oxfords instead of Reeboks."

You made a skeptical sound in your throat.

"I'm serious; I'm fast," I said. "And I can maneuver around obstacles, which is more than I could say for you."

"Fine," you said. "You want to race?"

I was fairly certain, despite my bravado, that you'd be faster, what with your longer legs and bulked-up leg muscles. So I dispensed with any on-your-mark preliminaries and took off, hoping to take you by surprise. And it must have worked momentarily, because I stayed ahead for eight or ten seconds before I heard you pounding up behind me like some kind of enraged buffalo.

My adrenaline kicked in and I swerved, dodging this way and that through a stand of trees and leaping over fallen branches. But it didn't even faze you for a second, did it? For you it must have been exactly like a football field full of opposing players. Dodge that guy, jump over that guy. It must have been pure muscle memory. Which is, I'm assuming, why you chose not to overtake me but to tackle me to the ground.

From here in the safety of my army tent I will admit that no, you did not hit me with your full strength. Yes, you did twist us both rather expertly in the air so that we landed with you underneath, taking most of my weight. No, the wind wasn't knocked out of me, nor did it really hurt when my cheekbone grazed the ground. Yes, there was a thick cushion of fallen leaves. But the surprise and indignity of it propelled me to play things up a little, briefly. Just a wince and a sniffle.

"You okay?" Laughter was right under the words. You pulled up on your elbow, panting, peering into my face.

"Well, a piano just fell on me," I said, trying hard to sound wounded.

"You asked for it. And I didn't *fall* on you. If I did, you'd be hamburger."

I perceived that there would be no sympathy forthcoming, so I changed tack. I may be small, Kurl, but I grew up with an older sister who, back in the day, used to love a good scrap. I swung a leg over your hips and straddled you. You brought your hands up by reflex—what did you think I was going to do, punch you?—and I grabbed your wrists and lunged my weight forward so fast that you didn't have time to brace, and you had to allow me to pin your arms to the ground above your head.

"Jack the Giant Killer," I crowed. "Brute strength is no match for agility—"

You bench-pressed your forearms, with me attached to them, an inch or so off the ground. I hovered. You tensed to throw me off. "You little punk," you said. Laughing, though. We were both laughing.

Kurl, I don't know who did what to whom. I felt you stirring at the precise moment I felt myself stirring. Forgive me the nineteenth-century terminology. I loathe the word *erection*. The only worse term for it is *boner*.

Stirring at least accounts for the fact that it's not always sexual, or not necessarily sexually motivated. It could have been the adrenaline still coursing through our veins. Or being physically starved for touch, for contact of any kind. You know those horrible studies where the baby monkeys will cuddle up to the robot mama monkey even though it's wired to administer electric shocks? That's the kind of starved I mean.

Anyhow. We were stirring, you and me, and it was obvious that you were noticing me noticing you noticing me, and so forth. Your ears were red, and I felt the blood rush to my face, too.

I mumbled something in the way of apology and let go of your arms. I was shifting my weight, looking for a way to fling myself into the leaves without making further accidental contact, when suddenly you sat straight up underneath me and grabbed hold of my waist.

I saw it on your face, the struggle, like some kind of internal fistfight. We were nose to nose, inches away.

I took a breath. "How about if I just kiss you," I said, "and you can see what you think?"

You shook your head. "No. No way," you said. Not even one second's hesitation.

So I apologized again, and shifted to get off of you, and again you tightened your grip. What is this behavior with you and belt loops, Kurl? You'd hooked your fingers into my belt loops like they were a harness.

I couldn't move, and your face was so close to mine. That shadowy, locked-down look was in your eyes—that same look you cast my way at Paisley Park that time, when I was slow-dancing with that guy Rogan. I know, I know. I'm not supposed to read anything into your expressions—but, Kurl, your lockdown look in particular is so excruciatingly humiliating! I turned my head away from you, looking for escape.

Shayna is yelling at me from downstairs. I'm late for school. I'll drop this letter by Ms. Khang's class after homeroom, if I don't decide to burn it before then. I understand the risks involved in rehashing scenes that you may prefer to forget, Kurl.

Yours truly,
Jo

Tuesday, December 1

Dear Little Jo,

Look. If you're going to give a play-by-play of the whole thing in the park you can't just stop at the exact moment where I come off looking like an asshole. Worse than an asshole—a psycho actually. My mouth saying one thing and my hands doing the exact opposite.

I mean I'm not saying you're wrong about that particular moment. I was in some kind of fog. Panicking, if you want me to be completely honest. That expression on my face, that *lockdown look* you hate so much? If you ever see it again don't take it so personally, Jo. It's just panic.

I guess I'd better finish the scene for you. So you're humiliated, as you said. Tears are starting up in your eyes. I'm hanging on to you so you can't wriggle away. And you *are* wriggling, by the way, and you're doing it right in my lap and it's not exactly making my head any clearer.

Wait, is what I say to you. It sounds more like a growl than a word. Wait. Will you please give me one second to think?

You sort of freeze. You sit there staring at the ground past my elbow, pawing at your cheeks to wipe away the tears. It's not perfect. I am aware it's not perfect and that I'm being a total asshole to hold you there after flat-out rejecting you. But I also

141

know that if I let go of you right at that moment it will be too late. You'll never get near me again.

If I let it happen, I don't know what'll happen, I say.

Your eyes move to mine and then away. Right, you say. I could lose control and overpower you. You're trying for a joke but it sounds more like misery.

No, I say. I mean me.

Your eyes meet mine, and it's surprise in them now. You almost smile.

It makes me so jealous, Jo, that you're not as terrified of this as I am. That you're settled with it somehow. Not necessarily comfortable but settled. How about if I just kiss you, is what you'd suggested. Just like that.

I shake my fingers loose from your belt loops. Focus on trying not to react to the jostling this causes. The truth is I'm breathing pretty hard by now. My quads have started trembling. I flatten my thighs to the ground, trying to hide the trembling from you.

We could set a timer, you say.

What? I ask.

A timer. For, say, thirty seconds. Or twenty. Just for a limit, you know. For safety.

You give my shoulder a little pat. You say, Either way I'm getting off your lap, okay?

I am pretty sure you're only kidding about the timer. I mean it's an insane idea. But at least you're not bolting away from me across the park or anything, so I just sit there while you arrange yourself on the grass beside me. On your knees facing me.

You're not kidding though. We'll have to find the right ring tone, you say. Crickets, or a dog bark, or something like that. Lyle's phone has a banjo riff, but if you really, really hate this kiss,

Kurl, it would operate like some kind of aversion therapy and you'll end up hating bluegrass too. And I won't be responsible for a tragedy like that.

You nudge my bicep. C'mon, give me your phone.

I don't have a phone, I say.

You frown. You look around in the grass like you might find someone's discarded phone conveniently lying nearby. Well, then, you say, maybe we can use a safe word. Have you heard of safe words? We could agree on a certain word, so that if either of us says it the other person knows everything has to stop.

By this point I'm barely listening. I can barely even hear you, the way my heartbeat is banging in my ears. I feel like every muscle in my body is flooded with waiting. Like I'm drowning in waiting.

How about *mandolin*, you say. Or *last time round*, like you say in a bluegrass jam. Or is that too complica—

You look at my face and cut yourself off mid-word. Then you lean in and lay your hand against my cheek and kiss me.

Well, you were there too, Jo. You know how it went. You came in lightly at first, like you were afraid I might bite you. Basically just brushing your lips over mine. You broke contact but stayed right there, so that the not-touching was part of the kiss too. Your eyes were open. You let out a soft shallow breath.

That's what did it I think. The feel of your breath plus all that caution. When your lips touched mine again I opened my mouth and kissed you back for real. Until your eyes closed and you swayed and I steadied your shoulders with my hands.

Oh my goodness, you said, but still not pulling away. Just saying it into my mouth. Your breath not soft anymore but ragged. You're good at this, Kurl.

I recognized that voice of yours. That turned-on, pitched-up voice from that time in my car. You said in your letter that your turned-on voice was whiny, but there was another word I liked better. *Undone.* That undone voice of yours.

By the way. No, I will not use the word *stirring.* I don't care who used it in the nineteenth century or how baby monkeys in experiments behave. I mean it doesn't even make sense. We're just going to have to think of other ways to describe it.

I wasn't completely crazy to worry what would happen though, was I? I mean it was a kiss but already it was more than that. My fingers in your hair but already sliding under your shirt, across your back. My tongue already in your mouth. Pressing deeper. My arms already around you tipping you off balance and turning you over onto the grass.

A word kept flashing in my head. One word, over and over, like a flashing neon sign. *Lucky.* I don't know how to describe it, Jo. *Lucky lucky lucky.* My whole body wanted to crawl inside your whole body, just to share all this luckiness with you.

At that exact moment a dog barked right next to our heads. We sat up so fast that your forehead smashed into my mouth.

It was a black lab puppy, barking like a maniac. Charging at us and leaping back, trying to get us to play.

Walter! Walter, come! this woman yelled, and ran up and grabbed the dog. She hooked the leash onto his collar. Sorry, she said. I'm so sorry about that.

They were gone before we could say anything.

Are you okay? you asked.

I checked my lip where your head had hit. No blood, I said.

No, I mean in general, you said.

I'm good, I said. I feel kind of amazing actually.

You laughed. Did you hear that? you said. Can you believe it? That dog's name was Walt!

sincerely,
AK

Dear Little Jo,

I am writing this sitting outside Mr. Abdi's office. Waiting on my so-called Decision on Disciplinary Action, otherwise known as sentencing. I've been here all afternoon waiting for the librarian to come by and give her report.

I'd really hoped not to see you at all this year, Adam, Mr. Abdi said, before putting me out here to wait. His whole face drooping with disappointment. I've been hearing such good things from Ms. Khang about your engagement with literature, your goals for the future. And now this.

Jo, you were the one who said we didn't need to talk it to death. Those were your exact words, remember? There's no need to talk it to death.

Monday when we were still in the park I said it would take me a while to figure out what kissing you meant and what to do about it, and you said, It doesn't have to mean anything. You don't need to do anything. Let's just let it be what it was.

Let it be. As if you've ever, in your whole life, let anything be. I mean I should have known you'd turn around and bring it up again within forty-eight hours. At school too yet.

We were in the library at lunch so I could show you the college information that Khang gave me. You were acting sort of nervous. I mean I could tell you weren't paying attention to what I was saying et cetera.

So I ask you what's wrong and you say, I can't actually not talk about it.

About what? I say. Walking right into it.

That kiss.

No, I say. We're not talking about that.

But you ignore me. You lean forward, all secretive. Come on, Kurl, you say. You can't just sit there and pretend it wasn't incredible. Extraordinary.

And then you put your hand over my hand. Right there, on top of all my notebooks on the table in the middle of the Lincoln High library. I mean it felt like stripping off all my clothes in public.

I get out of my chair and start shoving all my papers into my backpack. I say, No way. I'm not doing this.

You look up at me with this look. This sort of sympathetic look. Regretful. Like you knew I'd react like that, and had planned not to say anything, and then couldn't help yourself and said it anyway.

Like I'm that predictable, and you feel sorry for me.

So I turn and walk out.

I'm heading to my locker and I'm thinking how actually dangerous and psychotic you are, and wondering what I am doing spending any time at all with a person who can't even keep a promise for forty-eight hours. Maybe I'm sort of panicking. But I'm plain old angry too.

So it takes me a minute or two. I'm halfway across the school when I recall the fact that those kids had been in the library when I left. Some of those little jerkoffs you call the butcherboys. The blond girl and the stupid-looking boy, Dowell. They'd come in just as I was leaving, and I'd shoved right past them without registering it. But now it hits me. Why would they go to the library on their lunch hour except to find you?

By the time I walk back through the book stacks to our table, they've already got half your belongings scattered around on the carpet. The girl is scrawling all over your binder with a Sharpie. Hearts, *I love cocks*—the usual stuff. Dowell is waving something around, and you're trying to grab it away from him.

He shoves you away and starts reading: *Dear Little Jo, I guess I can tell you about heroes. Sacrifice et cetera. My dad died falling off a roof when I was ten.*

It's one of my letters he's reading. The one about Sylvan going to work for Uncle Vik and Mark joining the army. It's an old one, so it takes me a second to recognize it. And then it takes me a second to realize that you've been carrying it around. I mean I am so shocked that I just stand there for a few seconds listening.

You're hopping around going, Come on, give it back. That's my private correspondence.

Dowell stops. Turns the page over. Is this from your boyfriend? he says. Is this a love letter?

You know what you remind me of, Jo? I mean now that I'm stuck here outside the VP's office with all this time to think about it. You're like these Christmas ornaments that my babcia brought over from Poland and passed on to my mom. I hauled them all up from the basement last night because my mom wants to clean them before the holidays. They're these hollow red and gold shapes. Spheres and bells and diamonds, all made of the thinnest glass you've ever seen. They weigh nothing in your hand. You go into a trance staring at them on the tree, because the lights shine right through them and also bounce off the glitter-coated parts. They make amazing patterns on the walls.

Jo, you are exactly like one of those ornaments. Sparkly and delicate and fascinating. Go ahead and take that as a compliment if you want.

But here's the thing. You should see what happens when one of these ornaments falls off its hook. Once when we were kids Mark had an umbrella in the living room for some reason. He was swinging it around and its tip just barely brushed the tree, but one of the bells came loose. It made this tiny high-pitched pop against the hardwood. It just exploded. The shards were so small and scattered so far that we couldn't even properly sweep them up. We were trying to hide it, so Mark got a dust cloth and wiped the whole floor. But still for weeks after Christmas, if you walked around in there on bare feet, you'd end up with microscopic cuts in your soles.

Here is what I need you to do, Jo. I need you to figure out how to be less like a Christmas ornament some of the time. I'm not saying all the time. But some of the time. And in some places like school. Because there's no way I can keep catching you when you fall. And you are falling all the time, Jo. The goddamn tree is shaking all over the place.

To top it all off I promised Uncle Vik I'd show up this afternoon to help on a roof. Add that to a suspension or whatever Mr. Abdi decides to do with me. I'm just handing him an excuse.

That's not even what makes me so angry. None of that is. What makes me angry is that my life is so predictable. Everything that happened today at school, everything that'll happen when I go home. It's so routine at this point that it makes me sick. All your talk about Life After High School is bullshit, Jo. The truth is that nothing, none of it, is ever going to change.

sincerely,
AK

Friday, December 4

Dear Kurl,

I am positively reeling from the layers of irony in your letter. There are so many convoluted twists and turns of irony here that I nearly biked straight into the side of a bus on my way home today. That's how preoccupied I was, trying to sort it all out.

I love the part where you blame me firstly for touching your hand, *at school too yet*—as though it was a lap dance in the middle of the cafeteria!—and secondly for getting you into trouble with Ms. McGuire and therefore with the vice principal. How conveniently you overlook the fact that I was the one sitting there quietly in my chair while you were the one throttling Christopher Dowell right in front of the librarian.

He had your letter in his hands, yes. I'll concede your point about the carelessness of carrying any of your letters on my person, given my attractiveness to the butcherboys. But your reaction to the situation was out of all proportion. You were like the Terminator. You grabbed Dowell by the throat and slammed him so hard into the shelves that four or five books tumbled out the other side. No wonder Ms. McGuire showed up within mere seconds. The sound of falling books must be like a dog whistle to a librarian's ears.

You snatched your letter from his hand and flung it in my general direction.

"Whoa. Chill, man," Maya said. She had leaped up from where she'd been doodling on my notebooks and was backing away.

Dowell was choking, but you weren't letting him go. "Stay the hell away from him," you said.

"Kurlansky, we're sorry, man. We didn't mean anything by it," Maya said. I think Maya Keeler would like nothing more than to be a puppy at your heels, if only you'd grant her permission. Your very own apprentice menace.

I spotted Ms. McGuire marching toward us up the aisle. "Let him go," I suggested to you.

You let go, and Dowell clutched his throat and doubled over, gasping. But still he managed to tell you to go fuck yourself.

You hauled him back upright by his hair.

"Hey, Kurl," I said, trying to tip you off about the librarian's imminent arrival.

You leaned right into Dowell's face. "Now, why would I fuck myself," you snarled, "when there's a cunt like you?"

You'd delivered the sentence calmly enough, your lips right next to Dowell's ear. Your quiet-doom routine at its absolute finest. But when you uttered it, Ms. McGuire was standing all of two inches behind you.

You will remember I once mentioned that there are certain vocabulary words that tend to backfire on those who wield them? Jonathan Hopkirk Defensive Plan, phase three: Hope They Hang Themselves with Their Own Rope. Remember?

Well, the C-word would definitely qualify as one of those vocabulary words, Kurl. It's right up there near the top of the list.

The whole time you were choking Dowell, uttering those despicable words, listening to Ms. McGuire order you to the VP's office, your face never betrayed the smallest hint of emotion. Not even a flicker.

And seeing it—watching you stand there like a marble pillar while Ms. McGuire made Maya pick up the fallen books and then told the two of them to get lost so she could deal with you, watching you so carefully *not* glance over at me even once, not even when you slung your backpack over your shoulders and turned and walked out—I realized it's a completely different face than the one to which I've been getting accustomed. It was quite a jolt to see it and to remember that before we became friends, it's the only face I ever saw.

But my absolute favorite part of your letter is the passage about the glass orbs and the fascinating light patterns and the shattering into fragments. You've encapsulated the essence of my personality in a single, brilliantly elaborated metaphor. You've nailed it. You've got me in a nutshell.

Here's what I need you to do, Kurl. I need you to stop mixing me up in your head with yourself. Listen carefully now, because it's an established fact in the Hopkirk household that I am at my most insightful when I'm at my angriest:

Your glass ornament? It's not me; it's you.

Go ahead, take as much time as you need to recover from this revelation and think it through. Your brilliant metaphor describes yourself. Adam Kurlansky lives inside a shell. A perfectly smooth, hard exoskeleton designed to ensure that no influences from the outside world can possibly penetrate, and nothing can ever escape.

It is hardly a mystery why you wear this shell or where you perfected it. Just by way of a minor example, I am willing to bet any money that you borrowed this afternoon's degrading use of the C-word directly from the mouth of Viktor Kurlansky. I'm assuming that what you meant in your letter by *I'm just handing him an excuse* is that Uncle Viktor's going to holler at you for fighting at school again, and I'm willing to bet he won't use the politest language when he does so, especially if he happens to have been sampling the vodka. There you go, Kurl: your complete, complimentary family psych assessment, courtesy of

Yours truly,
Jo

Dear Kurl,

Aha. No letter from you in Ms. Khang's box today. Nor are you present at school. Here we go again. I'm starting to believe that my interacting with you in any format is bad news for your plans to graduate from high school this year.

Yours truly,
Jo

Dear Little Jo,

Well I guess I was lucky you were the only one home. When I got to your house just after dark I was positive Lyle or at the very least your sister would be there, and I didn't know what I'd do. I couldn't stand the thought of having to act normal around them. Having to make small talk. I mean I didn't think I could pull it off. But I couldn't delay it another second either.

You know when you're on a diving board and you can't decide whether to go in? You're at the very edge of the board looking down at the water and you still haven't made up your mind for sure. But the board is starting to bounce a bit with your weight. At a certain point you're leaning forward and you're up on your toes and your weight is gathering forward in your body. You know that if you don't jump you'll fall, and that falling will be worse than jumping. So you jump.

That's what this was like. You answered the door, Jo, and looked up at me. Oh, hi, Kurl, you said. You have a way of saying this—Oh, hi, Kurl—that sounds all casual, but meanwhile your eyes go really wide and your body gives a little twitch. The complete opposite of casual. I've seen you do this before when I show up somewhere you don't expect. Every time I see it I get a little flare of happiness.

I was also relieved that you didn't seem particularly angry or

156

upset. I knew from reading your last letter that you were pretty pissed at me. And I mean I deserved it for sure. But when I saw you face-to-face I suddenly remembered how you looked the last time I saw you. Pale and quiet while Ms. McGuire ordered me to the office. To be honest, over the last couple days I had already sort of forgotten that whole scene in the library. I was fully absorbed in my own mental crisis.

You stepped back and opened the door wider to let me into your house. I didn't move, couldn't.

What my mental crisis had looked like was this: I had been walking around since 7 a.m. staring at every boy I passed and asking myself, Do I want him?

Actually it was worse. As in more specific, and more relentless. All day, all over downtown, from one end of the park to the other, on the train, at the mall. I am walking around looking at every single male member of the human race over the age of sixteen, and I am asking myself these desperate, urgent questions: Do I want to have sex with that guy? How about him, do I want him? Do I want him to want me? Would I actually suck that guy's cock? Or that one. What about him? What about sex? What about kissing? Is it only kissing I want?

Once in a while some guy would stare back at me. I mean it was less like a stare and more like a series of quick looks, where each glance would get a little more curious. A little more interested.

And then it hit me that this is how it happens. This is how gay men hook up with each other.

And it wasn't only the ones who looked like they might be gay either. There was this security guard in the food court at the mall. I was pretty sure he was a vet. I mean he had the same shaved head and tattoos I remember from a lot of Mark's military friends. This guy looked me up and down and sort of nodded at me in this way that made me think he knew exactly what I was thinking about. I was positive I could have hung around the food court a few minutes longer, and he would have come over and talked to me.

Of course I didn't hang around. I was doing just fine freaking out all on my own. Thanks anyway.

What was the answer to all these questions I was asking myself? I don't know. I mean I honestly couldn't figure it out. I couldn't answer the questions at all. I just kept getting more confused and wanting not to ask the questions anymore but not being able to stop myself. I was like some kind of relentless Nazi interrogator with myself.

Finally I was so worn out from all of this questioning that I just thought, Go see him. Go see him right now, and see what the answer is when it's Jo you're looking at.

Now that I'm writing this after the fact I guess I knew what the answer was going to be. I mean I knew exactly. But I guess I needed to go through the whole exhausting experiment to prove it to myself or something.

And you answered the door: Oh, hi, Kurl.

Who's home? I asked you. It was maybe not the most polite greeting but I could barely speak at all. My heart was already beating so fast, walking up your porch steps, I thought I might pass out. And then seeing your face. Those wide brown eyes flying open even wider. That quick, uncertain half smile, with your one tooth on the top left turned slightly crooked and the rest perfect.

The second I saw your face after all those hours of mental torture, I fell. I mean I was off the diving board and falling.

You blinked up at me. Nobody's home, you said. It's just me.

I more or less shoved you back into your own house. I closed your front door behind us and locked it. I turned around, kissed you. And kissed you again, harder.

And within about five seconds we are stumbling up the stairs fumbling and tripping over each other's feet. I'm kissing you and pulling your shirt off over your head and you're undoing my belt.

And somehow you're also managing to talk the whole time. You're saying, Are you sure? I mean are you really sure? If this happens, Kurl, you have to promise not to hate me.

And I keep interrupting you with my tongue and murmuring Yes, okay, I'm sure, yes, against your lips and your ear and your throat.

We are winding our arms around each other and dragging each other against the wall and pressing each other into the railing, until by the time we've finally made it up to your room we're both breathless and laughing and completely confused about whose hands are where and whose skin belongs to whom.

We didn't do much, did we? I mean technically speaking. There was no time. We made it into your old army tent and lay down. We shoved our clothes out of the way and I pulled you on top of me, stomach to stomach. There was no time and no rhythm even. I pressed my spine into the mattress trying to kiss you and arch against you at the same time. You lifted away from me and gasped, said my name, said something about how you couldn't wait, couldn't stand it. You pushed down against me.

Those sharp hip bones of yours. That smooth hollow of skin

inside your hip where I held you. And that noise you made, that high little moan of yours. I mean that's all it took.

All those hours built up, and all those times I've said no to you. No. No. No. Since that first drunken time in my car when I touched you, weeks ago. I could feel all those hours of waiting like some kind of tornado lifting my whole body at once. All those stockpiled *no*s flipping over like dominoes into *yes*.

Yes. That was it. Just *yes*.

And directly afterward I started shaking so badly that you lifted your head from my shoulder and said, Whoa. You slid off me and wiped us both clean with the bedsheet. Are you cold? you asked. You tugged the blankets up to cover us.

My whole body was doing this violent trembling. For a minute or two I couldn't get a deep enough breath.

Are you panicking? you asked.

I tried to say no, it wasn't panic. But I don't know what happened. Suddenly I was bawling. Nothing like Jo Hopkirk style, a silent couple of tears here and there. More like painful dry sobs tearing my whole chest in half.

Oh, Kurl, you said. Oh, sweet one. You're so beautiful. You laid your hand at the base of my throat, right where the pain was worst.

Stop. Don't, I said, through the heaving and gasping. I couldn't stand it. *Sweet one*—nobody's ever called me something like that. Nobody's ever called me *beautiful*. I mean I couldn't stand it.

So you removed your hand and sat up and squinted down at me in the dim light of the tent. Well, you know, Kurl, you said, you were probably pretty backlogged.

For some reason this hit me as the most hilarious thing I'd ever heard. You sounded like a car mechanic or something saying that. Backlogged. So there I am, flat on my back in your army tent, suddenly laughing. Crying and laughing at the same time until I feel like my guts are going to implode from the pain.

And you're making it worse, because now you've grabbed your mandolin from somewhere, and you're strumming merrily away and singing the Ballad of Adam Kurlansky or whatever you called it.

You're still in there, Jo. In your tent. I'm sitting at your desk writing this letter while you sleep, which I am aware is a weird thing to be doing considering I could talk to you when you wake up instead. It's just that I've gotten used to doing this, writing things out as a way of sorting them out.

And this thing in particular seems important. I mean what I'm trying to tell you is that I'm not about to turn around and pretend nothing happened. Not this time. I promise. What happened tonight between us was important, Jo.

Anyway, you were playing your mandolin. Obviously giving me time to collect my wits. And eventually I did manage to get my breath under control, to get back to some sort of normal emotional state.

Don't leave, you said. You sang me a few bluegrass songs. I could hear how you were keeping your voice soft and low on purpose, trying to soothe me or trying not to remind me of your other, wilder voice. After a while it made me sort of ashamed of myself, so I finally reached out and put my hand over the strings of your mandolin.

Don't, you said. No, please. Don't leave.

I'm not leaving, I said. I sat up and kissed you.

So we started over. Slower, this time. It was too dark to see, now, so we got by with only our hands and our voices. Whispering. Laughing. Breathing onto each other's skin.

We played this sort of spontaneous game where we pretended to be researchers, explorers new to the human body. What do you call this? you said, circling my wrist bone.

There must be a name for this, I said, digging my finger behind your bent knee.

How does this work? you said, dragging your tongue along the rim of my ear.

Laughing, gasping.

What's this? I said, stroking the soft hair in your armpit.

You gave a shocked little grunt when I did that and shivered all over. Goose bumps roughened the skin of your arm and spread all down your side. That's...that's private, you whispered. Serious, suddenly.

I put my nose where my fingertips had been. I breathed in your scent—I could smell your haste and excitement from before, from when I arrived, sort of an acid tang, and under it a warmer, softer smell that was just you, just Jo. There you were, right under my nose. I mean I couldn't believe how lucky I was. I said this to you: I'm so lucky.

I kissed you there under your arm, kissed the scent of you, that private spot of you, so that you squirmed and moaned and your voice broke on the moan and wildness entered into it.

Lie still, I said. It really was research I was doing. I was set on discovering what your body wanted. Finding out where I could touch you to make you sigh, where you would shiver and gasp, where your voice would start to climb and crack and your words would fall apart. Hands versus mouth. Tongue versus teeth. The point after which it made no difference anymore, and you refused to lie still anymore and came back at me with your own hands and tongue and teeth and belly and hips. The point after which I stopped noticing any particular touch or taste, and it all tumbled together into that one word, that one thought, that *yes*.

Somewhere in the middle of all the research, though, I remembered these lines Walt wrote. I couldn't remember the exact wording, but the book was sitting right here on your shelf, so I looked it up just now. After what just happened in your tent, I think I get what Walt means. It's this part:

> *There was never any more inception than there is now,*
> *Nor any more youth or age than there is now,*
> *And will never be any more perfection than there is now,*
> *Nor any more heaven or hell than there is now.*

So I think this is the thing, Jo. This is why I can't agree with your life-begins-after-high-school-so-just-wait-it-out philosophy. I could never put it into words before tonight. It's not because things will always stay the same, or that time isn't going to keep passing year after year until you graduate. It's that now—right now, right this second—is the only actual time we're alive. I mean our minds can live in the past or worry about the future but our bodies are only alive and feeling things right here, right now. This is always true, but tonight I felt how true it is. You must have felt it too.

Walt says simple things but the meaning isn't simple. You have to understand them not with your mind but with your body.

It's getting sort of chilly out here in your bedroom. This has ended up a really long letter, probably my longest one ever judging by how cramped my hand is and how ice-cold my legs are. When I crawled out of the tent you were sleeping on my pants, and I didn't want to wake you up by pulling them out from under you. But now I'm freezing, so I'm coming back into the tent.

sincerely,
AK

PS: Did you know you talk in your sleep? Just now you said, It's only lightning. Loud and clear. It made me feel weird. Actually to be honest it made me a bit jealous. I mean I am actually a bit jealous of the person you're talking to in your dream.

Dear Kurl,

Good old Walt. He was writing about sex all along, wasn't he? You're absolutely right that you have to understand his poetry with your body, not your mind. I can't wait to reread "Song of Myself," after tonight.

I couldn't believe it when I read the lines from Walt in your letter just now. When we finally made it up the stairs and into my tent, the one clear thought I managed to form was Walt's line,

Urge and urge and urge. Always the procreant urge of the earth.

The word *procreant* doesn't make perfect sense here, I realize. Yet I did have the feeling tonight that we were creating something together, something frightening and precious and new. Maybe *co-creant* is a better word for it? *The co-creant urge of the earth?*

Anyhow. This happens to be the line that comes directly after the lines you said you were remembering. It's almost as though Walt was cheering us along from the sidelines, the voyeuristic old bugger.

I sat down to write this letter as an apology for not lingering longer when you crawled back into my tent and woke me up, for hurrying you out the door at one in the morning instead of asking you to stay. I was imagining my family arriving home any

165

minute, and Lyle coming in to check on me (not that he'd ever do more than call hello and good night from the doorway), and then breakfast in the morning (not that either Lyle or Shayna eat breakfast), and me suddenly being faced with trying to introduce you to them in this new context (not that we've decided there *is* a new context; despite your avowal that what happened between us was important, I'm not assuming there needs to be a new context of any kind, Kurl; we can talk about context later, or even not talk about it at all; the last thing I want to do is overanalyze this and start badgering you with demands to talk about it like before!).

As it turns out, it's now 2 a.m. and Shayna only just got home. I can hear from the way she is stumbling around in her room and singing, hoarse and slurring, that she is drunk. "Where were you?" I called, just now, and she called back, "Noneofyourfuckingbusiness."

Even for Shayna Hopkirk, this is unusually belligerent behavior. I'll have to ask Bron where they went tonight, or try again with my sister tomorrow when she's sober or the next day when her hangover has dissipated.

I sat down to write you an apology, and I found your letter lying on my desk. It truly *is* co-creation, Kurl, that's exactly what this is—what we did in my tent and what we're doing writing about it to each other, afterward. We are making something entirely new. In this case I'm grateful you took the time to write that long, eloquent account while I slept, because in case it's not obvious from *this* letter, I am never very lucid upon waking.

Anyhow. I am really sorry I didn't ask you to stay over. I'm sorry I didn't at least take the time to explain my anxieties to you, instead of merely tossing your shoes in your general direction and mumbling, "You have to go now."

I hope you had bus money. I hope you didn't feel used and discarded. I hope you know that it was just as raw and intense and glorious for me as it was for you. I hope you know that right now my tent is soaked in moonlight, and that I wish more than anything that you were here to see it, because it looks like this whole earth was just reborn into an entirely new universe full of possibility.

Yours truly,
Jo

Tuesday, December 8 +
Wednesday, December 9

Dear Little Jo,

I looked up from my desk in English just now and saw you at the window and caught your smile. You were gone before I had time to smile back or to feel the heat in my face.

I'd already spotted you when the bell rang, over by the flag-pole locking up Nelly with one of your gloves hanging from your teeth. Later I saw you again in the hall, digging through your backpack and pulling out a pencil, which fell to the floor while you were doing up the zipper. I saw you in the computer lab talking to Mr. Carlsen. I saw you through the gym doorway, leaning against the wall, staring into space. Oh, and I came by Khang's room right after lunch and read your letter.

That's the sum total of all my moments with you today so far, and I have to get the car back to my mom right after school for her visit to Aunt Agata, so that might be it. And I guess you only knew about one of the moments—the English classroom window—not counting the letter you posted.

I took this letter home instead of sticking it in the box. Khang kept me after class to tell me I have to take the SAT. There's no mini-mum score, but I do have to take the test and submit my score for the Bridge to Education people even to consider my application.

This is pretty bad news for me. I mean I haven't been studying like Bron and everyone else. I guess I never read the application forms that closely after Khang gave them to me. I thought it was only the forms to fill out and her recommendation letter and this other thing called the ACE, the Autobiographical Creative Essay, that I'm supposed to write. In other words things that wouldn't be comparing me to everyone else.

Now it's the next morning. I keep thinking about the news this morning. A Taliban strategy: Dress fifteen suicide bombers in US military uniforms. Sneak them past the NATO base perimeter. Blow up eighteen Harrier jets.

So I guess the math looks like this: fifteen Taliban lives equals $200 million and one gigantic eff-you to the USA. I mean they try not to say too much on the news for exactly this reason. Telling the world about it will just make it mean more.

In the middle of the night I woke up from a falling-off-the-roof dream. I lay there in bed listening, but it wasn't Uncle Vik. It was my own heartbeat. I dreamed it was saying, Help. Help. Help. Help.

I listened to it for a long time before I woke up for real.

Then I remembered you, Jo. Your tent. It seemed impossible that it was just over twenty-four hours ago. Impossible that it happened at all. I lay there trying to remember your body with my body. Hunting around for any sign of you on me. I mean I even stuck my nose into my elbows and armpits like a dog, looking for your leftover scent.

Don't say anything to Bron and Shayna about the test. I've heard Bron making study dates and talking about all these strategies for getting a good score, like an attack ratio et cetera. I mean I don't think I can handle them taking cracks at me about it, even if they are just joking around. Or if they don't think it's a joke, that might be even worse. Bron has this way of looking at me like she's trying to decide what to fix. I don't think I can handle her making me her personal SAT project.

sincerely,
AK

PS: What a pathetic way to end this letter. It's pathetic to end it talking about Bron. I mean I can't believe I talked about the Taliban after what happened in your tent. After us! I don't know how to talk about us, Jo, but I swear I don't want to *not* talk about us. I don't even want to talk about any of these other things.

Dear Kurl,

I owed Abigail Cuttler a letter today, so I don't have much time left in class for this one. I'm still writing to her as well as to you. I asked Ms. Khang before class this morning if I could possibly go back to writing only to you, but she said she's confident I can handle two correspondents. I only need to meet the minimum of one letter to each per week, she reminded me.

Once class had started and we were all supposed to be writing our letters, Ms. Khang came over to my desk, crouched beside it so that I had to lean over to her, and whispered, "Please don't think I want you to write fewer letters than you have been, though. I didn't mean that. What's happening between you and Adam is wonderful."

"What's happening between you and Adam." For a heart-stopping moment I was absolutely certain Ms. Khang had been reading our letters all along. I blushed so deeply that my scalp prickled, and the surprise sent tears filling my eyes so that I couldn't say anything, couldn't look at her.

I overreacted, I realized, a few moments later. Ms. Khang was merely referring to the frequency of our letters, not their contents. In my defense, it's always unsettling to have a teacher crouch by your desk and whisper to you, isn't it, no matter what she might say? You assume you've done something wrong. Then you worry you might have morning breath, or something stuck between your teeth. The whole time you can feel your classmates straining to hear what's being said.

The bell has rung, and I'm still sitting in Ms. Khang's classroom trying to finish this. What I wanted to say before I see you tonight—before we're with the girls and I don't have a chance to say anything privately—is that you needing to take the SAT is not bad news at all, Kurl. What you don't realize is how much I've been hanging around Bron while she studies, and how much that has taught me about SAT strategy.

Kurl, I can tell you with absolute confidence that you will get a perfectly adequate score on the test if you approach it strategically, and you will have no trouble approaching it strategically if you let me show you how. So long as you can stomach the idea of a sophomore SAT coach, the girls will never need to know.

Whoa! You just walked into the classroom. You're talking to Ms. Khang at the front of the room, and you're both glancing over at me and smiling.

"Hurry up, I have to work," you just called over to me. Now my face is overheated again and my heart is pounding and I'm scribbling like a moron, trying to finish. Bron told me you're coming with us to the Decent Fellows' gig at Rosa's Room, so I'll see you tonight.

Yours,
Jo

Dear Little Jo,

Sorry I was so late getting to Rosa's Room. Roofing went late and then my uncle made me do the dump run. By the time I got cleaned up and made it to the bar, the Decent Fellows' show was already at halftime. Intermission, I guess you would call it in the context of music. The band was sharing pitchers of beer around a couple of small tables. I didn't notice you there at first, because your scarf was over your head tied with a bow under your chin. Bron was sliding this pair of pink mirrored sunglasses onto your face.

I took a chair and said hey to everyone in general.

You ripped off the scarf so that the glasses clattered to the table. Oh, hi, Kurl, you said.

I was introduced to the band members I hadn't met yet: Derek the mandolin player and Scarlett the fiddler/singer.

So you're the football star, Scarlett said.

Something like that, I said. I was thinking again about how much I like the way you always say, Oh, hi, Kurl, like that, like it's no big deal, but meanwhile you pretty much jump out of your skin.

Cody said to Lyle, Dude, just a couple tunes, seriously. For old times' sake.

Lyle smiled but shook his head.

You've heard Shayna sing, right? Cody said to me. Back me up, here. We gotta let her up onstage tonight, right?

It's not going to happen, Lyle said.

You never let me do *anything*, Shayna said. Nothing I do is good enough. And she shoved back her chair and stalked off to the restroom.

So obviously there's some sort of family argument going on that I've just walked into. But meanwhile I'm noticing how your hair is sticking out all over the place because of the scarf. How you're trying to comb it back down with your fingers but you're just making it worse. How the whole time you're blushing and looking somewhere else, not at me.

Jo. I know you were embarrassed, and I'm sorry for staring. For not being able to stop smiling. I was close to laughing aloud. You must have thought I was laughing at you but I swear I wasn't.

I was just so happy for a second. I mean I was so happy it was making me light-headed. These little things you do. All the little gestures, your quick nervous fingers. I watch you do these things and I think, how could I ever be unhappy? How could anything ever bother me?

Lyle came around and crouched beside my chair. Hey, Adam, he said.

I looked down at him, and he turned away from the table a bit so I'd know he wanted only me to hear. I owe you an apology, he said, from last time I saw you. You know, at the Prince thing?

I wanted to pretend I didn't know what he was talking about but of course I knew exactly. So I didn't say anything.

174

That wasn't about you at all, Lyle said. It was about me—me and Shayna. I shouldn't have come after you like that. And I'm sorry for what I said.

Okay, I said.

You look good, Adam, he said. You look really happy. He stood up and patted my shoulder and went back to his chair.

I looked at you, Jo, and you were staring at me with a massive question all over your face. Of course I knew you must have talked to Lyle about the Paisley Park thing. I knew that's why he was apologizing after all this time. But it still worked, the apology. I mean it still felt like Lyle meant it.

I guess feeling so happy was why it was you and not me who was pissed off when Bron started grilling me with all those questions. She leaned over to us and told us she wanted to write about me for her blog. The Real Adam Kurlansky, or something. I mean I told you Bron sees me as some kind of project.

And then the waitress brings over that drink. This fizzy yellow drink with a skewer of melon balls in it. From the man in the black T-shirt over there, she says.

For me? Bron says, turning in her chair to look.

Nope, the waitress tells her, and points at me. For him.

The rest of you all whip your heads around to find the man in the black T-shirt. And then you all whip your heads back around to look at me.

I mean it's not that the guy is bad-looking or anything. Lean and tall, these craggy cheekbones. But he's got to be thirty-five or forty years old. And a *man*. A man has just bought me a drink.

He can't drink that, Lyle says, he's underage. They're with us, but they're not supposed to be drinking.

So she takes the drink away, and also the beer glasses in front of me, you, and Bron.

Holy gaybait! says Scarlett.

It's my face that's red now. I can feel it.

That's what you get for dressing up, Bron tells me. You finally show up somewhere in a decent shirt, and wham.

The band went back onstage and started playing. It got too loud to talk anymore, which I have to say by that point was just fine with me.

After a few minutes Shayna sat down again between you and me. Her eyes were red.

Are you okay? I asked her, but she just shrugged and kept playing with her phone. She pretty much ignored the band the whole rest of the night.

I was watching Lyle sing and thinking of you singing. Remembering you on the sofa beside Shayna with your mandolin and remembering you in your tent beside me with your mandolin. I was listening to Lyle's ordinary voice and thinking of your shivery, heart-scraping voice. I was watching Lyle's fingers and thinking of your quick warm fingers.

The whole time the band played I kept sneaking looks at you, Jo, and thinking: How could I be unhappy? I mean how could anybody be unhappy? And also: How is anybody supposed to hide happiness like this?

sincerely,
AK

Dear Kurl,

I realize we're probably going to cross letters today, but I woke up this morning still irritated with Bronwyn for her despicable rudeness to you at Rosa's. Frankly, I don't care what kind of writing she's aiming to do, with all her talk of "exploding the line between fiction and reality" and "getting under readers' skin." She's calling these new pieces on her blog "Dispatches," as though she's sending exciting news out to the world from her special place at the epicenter of it.

Bron crossed her arms and leaned her elbows on the table. "So, Kurl. Adam Kurlansky."

You leaned back a little in your chair. "So, Bron. Bronwyn Whatever-your-last-name-is," you said.

She grinned. "Otulah-Tierney. So who is the *real* Adam Kurlansky?"

"What do you mean?"

"Let's start with that cut healing up on your face," Bron said. "Who would you say are your current enemies, Kurl? Why do you feel the constant need to press up against the rest of the world? Why do you think physical conflict is such an integral component of your identity?"

You frowned a little, sipped your beer, and glanced around the bar.

"Mind your manners, Bronwyn," I said.

She ignored me. "Kurl, are you poised between fight or flight right now? Are you experiencing an urge to hit me?"

"What kind of an interview strategy is this," I asked her, "asking seventeen questions in a row?"

"It's not fighting," you said. "I don't actually fight."

Bron laughed. "I've seen you fight."

"I mean this." You pointed to the scratch along your cheekbone, something I'd noticed the other night when you came over but hadn't had time to ask you about. "It's not from a fight."

"Did you bump into a telephone pole?"

"Something like that."

Bron sat back, crossed her arms, and shook her head. "Well, that one's *never* true. I've been researching this topic. Self-injuries to the face are extremely rare."

You leaned forward and put your elbows on the table, imitating Bron's earlier pose. You gazed at her steadily, serenely. I recognized this tactic of yours, this aggressive expressionlessness.

"Come on, you have to admit there's a mystique," she said. "I'd like to dispel it a little, if I may. Shed some light on the fog."

"You're mixing your metaphors," I told Bron. "You don't *dispel* a *mystique*. And you can't *shed light* on a *fog*."

"Everyone's a critic, Jojo," she said. She was trying to hold your eye.

"If you want to be a writer, though," I persisted, "you should practice writing *well*"—and was rewarded, finally, by her turning to me with a glare.

And then the waitress brought over that drink for you, and Bron was forced to give up on her interrogation.

The girls departed just before the end of the show. Shayna

seems fully convinced that open mic night at the Ace is going to prove her big break. They swore us to secrecy about their destination and slipped out before Lyle finished playing.

I was glad the group split up, not just because of Bron's annoying behavior but because if I had one personal goal for the evening, it was this: to have the ride home with you alone, Kurl. I'd had no idea how to accomplish the goal and spent nearly the whole last hour of the evening fretting about it. I was worried you wouldn't offer a ride—wouldn't think to offer, because you'd make the logical assumption that I'd go home with Lyle after they packed up.

But you did offer, and the girls had already left, so it was just you and me in the car. I love how normal it feels, the two of us talking. All the awkwardness of when we're together in public just falls away. We didn't discuss the show, or Bron's heckling, or Lyle, or school, or anything immediately relevant.

What did we talk about? Food. We discussed our favorite foods, which vegetables are most often overcooked, how spicy is too spicy. You told me about this Moroccan stew you saw in a magazine, which they cook in a clay dish shaped like an upside-down funnel.

We forgot entirely about having to say goodbye until we were already in my driveway. You turned off the engine, and we sat there a moment in silence.

"Lyle could be home in twenty minutes," I said.

You started the car again and put it in reverse. "I'll just drive around the block," you said. And you did drive, literally, around the block, and parked at the curb one street away from mine.

"This is going to sound stupid," you said, "but do you think I look gay now?"

I laughed, but you were serious. "What do you mean?" I said.

"I mean do I look gay? Do I come off as gay now?"

"Because of your shirt?" I asked.

You glanced down at your blue button-down as though you'd forgotten you were wearing it. "Is it a gay shirt?"

I laughed again. "No, it's not a gay shirt. It's a completely neutral shirt. Neutral to straight, in fact."

You frowned.

I made another guess. "Because of that man at the bar?"

"I just feel like maybe I look gay now. I told you it was stupid." You looked out through the windshield, up at the sky.

"When you say 'now,' do you mean—" I stopped. "What do you mean?"

"I mean now compared to before you and I fell in love."

I stared at your profile. "Is that what we did?"

You didn't answer, and I decided I'd misheard. I decided I was doing it again: I was making an issue out of something that wasn't an issue. I was cornering you like I'd done in the library that day after we kissed. Forcing you to rethink, retract, and withdraw what you'd said. I was an idiot. I wanted to bite my tongue off.

Yet for some reason I kept going anyhow: "Fell in love. Is that what we did, Kurl?"

You looked at me. Shrugged. "I did," you said, as though it should be obvious. As though it was as simple as the stars out there in the night sky.

"Me too," I said.

Yours truly,

Jo

Friday, December 11

Dear Little Jo,

Today this girl had a sudden nosebleed in the cafeteria. Some freshman girl I think. She sort of panicked, stood up saying, Oh my God, oh my God.

There you were, Jo, next to her like a shot. You pulled this giant white handkerchief from your pocket. You put your hand to the back of the girl's head and the hankie to her face. Sat her down gently and spoke to her quietly.

I thought, There it is. The bright flag of your disposition. How you give things to people without needing to stop and think. How it goes straight from your heart to your hands.

I mean you told me this about yourself in one of your first letters. Quoting Walt to describe your personality: spending vast sums, bestowing yourself on the first that will take you. I can't remember Walt's exact words, but I was reading over your first letters last night, remembering. *Be real and be true* et cetera. I can't believe how long it took me to see how amazing you are. And now I can't stop seeing it all day long.

sincerely,
AK

Dear Kurl,

As you know, we're meeting tomorrow morning at the public library for our first SAT-coaching session, so I'm enclosing a test-strategy sheet I printed out last night. It describes how to calculate the ratio between your "attack" percentage and your "get" percentage in order to know the minimum number of questions you'll need to answer in the allotted time to achieve your target score. I know, I know—it makes for riveting reading, doesn't it? But you should review it nonetheless before we meet, to save us time.

On another note, I lost my scarf the other night at Rosa's. Remember that burgundy patterned silk one Bron was tying in a bow under my chin? I'm wondering if you happened to find it in your mom's car. It's not a vintage item, but it has sentimental value to me, since it used to be Lyle's, back in his 1980s paisley phase.

Yours truly,
Jo

PS: One more point about the SAT: I read that they grade for punctuation on the composition section of the test. I think it would probably be prudent for you to start practicing using quotation marks for dialogue, Kurl. I could help you by inserting them in your letters from now on wherever you've omitted them, if you want.

Saturday, December 12

Dear Little Jo,

Half the time we were supposed to be talking about the SAT in the library today I was thinking about other things. Specifically I was thinking about how, that last time in the school library, I got so angry with you for bringing up our kiss in the park. And how now I'm the one who wants to bring up that topic. Kissing, I mean.

You kept saying, "Are you even listening?"

And I'd say, "Yes, of course. Keep talking."

And you'd tell me how to eliminate the two least-likely multiple-choice options right out of the gate.

And I'd be thinking how there were only two or three other people in the library anyway, and would it be such a big deal if I just leaned over, just for a second, and pressed my mouth to yours? I mean I felt a sharp little thrill just thinking about it.

You'd say, "Are you paying attention?"

And I'd say "Yes," but I'd be thinking about how you had to finish your letter to me in a huge hurry that time. I was standing in the classroom with Khang waiting for you to hand it over. Remember? You signed your letter differently that time. You left off the word *truly* and wrote, *Yours, Jo.*

I know it was just a slip of the pen. But I couldn't help it. He's yours, I thought. Just go ahead and kiss him already.

So finally I stood up and said, "Follow me," and led you

around to the back corner section of the library, the section on Reptiles & Amphibians where I know for a fact nobody ever goes.

"What?" you were saying. "We don't have much time before we have to—"

I turned around and caught your words in my mouth. Caught your waist with my hands and snaked my arms around your ribs and pulled you against me and kissed and kissed and kissed you.

Sincerely,
AK

PS: As you can see from this letter I pretty much know exactly how to use quotation marks for dialogue. I just always think they get in the way of telling the story somehow. To be honest when I first noticed you putting them in your letters I thought it was sort of pretentious. These are letters, not novels, I thought. But I get it. It's a good idea to practice for the SAT at least. So okay, I'll do it from now on.

Monday, December 14

Dear Kurl,

Did you know that you have a freckle under your left ear, about an inch below and a quarter inch behind your earlobe? Today at lunch, when you stopped by the art room to hang out with me and the girls, I noticed this freckle for the first time.

Bron had called us over to the window to see how beautiful the rain looked bouncing off the flat roof outside.

"That's a bad seal on that skylight," you pointed out. "That'll be leaking in a couple months." And Bron teased you for focusing on practical rather than aesthetic concerns despite standing in the art classroom.

I was standing next to you, noticing how the light from the window cast raindrop-shadows across your cheekbone. The freckle under your left ear surprised me: How could I never have noticed it before? I'd always believed your skin was uniformly pale. Were there more freckles I didn't know about? Was there a matching freckle, for example, under your other ear?

The three of you discussed that photo in the hallway by the restrooms at Rosa's Room, the one of Raphael and Lyle onstage together. You told us you'd thought it was a picture of Shayna at first, and that you'd had to look twice.

Shayna said, "Seriously, if it wasn't for that one picture, I don't think I'd remember I ever had a mother. I'd believe Lyle found us in a forest or something."

Meanwhile, I'd snuck around to your other side to see if I could find more freckles. My sister was in the way, so I squeezed in and hip-nudged her off balance, pretending I wanted the view from her side of the window.

"Screw off, you little worm," she said, and dug her knuckles into my ribs, whereupon the whole scene degenerated into a sibling tussle upon which you and Bron looked with detached amusement.

Yours,
Jo

PS: I must have been about six months old when that photo was snapped at Rosa's. My mother is decked out in full grunge-maiden regalia: long floral dress, motorcycle boots, a choker with some kind of polished stone or shell, lots of rings on her fingers. I've got that photo committed to memory, Kurl. Lyle is playing the banjo, but he has sidled up beside her and leaned way over and is resting his temple against her shoulder. He's smiling wide, and her head is thrown back in the biggest, happiest laugh....

I always wanted to know what song they're singing in the photo, but Lyle was never sure. "It was all pretty much a green haze," he would say. How I hated that! I have no memories of Raphael, so I can't help but feel that Lyle needs to be responsible for all the memories. How could he have been that happy in the photo and not recall every single detail about the moment it was taken?

Tuesday, December 15

Dear Little Jo,

Regen. I keep waiting for it to finally snow so there won't be any more roofing until spring. But instead there was light rain all day and then it came pounding down after school. You were standing there at the bus stop when I drove by. I wasn't sure if it was even you at first. I mean I've been doing that a lot lately, thinking it's you and then it's not you. Your hair was slicked flat and your shoulders hunched in trying to protect your backpack wrapped in your arms. Not standing with the other kids inside the shelter.

My foot was already on the brake and I was already pulling the car to the curb before I even considered how it might look, me picking you up in my car. I mean we haven't talked about it, Jo. We've just assumed we're not telling anybody, not even Bron and Shayna, let alone the general public at school.

It was my body making decisions for me faster than my brain. My foot on the brake, my hands turning the wheel. The sight of you shot something strong and bright through my veins. I swear my mouth started to water. It must be how a dog feels when its master comes home. Joy coursing through its whole body.

I guess it must have spooked me a bit, how strong it was. How it got even stronger when you climbed in and slammed the passenger door with the water puddling on the floor mat. Shaking drops off your hair and saying, "Oh, man, you are a

187

lifesaver," and the whole car filled with the smell of wet Jonathan Hopkirk.

Your scent, Jo. It's like wool and bread and something else. I don't know. A scent like if laughter had a scent, or daybreak. You filled the whole car with a yellow light like daybreak. I swear it felt like light pouring into my veins.

I was sort of absorbed in this I guess, and you were talking about normal things. How all this rain reminds you of Prince's Super Bowl show—"Have you ever watched it?" you asked. "It's earthbreaking." That was your word, *earthbreaking*.

How Ms. Deane, the art teacher, wants Bron to apply to art college instead of journalism school. How Shayna cut class and disappeared this afternoon.

Normal things, you talked about. Everyday things.

And suddenly it all seemed really uneven to me. Unbalanced. Which is why I pulled into that grocery-store parking lot.

"Are we doing errands?" you said. You were shivering a bit, so I left the car on and turned up the heat.

It took me about five minutes to spit it out. And still it was completely faltering and awkward. "Do you think you like me as much as I like you?" I asked.

Total silence. You looked sort of shocked. You said, "Kurl, I think...I think it's basically a miracle you like me at all."

I tried to explain what I meant. I said, "It's just that I can't really remember what my head was like, before. What was in my head."

"Before what?"

"Before you," I said. "I mean I think about you all the time. From the second I wake up, all day long. At school I see something going on in the hall, a crowd gathered, and I think, Oh, Jo would say that's the *crux of the dilemma*. Or I will read something in class and I think, I have to remember this for Jo; Jo would love this phrase, or whatever."

You were smiling. "Jo would love this phrase?" you said. "Really?"

"Or in the caf, they have those vitamin C cough drops you like, and I'll want to buy them for you."

You said, "Can I have one now, actually? My throat is sort of—"

"I didn't buy them," I said. "I just wanted to." You were missing the point. I said, "I don't know what was in my head before I met you. What did I even think about? Because whatever it was, it's not in there anymore. It's gone. I am completely, one hundred percent all the time filled up with you."

You were quiet.

"It doesn't feel entirely normal," I said.

You frowned.

"I mean I'm not complaining," I said.

"You're sort of complaining though," you said.

The heater was making an irritating clicking sound. I shut off the engine. "That's not how I meant it, I guess." It sounded wrong even to me. It was joy I'd felt, seeing you at the bus stop. What was my problem? Why did I have to switch joy into something else?

"Maybe you're looking at it the wrong way," you said. "Maybe it's a beautiful thing to be filled up with someone else."

I said, "Sure. So long as it's two ways. So long as you're not deluding yourself."

You turned to face me then. Nudged right up to me. Hooked your knee over my thighs and wrapped your damp arm across my ribs until your mouth was next to my ear. The scent of wet Jonathan. And now the feel of you.

I jerked back and looked around to make sure no other cars were pulling into the spot next to us. It was raining so hard I couldn't see much.

"You're delusional, all right," you said, "if you think it's not two ways. You think I don't like you? Do you need me to tell you how I want you?"

Of course I could feel that you did want me. But I wanted you to tell me too. Your lips were cold on my ear but your breath was hot.

You started to say filthy things, Jo. X-rated things. Unrepeatable things. "I want you on your knees, Kurl," you said, and "I want you flat on your belly."

You took me through it step-by-step: what you'd make me do to you, what you would do to me, what we would do together.

It was just talk. I mean you were pushed up against me, and we must have been moving. We were moving a bit and you did kiss me at one point, now that I'm thinking back. Toward the end of your speech you were kissing me. My head was tipped back against the headrest. I was breathing your breath and not even hearing the words you were saying anymore but just the command behind the words and the kisses. The command was *Surrender.*

"You think you're filled up with me now?" you said. "You're going to be so full of me that you won't even know where you end and I begin. You're going to be so full of me that you'll think you're going to die with the pleasure of it."

And of course I was dying with the pleasure of it right then, exactly like you were ordering me to. *Surrender,* I heard in your words. *Surrender.* And I did.

And then without another word you lifted yourself off me

190

and plunged back into your seat and I was torn from you and from myself too, it felt like. Hovering there, shaky and sticky and embarrassed. You cracked open your window to let the steam out.

I crossed my arms on the steering wheel and rested my forehead on them.

"Are you okay?" you asked.

I waited until my voice was back in my throat. Then I waited until my brain found the words. It seemed to take a long time, a couple of minutes at least.

"Those things you're describing," I said. "Have you done all those things?"

"No," you said. "I told you what I've done. Just groping, basically. Clumsy stuff."

"Then how can you say it? How can you even think the words and get them out of your mouth?"

You laughed. "Are you shocked? I just wanted to turn you on, Kurl. Words are sex too," you said. "There's no difference between describing it and doing it."

I turned my head to peer at you past my arm.

Another laugh. "Well, okay, there *is* a difference, of course, but maybe it's a spectrum. Maybe describing it is part of doing it."

"Would you want to actually do it though?" I asked.

"Which part?" you said.

"Any of it. All of it."

"With you? Yes," you said.

That was all, just "Yes." I lifted my head all the way off my arms and looked at you. You were doodling in the fog on your window. Your ear was bright red, and noticing that made me suddenly a bit less embarrassed.

"Me too," I said.

Why am I repeating all of this? Why did I just sit here in my bed with my babcia's ugly orange quilt wrapped around my shoulders against the chill, staying up late, trying to remember how the words went, who said what, how we moved against each other, how it felt?

Well, I know why. Because remembering it brings some of it back, sensation-wise. But also because I have this idea that it needs to be written down. For the record, for some kind of record. No one knows about us, Jo. There's an entire universe that we've created from scratch, just you and me. And I mean I would like to live here full-time. But the outside world doesn't match up to the inside one, so I keep feeling like you and I are a dream.

No. It's the opposite. I feel like I walk around all day in a dream and then, when I see you, I wake up.

Kurl, you wrote in the steam on the car window.

So I wrote on my window too. I wrote, *I am large, I contain multitudes.*

You squinted, trying to read it. "I didn't know you could write backward."

"It's Walt," I said.

"But why backward?" you said.

"So it makes sense from the outside," I said.

Sincerely,
AK

Friday, December 18

Dear Kurl,

Maybe it is always like this. We are granted these tiny windows of time, these small pockets of space, where nothing else intrudes. Maybe that's all we can ever hope to get, together. And maybe, just maybe, it will be enough.

I'm referring here to your bedroom, Kurl. Your un-Inner-Sanctum, with the bare walls and your babcia's pink-and-orange quilt on the bed.

More specifically, I'm referring to me in your bedroom, with you, last night for the first time.

Can I write about this, Kurl? Or is it a topic—a memory—that belongs only to the secret universe we've created and therefore should stay there? To which universe do our letters belong, do you think: to our own or to the one outside of us?

I'm going to wait and see what you write, to see if it's okay with you.

Yours,
Jo

Dear Little Jo,

Well, I guess now you know where your scarf ended up. You did leave it in my car that night after Lyle's show. Sorry I didn't say so when you asked about it. Actually, you didn't even leave it. When we were parked at the curb around the block from your house, the scarf was slipping out of your collar down the back of your seat. I reached around and gave it a little tug so it dropped onto the floor in the back seat.

I'm aware it was weird of me. It wasn't straight-up theft. I mean I didn't want Lyle's old hippie scarf for myself or anything. I just wanted some kind of souvenir of you, something that smelled like you, Jo. I'm aware it's a little weird.

"I feel like I should have brought flowers," you said, at my front door. I was thinking I should have changed into something better than jeans and a T-shirt at least. I'd been roving around the house all evening looking at everything through fresh eyes—through your eyes—and trying to hide all the most obviously horrible things. Elementary school photos, my mom's prescription bottles, my bathrobe with all the strings hanging down at the hem. I mean I'd started to regret inviting you over, even though it was a once-in-a-lifetime opportunity that my mom and Uncle Viktor were away overnight. A once-a-year opportunity, anyway.

It's how they first got together, actually. The year after my father died, Mom skipped her orchid show in Chicago, and the next year Uncle Viktor offered to go with her.

I don't know if I ever told you that my mom works for a plant-care company that does most of the big office buildings downtown. But her hobby is orchids. She has grow lights in the basement and a little fiberglass greenhouse out back. They go to the orchid show every year, Mom and Viktor.

You came into the house and put down your mandolin case, and for some reason I unzipped your coat for you and took it off your arms like you were four years old. Tugging one sleeve and then the next so you turned a complete circle to release it. You closed your fist inside your cuff at the last second and pulled the coat, and me, toward you. Went up on your toes to kiss me with your cold mouth.

I offered you a cola, and then we didn't have any, which for some reason made us laugh. Everything seemed funny, even not having cola. We drank water and joked around.

You went around looking at everything in my house, but somehow none of it looked as horrible as it did before you showed up. You asked me to plug in the lights on the Christmas tree. We sat with our feet up on the coffee table and my arm around your shoulders. We talked about how they used to make those ornaments by hand with a glassblower and a fire. We laughed about that stupid Christmas-ornament argument we had that time, about which of us was the sparkly glass object that would break under pressure.

You said someday we should take a workshop together, a class in glassblowing.

"When?" I said. It was hard to picture a class like that with both of us in it.

"Someday," you said. "After high school? I don't know."

For the space of maybe fifteen seconds, I was completely and perfectly happy. I mean imagine if you and I still knew each other someday and it wouldn't be a big deal to sign up for a glassblowing class. Imagine if there was even such a class.

Sincerely,
AK

PS: I just read your last letter, which you handed me this morning in the hall but I forgot to open until just now. On the back of the envelope you wrote the phone number of your grandma's house up in Moorhead, since that's where you'll be staying over Christmas. I'm going to drop this letter off at your house tomorrow and see if you have another one for me by then too. I have to say I'm not really looking forward to the holidays this year. Two weeks seems like kind of a long time without any mail.

Yes, you can write about it. Actually I want you to write about it. I mean it's something I wish wasn't part of our universe at all. But it's in there. Maybe if you write about it I will quit feeling like it crowds everything else out.

Dear Kurl,

I'm going to go ahead and write about Thursday night in hopes you'll give me permission, but I'll wait to give you this letter until I hear back. Here goes. We were standing there in your bedroom, kissing, and I noticed that you suddenly weren't quite kissing me back. You weren't even really quite breathing. Somehow my clothes had come off but yours hadn't. Your jeans were open but still on, and when I lifted the hem of your shirt, you pulled away.

"What's wrong?" I said.

"Nothing," you said, but you looked everywhere except at me. You leaned in to kiss me again, and I could sense the awful change as you tried to do it but didn't really want to do it.

I pulled back. "We don't have to do anything. I just came over to see you, not to—"

"No, I want to," you said, but I spotted that panicky look in your eyes, the lockdown look.

"Oh, no," I said. I stepped away from you. "I swear I didn't assume anything in particular would happen, when you asked me over here. It's not a big deal."

In retrospect I will admit I was a little hurt—well, it was a little humiliating to be naked and not wanted—but I truly was resigned to the idea of getting dressed and going back downstairs to hang out, playing some mandolin tunes for you, talking more, maybe ordering pizza. I kicked my boxers free of my trousers and picked them up.

"Don't." You snatched them from my hand. "I don't want you to get dressed."

"What do you want me to do, then?"

You paced a little circle on the rug, looking wildly around the bedroom. Then you opened a dresser drawer and took out my paisley scarf. "I want you to wear this," you said.

"Oh good, you found it." I slung it around my neck. "You want me to wear it? Really?"

"No, I mean over your eyes."

"You want me blindfolded?"

"Yes. I mean, not like that—it's not some kinky thing. It's just...if you wear it, we can do anything you say, anything you want."

It's possible I was curious what you had in mind, but mostly, I think, I just wanted to put you out of your misery. And maybe already then, at some subconscious level, I knew it without really knowing I knew—I knew what you were so worried I might see.

Whatever the case, I held the scarf to my eyes and turned around for you to tie it behind my head. When it was done I said, "Now will you please take off your clothes?"

I didn't touch you, just listened for the sound of things hitting the floor. When I felt you closing in, I stepped back. "Now get on the bed."

And then I exercised my right to do whatever I wanted, which involved, first, jabbing you clumsily with my knees and elbows and apologizing repeatedly, until we were both laughing and cracking jokes about the not-sexiness of being blindfolded. Second, slowing down and telling you to lie still so I could figure out where my limbs ended and your body began. Third, sensing instead of seeing how you were responding to my touch, my kiss. Allowing my fingers and tongue to speak directly to your skin, to make you gasp and arch.

Then we lay side by side. I let you take me into your hands, Kurl, and the blindfold made everything a surprise. I was never sure where I'd feel you next. You laughed at the way I quivered—"like an amoeba," you said, "only louder."

But afterward, when I could think clearly again, I decided it was time to face up to reality. I'd received a few clues already, by then—I'd felt you wince once or twice when I was touching you, and I'd found a raised line of skin at the small of your back when you lifted your hips.

I slipped the scarf off my eyes and blinked in the glare of the side-table light. Your chest was broad and smooth, scattered with a handful of freckles matching the one under your ear. I rested my cheek against it.

"Roll over, Kurl," I said.

You noticed I'd taken off the scarf, and you stiffened. "What for?"

"I need to see," I said. I tried to keep my voice very gentle. "Blindfolding me isn't going to be a long-term solution."

For a minute I thought you would shove me away and bolt from the bed. Your ribs leaped against mine with the force of your heartbeat, and you were staring at me with your lockdown look again.

I was just about to retract. I was thinking, Jonathan, you moron, you are ruining, ruining everything!

But then, abruptly, you rolled over onto your belly, your face turned away and hidden against your pillow.

"What...?" I got my voice under control as soon as I could. I knew I needed to say something, and I knew it mattered to you what I said. "What...did this?" I finally managed.

"Belt," you said. Your voice was muffled by the pillow.

I touched a scab under your shoulder blade. "What about this?"

"Belt buckle."

There were red and blue marks, a few awful, scabbed-over gouges, but there were scars, too. Older wounds.

"Fists, sometimes," you said. "Occasionally a steel-toed boot."

I remembered something and lost my breath for a second. Then I said, "You weren't in a fight, were you."

A whuff of sound into the pillow—amusement, almost. "No."

"I mean your face. That time in your car, the first time you touched me, when you were drunk."

A pause, as you realized what I was asking. "No," you admitted.

"Ever," I said. "You don't ever get in fights, do you?"

"No."

"And that time your back was sore, and you missed school. It wasn't sore muscles you were referring to, was it?"

"No."

"Okay," I said.

You half lifted your head from the pillow. *"Okay?"*

"Not *okay*, okay. Just—" I stroked your hair. I splayed my hand at the top of your spine, my middle fingertip just touching the line of bristle on your neck where your hair stopped—"Okay, Kurl, I'm seeing this. I'm seeing you."

I touched some of the scars. I felt you getting more and more tense, trying to not react to my touch, trying to tough it out. I could tell you'd made a pact with yourself not to pull away, not to try to hide. I kissed the scar on your shoulder. I was crying, but it wasn't pity, Kurl, I swear it.

"Stop, now," you said. "I can't stand it anymore."

"You're beautiful," I said.

"No. This does not make me beautiful."

"It's part of you, though." I traced an older, nearly healed bruise on your ribs, curving down to your hip bone.

"It isn't like laugh lines, for God's sake. It's ugly."

"It's ugly what he does to you," I agreed. "It's hideous what he does. But you, you are beautiful."

"Stop," you begged. "Jo, just stop. Stop."

So I stopped, and I climbed on top of you and pressed my chest to your ravaged back. I tugged your wrists out to each side and pressed my arms along yours, pressed my temple to your cheek, pressed my knees into the backs of your thighs. We lay together like that a long time, until it felt as if there was no longer any skin between us, just bones twining like vines around each other's bones.

Yours,
Jo

Dear Kurl,

Your brother Mark is almost exactly how I'd pictured him from your description, except his curly hair is cut short now, and he is extremely, shockingly thin. Did you even know Mark dropped by your house the morning after I slept over? He said he was waiting on a VA check and hoped it had been delivered there by mistake. You didn't wake up until after he'd left, Kurl, and I don't think I remembered to tell you about his visit. Mark was surprised to see me playing the mando at your kitchen table, of course—fear not, I was fully dressed except for my socks—but I simply told him I'd been over the night before helping you prep for the SAT, and you'd fallen asleep midway through the session. I think he was more taken aback by the notion of you planning to take the SAT than by the notion of me helping you, although he did ask how old I am.

I will admit I was a little nervous, talking to your brother. Thanks to the mandolin, though, the conversation moved swiftly to music. Mark told me about this banjo player named Davey at one of the bases in Afghanistan who taught everyone to sing "I'll Fly Away" in four-part harmony. Kurl, did you know that your brother learned to play harmonica over there? "I did a mean little solo on that song," he said. Sometimes they were ordered to patrol on amber status, and everyone would be so nervous they'd beg Mark to take out his harmonica just to break the tension. "Can you picture us idiots? Strolling around a combat zone playing the harmonica?"

I asked him what *amber status* meant.

"Cold weapons," he said. "The magazine is loaded, but the safety is on and there's no round chambered."

I thought of your letters about ambushes, surprise attacks, suicide bombers, and I found myself wondering whether guns would have been any help to Mark and his friends at all, in an explosive attack.

"So did you do it?" I said. "Play the harmonica on patrol?"

"Yep." He didn't smile, exactly, but I thought he sounded proud.

I better go walk this down to the mailbox, since the pickup time posted on it is 5 p.m. I looked up your zip code online, and I think Lyle has stamps somewhere in the basket above the fridge. I wonder if you'll even receive this letter before Christmas, given the holiday postal crunch. We really are authentic pen pals now, aren't we, Kurl?

Yours,
Jo

Dear Little Jo,

Merry Christmas. Do you know about Polish Christmas? I mean I don't see us as all that traditional or ethnic in other ways. But Christmas at the Kurlansky house is very, very Polish.

First is the fish. The morning of Christmas Eve I go with my mom to the deli and line up with twenty other people to choose a fish from the tank. Mom has had the bathtub filled with water since the night before so the chlorine will evaporate out of it. None of us can shower Christmas Eve morning. One of those things that would be weird and irritating except it's been true since I was born.

So our fish swims around in its new home for six or seven hours, and then Uncle Viktor chops its head off and filets it. With the fish, we eat this beet soup. Borscht. And pierogi, of course, and this syrupy drink with fruit soaked in booze called *kompot*.

Aunt Agata gets dropped off on Christmas Eve by a wheelchair van from her nursing home. She's actually Uncle Viktor's aunt, my dad's aunt. My great-aunt. Aunt Agata is bent over so far in her wheelchair that she has to lift her brows and open her eyes wide to look up at you. She always seems surprised and sort of skeptical. She just sits there and has to wait for people to move her around.

Sylvan and Julia, his girlfriend, and Mark came for Christmas dinner too. Sylvan announced that he and Julia are getting married next September, so there were lots of toasts and we all drank a bit more *kompot* than usual. Dessert is noodles with this sweet caraway sauce. It sounds disgusting but it's delicious. I'll have to make it for you sometime, Jo.

After supper was cleaned up and gifts were done, we all sort of sat around wondering what to talk about. Aunt Agata's arms looked more blue than before the meal, so I went up and got my quilt for her.

Sylvan says, "You shouldn't let her have contact with your bedding. Those nursing homes are crawling with bedbugs." And Julia shushes him.

Meanwhile I'm not really listening to the conversation because I'm thinking about that quilt on my bed and you with your scarf tied over your eyes. That quilt with you lying across it.

"I know you," Aunt Agata suddenly says to me, out of nowhere. Staring straight up at me suddenly with those peeled-back eyes. My heart pretty much stops for a second because I'm thinking what she means is that she knows about you—about me and you, Jo. Which is an important lesson in not letting myself drift off like that into thinking about you.

But of course that's not what Aunt Agata means. She says, "You're Zladko's boy."

And now it's not just me tensing up. For a second everyone's dead quiet. We're all holding our breath because nobody has mentioned my father's name all through dinner, all through this whole Christmas. No one has said his name aloud like that, in front of other people, in ages. Especially not in front of Uncle Viktor.

"You're the smart one, aren't you?" Aunt Agata says, and she turns to my mom. "Isn't this the smart one, Ewa?"

And now everyone sort of chuckles, *heh heh, crazy old lady* et cetera, because Ewa was my dad's and Uncle Viktor's older sister, who died before my parents even met. Aunt Agata says to me, "Such a smart little boy you were. So tall, now!" And then she looks down at the quilt in her lap, and a few minutes later she's asleep, and that's it.

Uncle Vik falls asleep for a while too, until Mark stands up and turns off the TV. You never turn off the TV like that when Uncle Vik is asleep in case it wakes him up. And sure enough, he wakes up and stomps out to the garage, which is where he keeps his vodka. Mark doesn't know about any of this, of course, about any of Uncle Vik's habits or the rules for how to handle him.

We go to midnight mass every year, but this time Mark says he has to bow out, because believe it or not Christmas Eve is one of their busiest nights at the Texas Border. And then Sylvan and Julia do some whispering and say they can't come to mass either. My mom is upset by this, tears in her eyes and sniffling as they start gathering their stuff. Saying, "No, no, I'm just so glad you were here for dinner, thank you, merry Christmas."

Looking back I realize it was her being upset that got him upset, probably. Uncle Vik. I mean she was already upset by Uncle Vik being out in the garage on Christmas Eve, and then he came back in and saw her crying and it pissed him off I guess.

The van was coming for Aunt Agata soon, so I started steering her chair around the coffee table. And Uncle Viktor starts in on me. "Look at him; can't you just see his future? Some kinda nursemaid. A nurse, right? But the kind that don't gotta go to school for it." He's laughing and laughing. "Little blue uniform, and them paper slippers. I can just see it; it's perfect."

I'm almost to the hall with Aunt Agata. "Surgeons wear those slippers, actually," I say. "In the operating room. Because they're sterile."

Uncle Vik is up like a shot and follows me down the hall. "Don't be smart," he says, and then he surprises me with a punch to the ear that sends my skull into the hall mirror. The impact makes a long crack in the glass.

Aunt Agata tries to see what's going on, but she can't turn that far in her chair. She's just staring sideways at the wall beside her, and suddenly it is the most awful thing I've ever seen. That frightened craning neck. Those wild eyes. I mean she can't even turn around to face what might be coming.

My mom follows us out from the living room to see what the noise was and then backs up again fast. Backs up and veers into the kitchen.

I turn around and run. Well, I sort of stumble because my head is exploding with pain. Straight up the stairs to my room.

There's something that happens to me in these situations, Jo.

I mean you know. I'm writing this story differently because you know, now. I'm aware that just because you know about Uncle Viktor and me doesn't mean you want to hear all the gory details from now on. But being able to write the story unedited, writing it straight like it happened, like it's happening, feels different. Faster. Not easier but faster.

Something happens to me when I'm alone and hurt. I can't sit down or lie down. I stand there in my room without moving for hours sometimes. Sometimes all night. Sometimes I go for a run instead because even though it hurts more, it's movement at least. That's what I did that day I ended up at your house when you weren't home, that time Lyle noticed I was acting squirrelly and gave me weed to calm me down. What happens is a belief that if I rest I'll die. If I sleep I won't wake up. In words like this it sounds ridiculous but there aren't words when it happens. There's only the belief.

Sylvan knocks and then opens the bedroom door before I can say anything. "What the hell happened to the hall mirror?" he says.

"It was an accident," I say, "when I brought the chairs up." We hadn't needed any extra chairs from the basement but I figured Sylvan wouldn't have bothered to count.

He says, "If Mom's Christmas wasn't ruined before, it is now. I told her I'd take it with me, get it fixed, but you're paying for it."

"Okay, thank you," I say to him. "Merry Christmas."

"Merry Christmas," he says. "See ya."

That's when I called you, Jo, at your relatives' house in Moorhead. I was still sort of hanging there in space, still certain I would die if I didn't stay on my feet and watch out. There still weren't words for it.

That's why I couldn't really talk, and I said so, and you said, laughing, "So you called me not to talk?" In the background I could hear Shayna and Lyle and a bunch of other voices. It was Christmas Eve.

I said, "I just really wish we could..."

I don't even know what I wanted to say. I mean I wanted to say, "I wish we could be alone," or something. "I wish we could be together." Like that time you were half-asleep and rolled with your shoulder in my larynx and said, "Can you breathe?" And I couldn't really but didn't need to either, because air seemed unnecessary with all that happiness in my chest.

I couldn't say any of this to you. Yet you somehow understood it anyway. "I know," you said. "I wish we could too."

sincerely,
AK

Dear Kurl,

A confession, Kurl: I am utterly weary of Christmas, and it's only the second night of our four-night stay up in Moorhead. I've often wondered how a person can have so little in common with his extended family. Perhaps it's because they're not actually related to us, except for my maternal grandmother, Gloria, whose house we stay at every year. Every year, we three Hopkirks and Gloria are joined by the Hanssen family. Tony Hanssen is Gloria's stepson from her second marriage. He's one of those red-faced, round-stomached men who wear watches that were supposedly designed for Navy SEALs or NASA engineers but are only ever worn by men like Tony Hanssen. His wife, Andrea, is so yogacized and blow-dried and made-up that she looks her age only close up, or under the halogen lights in the kitchen. Their kids, Calder (twelve) and Jonah (ten), went to Montessori and Waldorf and Junior Juilliard and puppetry camp and all the other programs that make children impossible to talk to.

I never feel I have anything to contribute to all these people's endless small talk—Tony Hanssen collects model boats, Andrea hates her boss, Gloria wants to remodel the kitchen—so I sit there silently, awkwardly, while Shayna and the Hanssen boys stare at their phones. This year I also find myself thinking about you, Kurl, missing you: your broad scratchy palms. That heat coming off your skin. And then one of the adults will direct a question my way and I'll miss it entirely and snap to attention, embarrassed. It's exhausting.

Tonight I'm feeling homesick and forlorn, lying here on my inflatable cot across from Shayna's pullout sofa in the study. My sister just fell asleep holding a family photo of the Hanssens that includes Lyle and Shayna and a very pregnant Raphael.

"Everyone always says she looks like me, but she doesn't," Shayna commented, when she pulled it off the desk.

Gloria had said it, too, when we first came through the door. She'd grabbed Shayna's shoulders, stared hard into her face, and teared up. "Oh my good Lord, it's like seeing a ghost," she cried. "Spitting image. *Spitting* image. Darling, you are the *spitting* image of your mama."

Shayna passed the family photo over to me for my opinion, but I couldn't tell one way or the other. My mother wears heavy bangs in the photo, and her face is round and soft with all the extra weight she's packed on, carrying me. It looked to me as though a stranger off the street had stepped into our group right before the picture was snapped.

You sounded forlorn, too, Kurl, on the phone last night. It was nothing you said in particular, just something faraway in your voice, as if it were coming from a smaller body than yours. I wanted to call you back right after we said goodbye, but I didn't know who would pick up. I wish I had the money to buy you a phone for Christmas—to buy us both phones with only each other's numbers on them. But I suppose there is already enough you have to hide.

Yours,
Jo

Sunday, December 27

Dear Little Jo,

Another letter you won't receive till you're back in town. It almost seems like there's no point to writing except that what else am I supposed to do when I get torn awake from a nightmare? I have this one repeating nightmare of a fire burning down a barn, and I have to rescue a horse from it. This horse won't come out of his stall. He just stands there looking at me while my lungs fill up with heat and smoke, and the look in his eye is what finally wakes me up because it's so awful. That look says, *This is your fault.*

Sylvan told me that once Mark jumped out of his car right in the middle of traffic on South Eighth Street. He yelled at Sylvan to take the wheel, and then he limped right through all the cars, right across to the sidewalk. He still used his cane back then, but he didn't wait long enough to grab it from the back seat. It took Sylvan a few minutes in the middle of all those honking cars to pull over and pass the cane to Mark through the passenger window. Then Mark puked in a flower box in front of the Gap. Sylvan said he wouldn't get back in the car. Couldn't.

Why do I dream about this horse? I mean I'm pretty sure I've never even seen a horse up close like that, in real life. I've never even been inside a barn.

Most veterans can't afford cars, Sylvan says, but even if they have them they don't drive them. In traffic is where people in

Afghanistan got killed. A traffic jam meant a roadblock, meant suicide bombers or grenades dropped from the rooftops. Honking cars meant here it comes.

Sincerely,
AK

Dear Kurl,

Back home at last, and I found both your letters waiting for me
in our mailbox. Thank you, Kurl! It's by far the best Christmas
present I've received this year. Your letters are heavy in content,
I know, but it's such a joy and relief to hear your "voice" that I
felt lighter reading them. I'd like to deliver this reply, and my
previous letter, to your house, but I worry about possible inter-
ception. Did you receive that one letter I posted in the mail,
the one about your brother Mark? I hope it found its way safely
into your hands, though I don't think it contained anything too
incriminating, if your Uncle Viktor did happen to read it.

At 3 a.m. this morning in Moorhead, Shayna shook me awake.
She'd switched on the halogen lights in the study, and once my
eyes adjusted to the glare I saw that she had spread photographs all
over the rug between my cot and her sofa bed. "Get up," Shayna
ordered. "Come look."

It was so cold in the room my nose was numb. Gloria likes
to economize on heating at nighttime. My sister had swaddled
herself in all her blankets. Rather than unzip my sleeping bag,
I wormed to the edge of the cot and flopped over onto the
floor.

"Watch it!" Shayna hissed. "You're messing them up."

"Where did you find all these?" I said.

"In this thing"—she toed a floral-print file folder—"underneath all that crap in Gloria's basement."

"You snooped in Gloria's basement?"

"Look, will you?" Shayna said. "They're all of Mom."

She was right. Raphael with eight candles on her birthday cake. Raphael missing her front teeth. Raphael in a church choir.

"She looks like *me*," I said, surprised. I'd always thought I took after Lyle. "Like pictures of me as a little kid."

Raphael crouching on the grass with her arms wrapped around the neck of a German shepherd. Raphael in a soccer uniform, one foot proudly poised on the ball. Raphael in a turquoise satin prom dress.

"Well, she looks like you more," I amended. Teenaged Raphael had Shayna's light brown hair, her pointed nose, her arched brows. Raphael and a friend wearing matching acid-washed jeans, jean jackets, and little bright-colored vinyl purses with long straps. Raphael and two friends posing like models on the steps of a museum or library.

There were so many pictures. Raphael sitting behind a boy on a motorcycle, lifting her helmet high in the air. Raphael on the sofa beside another boy, holding a bottle of beer. Raphael wearing dark eyeliner, her hair dyed black like in the picture at Rosa's Room. After a while I found myself scanning the array for images from the less distant past. "Is Lyle in any of these?" I asked.

"Lyle?" Shayna exploded. "Who cares about Lyle? This is Mom's whole life, right here, and we've never seen any of it."

"But they met really young, right?" I said. I picked up a photo of black-haired Raphael playing guitar and held it up for her to see. "She might have been singing with the Decent Fellows already by this point."

Shayna lunged to grab a photo from the far side of the display, moving so violently that her blankets swept a half-dozen others under the sofa bed. "Do you remember this?" she asked me.

It was Raphael in a hospital bed with her leg in a cast, in traction. Her arm was wrapped around a small child curled beside her, asleep. "That's you?" I guessed.

"It's *you*. Remember? You would have been three or four. I think she slipped on some rocks or something when we were swimming. Maybe at a festival?"

I looked closer. The child's face was wide and pale, the hair long and feathery. I didn't recognize myself.

"Don't you remember?"

I shook my head, and when I looked up Shayna was crying. "I'm sorry," I said.

"It's not that," she said. "It's like he just *erased* her."

"Lyle?"

"Yes. Like, maybe you actually would remember some of this stuff, if he hadn't gone and destroyed all the evidence of her existence."

She wiped her face with her blanket and was quiet a minute as I looked at more of the photos. Then she said, "You know that place called the Ace? So it turns out that guy Axel, the owner, is pretty cool. He really liked me, that time Bron and I went to the open mic night. He says he might give me a gig."

"Like Raphael, on that postcard," I said.

Shayna nodded. "Mom played there a lot, apparently. Just her and her guitar. Axel says she used to pack the place."

"Cool," I said, to make her feel better. But I knew Lyle

wouldn't think it was cool, that my sister was frequenting the Ace. In fact, I strongly suspected that Lyle had never thought it was cool that Raphael played there, either, although I didn't know why not. Maybe she'd had a falling-out with the Decent Fellows and went solo, and there'd been hard feelings.

I kept all this speculation to myself, though. Things are heated enough between Shayna and Lyle these days; I didn't want to add fuel to the fire.

Yours,
Jo

Dear Little Jo,

Who would have thought in a million years I'd be so happy to be back at school? There you were at lunchtime wearing some kind of heavy goat herder's turtleneck sweater under your Loaghtan tweed jacket. And those knitted gloves that only reach your knuckles.

"Oh, hi, Kurl," you said.

Do not press Jo's icy red fingertips between your hands and blow on them, I told myself. Do not put Jo's fingers into your mouth. I mean Bron was standing right there.

It's actually hard to think of things to write when you just invited me home with you after school. What are we going to write about, Jo, now that we can say everything to each other in person?

Sincerely,
AK

Dear Kurl,

We must have picked the coldest evening of the year to visit your Outer Sanctum. I could see the potential of the place under the skeletal trees and knee-deep snow, but this particular trip was all business. Bron and Shayna needed to see a train up close, as research for their Civics presentation on crude-oil transportation safety policies.

As she drove, Bron lectured us the whole way: The spill-cleanup contingency plans are laughable, she said. Even the so-called safety tankers are vulnerable to explosion in the event of derailment. They roll right through Minneapolis, these firebombs-in-waiting, 170 tanker cars at a go.

I kept sneaking looks at you in the back seat. At first I was looking for a way to take your hand, maybe by spreading my extra sweater and gloves between us on the seat, but there was about four feet of space between us in that monster vehicle, and in any case you were staring out the window into the dark, lost in thought.

I wondered if it was Bron's talk of explosions silencing you—you have some expertise in that subject, I know—and then I started thinking how often it is that I see you *not* jump into a conversation even when you know something about the topic, how more often than not you get quieter, not more talkative,

218

when the rest of us are discussing a subject you know all about. I thought about how I would never have any idea what you know—how much you know—unless I read it in your letters.

The whole thing took my breath away for a moment. How lucky I am that you write to me. How, even if you and I were able to talk together openly about any subject we wanted, anywhere and in front of anyone in the world, I would still want you to write to me as well, just so I could be sure I was getting the whole story.

Anyhow. We parked the car (Bron: "This is the sort of spot my parents always tell me not to park the Escalade.") and you broke trail for us, flashlight swinging through the brush to find the path. The snow went directly down the cuffs of my boots, so I tried to step only where your footprints had broken the crust. I saw you half turn, notice my struggle, and shorten your stride for me. Then you started dragging your boots instead of stomping, making a kind of ski track for the rest of us to follow.

Bron and Shayna started bickering behind us. Bron said, "You didn't read any of those articles I sent you, did you?" and Shayna said, "Did you bring us any green, Bron? A couple of beers?"

"I need you to take this project seriously," Bron said. "I'm starting to get really sick of carrying you at school."

We were at the tracks. The girls burst out into the open white stripe of snow, and you held me back under the trees. You took off your glove, dragged a hot finger to my cheek, pushed it between my lips. "You're quiet," you said.

I kept my eye on the girls and bit down until you pulled your finger back. "*You're* quiet," I said.

"C'mon. They're fighting. They're distracted." You tried to kiss me.

I was distracted by the fight, too, though. "Excuse me for wanting a decent grade on this," Bron was saying, and Shayna retorted, "It's not just the grade, though, is it? It's this whole other agenda with you. You want to write a story on this for the paper, for your portfolio."

Port-FOH-lee-oh: Had you ever heard someone put so much sneer into a word?

I have to say I'm fully in agreement with Bron about my sister's attitude these days. Shayna's been on a steep downhill slide since school started again: going right back to bed after Lyle leaves for work, slumped in front of reruns when I get home from school, skipping all her SAT practices, sneaking out at night.

Bron had somehow consulted the train schedule and timed our trek around it. I see now why that long, straight run of track is such an important feature of your Outer Sanctum: We could hear the train coming, and see its headlight, for four or five long minutes before it was upon us.

Anticipation! Which my sister decided to amplify for the rest of us by plowing straight up the slope to stand on the tracks.

"Really?" Bron hollered. "You're doing *that*? Give me a break, Shay."

Immediately, you were up there on the tracks beside Shayna. I heard you murmuring to her, one hand raised to stop us from joining you.

"Congratulations. You're in the fucking *Breakfast Club*, all right? You're officially a teenager cliché." Bron was stomping little circles, clutching her arms around herself, swiveling her head from the oncoming train to her friend and back. I said, "Shh," and tried to take her arm, and she shoved me nearly off my feet.

Each of us reacts in our own way to danger, don't we? Bron

short-circuits straight from fright to anger. I focus on whoever is closest to me and try to divert them, draw their fire, pacify. And you. You stand directly in the path of the oncoming train, murmuring comfort.

It's morning, and time for school now. I suppose you'll have to tell me the rest of last night's story. Or maybe you've already written it, and in that case I wonder which part you chose. Maybe I can guess: the very last part, the best part.

Yours,
Jo

Dear Little Jo,

You write me up as such a hero with that train situation but I didn't feel it to be dangerous exactly. I mean Shayna may be pretty unhappy these days but she isn't suicidal. Also the way I got her to come down off the tracks is I used you. Told lies about you basically. I said you were scared to come down here with us because being hit by a train is your worst nightmare. You had only agreed to come along because you didn't want to look like a coward. I said you were back there shitting your pants probably. So would Shayna mind please showing a little mercy for your sake?

She smiled finally, and pouted her lips and put her arms up around my neck. I carried her down the slope like some rescued princess. Until I stumbled and we both went face-first into a snowbank. It loosened things up though didn't it? You're welcome for that part, because that *was* heroic. Even Bron laughed.

And we still had just enough time for Bron to remember the magnet lights in her bag and hand them out. You're supposed to stick these magnetic LED lights on your car bumper if you break down at the roadside so the tow truck can find you. Or I guess so nobody mows you down. Bron had read that people throw them at passing trains at night. I like Bron for that. I will read something and think about it, but Bron will read something and go do it.

So the train came past and it was shorter than we thought, only about ten or fifteen tankers. We all tossed our lights but only mine stuck. It lit up right near the top of the very last car.

Bron said it would look like a flare going up, but this was better than any flare. This was a blind throw and then a sudden red sword cutting its way through the night. This was the muscles of my arm, my ribs, my guts, my groin, all flung out of my body at once so that only space was left inside. It was like watching Prince onstage that time. Like empty space filling me up to bursting. Filling up the moment with *now, right now.*

I gave a sort of whoop. A laugh, and then I couldn't stop. Laughing and shouting and running along the tracks after the disappearing train with its red beacon. The rest of you came running and yelling too, up and down the slope, and none of us stopped until the train was completely out of sight and it was quiet. Then we went back and searched without much hope for the three lights that had missed the mark, until Shayna said, "Fuck it's cold, let's get out of here."

Nearly at the car I said I had to piss. I yanked at your sleeve until you caught on and said, "Me too."

I pulled you behind some bushes. I looked all around to make sure, even down at the ground and then up. There was nothing but shadows and pockmarked snow and a flat black sky.

You yelped at my cold hands down your pants but then you did the same to me. We rocked and swayed, swore and laughed. Touching you was like finding myself in the dark, Jo. That one moment stretching itself out again like *now now now*, like steel wheels on tracks. I mean the train was long gone but I swear I could still hear it when I came. Me first and then you right after me, shuddering, leaning into each other, your nose pressed hard

223

into my neck and both of us laughing and gasping in the freezing dark. We could hear Bron yelling for us to hurry up. We wiped our hands with snow and found our dropped gloves and ran.

In the car Bron asked what took us so long, and weren't we aware how brutal the Escalade's idling was, in terms of emissions?

Emissions. I didn't even look at you, Jo, for fear of laughing. We laughed anyhow, both of us helpless with it. That swift secret. That joy.

Sincerely,
AK

Dear Little Jo,

A quick note that I'll give to you directly since you're likely not checking Khang's box anymore. I have to say I always have a tiny fumble of disappointment walking into her classroom and seeing the mailbox. It takes me a second to remember that the letter-writing assignment is officially over and there won't be anything from you waiting for me. Half the time I still check. I mean it's not like we don't see each other pretty much every day. It's just reflex.

So at lunchtime I was studying math in the art room with Bron. The art teacher, Rhoda, said if we ever want to use the room when she's not there, we can get the key from her ahead of time. Did you know there's also a little art-supply room with a lock? I saw Rhoda put the key in the drawer of her desk.

Sincerely,
AK

Dear Kurl,

Lyle asked me last night about the butcherboys. He noticed that the collar point of my rough-spun linen shirt had been snipped off and guessed, correctly, that it hadn't been a slip of *my* scissors.

He said Bron had mentioned that maybe it was worse for me this year at school than last. "Are you suffering?" he asked.

I told him it was indeed worse, actually, but that I didn't feel I was suffering, exactly. I couldn't tell him about you, of course—about how your presence at school more than compensates for the presence of the butcherboys. It's been months now since I last left for school carrying dread like stones in all my pockets.

"And what about your sister?" he said. "Do you have any thoughts on what's up with her lately?"

I shrugged. "She seems okay to me."

"Okay? She's been cutting school almost every day. They leave automated messages on my phone, you know."

I did know. I also know that Shayna and Lyle argue constantly these days. When she dyed her hair jet-black on New Year's Day, they yelled at each other for nearly an hour. Lyle has worlds to say about Shayna's clothes, her hair and makeup, her attitude, her habits; Shayna has nothing to say in return but "Get off my case" and "Leave me alone, Lyle."

I said, "I thought you were asking me whether she's happy."

"Well, does she seem happy to you?"

"Happy enough," I said. Happy being Axel's newest rising star at the Ace, I meant. But I kept that tidbit to myself.

As you know, Kurl, Lincoln High is supposed to be a place of learning. What I learned today at lunchtime, in the art-supply closet: There is a three-inch section of skin over your spine, just above your shoulder blades, where the fine hair forms an almost-invisible furrow. Brushing my lips along it generates the softest, most delicate sensation any part of my body has ever experienced.

Yours,
Jo

PS: I'm going to put this letter in Ms. Khang's box regardless of the fact that I'll (hopefully!) see you today after school. Now that the assignment is finished, Ms. Khang will give you the combination so you can access the mailbox whenever you want. I don't want you to feel disappointed when you check the mail, Kurl! I don't want you to experience any disappointment, in any context, even for one second. And anyhow I'm still exchanging letters with Abigail Cuttler from time to time. She and I enjoy some interesting philosophical debates, so we've agreed to keep corresponding.

Dear Kurl,

A good reason to write a letter: to tell a story.

Once upon a time, Christopher Dowell and I used to be friends. I know I've mentioned this before, but I never told you our story. For several months in the spring of fifth grade, we would walk home together after school once or twice a week and play video games or jump on his trampoline. He was roughly twice my weight back then, too, but the only practical result of the size difference was that Dowell liked to give me piggybacks. He was terrible at reading and writing, so I used to read aloud to him often—school handouts, comic books, even the onscreen scripts from *Pokémon* while we played. He was called "Christopher" by everyone back then. Never "Chris," only "Christopher."

For some reason Dowell always had about twenty or thirty golf balls lying around his backyard, and once we made up a hilarious game in which we'd stuff all the golf balls into our shorts and jump off his shed roof, over the edge of the safety net, and onto the trampoline. We would film each other's jumps on his sister Laurie's phone. On impact the balls would fly out the cuffs of our shorts and bounce violently up into our faces and come raining down onto our skulls. Sometimes they'd ricochet right back into our crotches or leave bruises on the undersides of our arms.

Recounting this to you, I'm finding the pseudo-sexual nature of the game glaringly obvious. But at the time it was simply fun. Normal.

Dowell went to a different junior high than me, so we didn't cross paths again until last year, by which time I was wearing my Walt Whitman garb and he was a butcherboy. I suppose fond memories weren't enough to overcome the social gulf between us. Or maybe it's more directly correlated than that: Maybe remembering the piggyback rides and the golf-ball game fills Dowell with retrospective loathing and intensifies his will to violence.

Yours,
Jo

Monday, January 25

Dear Little Jo,

Khang caught my attention on my way out of English class and
sort of nodded in the direction of the box so I'd know you'd left
me a letter. You can tell she gets a kick out of the fact that we're
hopelessly addicted to mail.

I know I'll see you in Rhoda's room today—at least I hope
I will—but this note is to formally thank you for all your help
with the SAT prep. I did okay I think. I mean there were lots of
questions I had to skip but I managed to stick to the strategy and
everything.

Thank you, thank you, thank you, Jonathan Hopkirk. A couple of letters ago you mentioned that I make school easier for
you. Well you make it easier for me too. I mean everything, all
of it. You make everything easier. You make me feel like I can do
pretty much anything.

Sincerely,
AK

Dear Kurl,

I meant to tell you today that when Shayna arrived home Saturday from taking the SAT, hours before I expected any of you, she stomped straight up to her room and slammed the door. At first she wouldn't even answer when I knocked. Then she said, "Now we know why you were so interested in that goddamn test. You were prepping Kurl, weren't you?"

"Can I come in?" I asked.

"No."

"What happened? Why are you home so soon?"

"I should never even have registered," she said. "There was no way in hell I was going to score high enough to bother."

I rested my forehead against her door. It was exactly what Bron had been afraid of: Shayna giving up and not even taking the test.

"Kurl seemed to be killing it," she said. "He was filling stuff in like a demon. Didn't look up from the page once."

"Are you mad we kept it a secret?"

"No, Jojo, I'm not mad. God. Why would I even care?"

"Do we really have to conduct this entire conversation through the door?" I asked.

"There is no conversation," she said. "Go away."

Go away. Leave me alone. I've been getting a lot of that from my sister lately, on the rare occasions she's been in the house. Lyle found a pack of matches from the Ace in her bag the other day and hit the roof. She confessed to him she and Bron had been to that open mic night before Christmas, which is technically true, but she did not divulge that she's been spending most of her time there ever since.

Lyle tried to say that she's not to go there again, ever, or else. She kept asking him why not: What is his problem with that place in particular, why does he get so worked up about it, why can't he give her a single logical reason she shouldn't go there? "Because you're underage" is clearly not holding water with her.

Yours,
Jo

Dear Little Jo,

Well that wasn't exactly how we planned it. I hope you're not mad. I mean I didn't plan on it at all. Sylvan and Julia were coming for dinner, so I'd promised Mom I'd help her cook. I only had half an hour left after we came downstairs from your room.

By the way I didn't mean to make it sound like I thought you should have let me come into your tent with you. Not with everybody downstairs like that and the girls likely to barge in any second. At least standing behind your bedroom door we could do what we liked, or some of what we liked, and still not get caught if we heard someone in the hall outside.

Well not getting caught was the theory, anyway. I guess we didn't account for my big mouth. Everyone was sitting around in your living room: Bron, Shayna, Lyle, Rich, and me. You were only out of the room for two or three minutes, Jo. Somehow the conversation had drifted to the topic of body smells. Rich said his father's hat still smells like his hair, even though he's been dead for twenty years. Bron swore she could tell Isaiah and Ezra apart by smelling their necks.

Lyle and Rich were already getting their coats on. They were just about to leave for rehearsal. I mean the conversation was basically over.

Then Shayna said, "Jojo's feet smell like peanut butter."

And without thinking at all I said, "Hazelnut."

"What?" she said, and I repeated it: "They smell like hazelnuts."

There was total silence, but it wasn't too late. I mean there were so many things I could have said. "He told me himself, in a letter," or "He shoved his feet in my face one time," or even "It's his vintage shoes." There were so many simple things that could have explained it away, or at least made it seem sort of logical that a teenaged boy would say a thing like that about the scent of another teenaged boy's feet.

But none of those things came into my head. Or at least not fast enough to dodge Bronwyn Otulah-Tierney.

And of course it was Bron. She knew instantly. She said, "How is it that you've become the authority on the smell of Jonathan's feet, Kurl?" Her voice all chirpy. Her head sort of tilted to one side, her lashes fluttering. Letting me know she'd figured it out.

I sat there, dead silent. Speechless. Heat crawling up my neck to my face. I mean I could feel the heat burning behind my eyelids, even.

Bron looked at Shayna, and Shayna's eyebrows disappeared under her bangs. "No way," she said. "You and Jonathan? No *way*. Since when?"

"Are we talking about what I think we're talking about?" Lyle said.

"I wasn't supposed to..." I stuttered. "I mean, he didn't want to..."

And then you walked into the room. You looked around at the gaping faces, and asked, "What's up?" And then at me, with my hot face: "What's the matter?"

Everyone cracked up. You have this way of smiling, Jo, when other people are laughing and you don't know why. Your eyes crease at the corners and your mouth turns up, but only for a second. Then it flips into a half frown, and then back to smiling again. Like you're testing which one might be the right answer. It's one of those things about you that pumps adrenaline straight through my guts. Makes me want to punch anyone not sharing the joke with you.

"I told them," I said, before anyone else could say it, "about us. It was an accident."

Bron leaped up and hugged you. It was kindness, I think. Holding you in case you fainted or something.

"Well, no wonder you're such a good cook," Rich said.

Shayna punched him. "Rich!"

You sank into Bron's chair, and Shayna sat next to me on the couch. "So, how long? Weeks? Months?"

"A couple months," you said. A bit teary from the shock.

Lyle and Rich gave us a big round of congratulations on their way out the door.

"You're not mad, are you?" you asked Shayna. "Lying by omission?"

"No. I mean I wish you could have told me sooner. But no." Shayna laughed. "Hazelnuts! Oh my God, Kurl."

So I had to explain it to you, about your feet smelling like hazelnuts. It was the first time I was talking about our universe, our secret dream universe, out loud. It was still a dream but suddenly also real life. This realness made everything so much sharper. Honed the edges of everything.

You laughed at my stupidity and dragged my hand to your lap and lifted it and bit my fingers, hard. I snatched my hand back and dug my knuckles under your ribs until you yelped and squirmed. It was the first time we'd touched in public. The first time people were watching us. Seeing us. It felt like something striking sparks in my chest. The sharpness of it! Grinning. Both of us grinning like idiots, and Bron saying, "Oh my God, stop it. Stop, I can't take it; my brain is exploding."

I had to go. You walked me to the door and we kissed as quickly and quietly as possible. You whispered, "Don't leave me to this pack of jackals."

I brushed the side of my face against your face: mine rough, yours smooth. "I won't sleep," I promised, for no reason at all.

But you understood whatever I was trying to say. "I won't either," you vowed.

Sincerely,
AK

Dear Kurl,

I'm writing to formally request a do-over of something I botched yesterday in the art closet. In the heat of the moment you said, "Ask me for anything, Jo; the answer is yes." I was light-headed, laughing, but itchy with sweat, so I asked you to scratch the back of my thigh for me. I was just like the old woman in the fairy tale who squanders her three wishes by sticking a sausage to the end of her husband's nose and then wishing it off again.

Yours,
Jo

Thursday, February 25

Dear Little Jo,

It wasn't just the heat of the moment. Ask me for anything. The
answer is yes.

sincerely,
AK

Dear Kurl,

It's an amazing phenomenon: Every time I reread your letter that says "Ask me for anything," I find there is nothing more I need or want.

Yours,
Jo

Dear Little Jo,

I came down the path by the railway tracks after school today. My Outer Sanctum. On the asphalt right before the gap in the fence, someone has spray-painted the word BREATHE. Probably a coincidence, but I have to say it felt like some kind of sign. I found a lawn chair someone tossed down here beside the tracks, and I'm sitting in it writing this letter.

So in the art closet today I found my jeans, pulled your last letter out of my pocket, and waved it in your face. "Come on," I said. "There must be something you want from me."

You dug your chin into my belly. "What would *you* want?" you asked.

I was ready: "A house with lions in front of it. A pair of life-sized lions. Made out of marble."

"I've seen your front lawn." You laughed. "I don't think there's room."

"No, I want the house too. My own house."

"Okay. Those lions are going to be hideous. But okay."

"Ask me now," I said, reaching down, wrapping my arms around your shoulders, and dragging you up so that your cheek was on my collarbone.

"I want the Stanley Brothers to sing 'White Dove' for me," you said.

"Isn't one of them dead?"

"Yes, and the other is terminally ill. But if I can get you a house, you can bring a couple of singers back from the dead to sing for me."

"Why not bring Walt back, then, to read you *Leaves of Grass*?" I asked.

Your palm stroked my ribs. "Did he even do public readings?"

"I can grant *anything*, Jo. I can get you into Walt's house, if you want. You can hang out with him."

"No, thanks," you said.

I had to think about this. "Is it that Walt might be better on paper? He wouldn't measure up in real life?"

"*I* wouldn't measure up," you said.

I pressed a hand against your hot ear. "Walt would love you. Walt is going to love you."

There was silence. Then a sniffle.

"Are you crying?" I asked.

"No," you said, but I felt a tear roll onto my sternum, which made me laugh.

I wiped your cheek. "Walt Whitman is going to adore you."

You were still quiet.

"I adore you," I said.

You sat up and smiled, teary and flushed. "You do, don't you?"

"I really do," I said.

sincerely,
AK

Dear Little Jo,

I know we're not really writing anymore, and I know I already said I was sorry a few times in person. It still doesn't feel like enough somehow, so I'm just going to write it out. Get it down hopefully once and for all. Maybe this is what they mean by a formal apology: It doesn't feel like it sticks until it's written out.

We were in your bedroom, sitting on the floor just inside the door. Not in your tent yet, although that's where we were headed. You were kissing me and you stopped and said, "Are you okay, Kurl?"

"Why?" I said.

"Sometimes I get the sense that you check out for a few seconds. As though you suddenly jump ship, and I'm the only one here with our two bodies."

I said I didn't know what you were talking about. But of course, Jo, of course I knew. I'd felt it—exactly what you described, like I'd gone somewhere else.

"Maybe it's related to your uncle in some way," you said.

I didn't move a muscle and I didn't say anything. But I mean you must have felt me pulling away even further because you rushed in to say more: "But my point is that I don't care what it's related to," you said. "I just don't want you to worry about calling a limit, or saying 'no' to me. Ever. I don't want to hurt you."

"You're not hurting me," I said. I tried to add in a laugh to it, but we both knew it wasn't a real laugh.

"Can we change the subject, please?" I said.

"Okay," you said.

So we sat there a minute totally silent while I tried to think of another subject. My brain had nothing in it though. Just white noise. Static.

"Have you started writing that autobiographical essay for the college application yet? The ACE piece?" you said, finally.

"It's under control." Small talk, I thought. We were making small talk, like distant cousins or something.

"I can help you with it, if you want."

"Nah, I'm good. Thanks though," I said.

"It's just that I sometimes worry a bit when we're together," you said, rushing the words, "that maybe you'd let me push you past where you're comfortable, or where it's feeling good to you. You know, because you're used to Viktor doing it."

I swung forward onto my haunches and spun around to face you. "I'm not fucking broken, all right?" I said. "I'm not like some broken thing you have to hold together."

"I know that, Kurl. I just wanted to have it said."

"Stop acting like a fag for one second, would you?"

Your head snapped back so hard that your hollow bedroom door gave a loud thwack.

"Seriously," I said, "you can be such a fucking pussy some-times." My voice was terrible. Terrible.

You got up off the floor, backed over to the chair by your desk, and sat down. The worst thing of all was how you were trying to not let me see you were crying and also to not take your eyes off me, both at the same time.

243

It was like a contaminant had leaked out of my mouth. A chemical spill. There must have been a stench. I mean I've inhaled this exact poison for five years now from my uncle. No surprise really that eventually it would build up and boil over.

So that's when I started saying I was sorry.

Right away you said, "It's okay," but I said, "No, I'm serious, Jo, I'm really sorry. I didn't mean it."

"I know you didn't," you said. "Ignore the crying."

I kept apologizing, and you kept saying to forget the whole thing. Finally you asked if we could please pretend it never happened. We went downstairs and made ourselves dinner from the stuff we found in the fridge: eggs and oven fries and eggplant and peppers.

But I know the night was ruined because of me. And I know it's not going to go away. A chemical spill doesn't just soak into the dirt and disappear. I don't know what it'll take to clean it up, but maybe a formal apology is a place to start.

Jo, I am sorry for what I said. Forgive me?

Sincerely,
AK

Sunday, April 10

Dear Kurl,

Yesterday was amazing, wasn't it? It was hands down the best birthday I've ever had. Thank you for my lantern! The LITTLE WIZARD from Detritus, which you fitted with an LED/battery mechanism so that I don't burn the house down in a kerosene fire.

You confessed that you'd had it since before Christmas but had been too shy to give it to me back then. "It's for the tent," you murmured, when I unwrapped it, and laughed at me when my face heated up at the thought of my tent with this red light glowing over our skin.

It was my first civic protest, but I'm fairly confident it won't be my last. The whole day felt like the future. The warm sun on our backs promising summer. The whole Otulah-Tierney family pitching in—Bron's mother, her sister, and the twins handing out leaflets, her dad passing around a thermos of hot chocolate to our group. I loved all the chanting: "No spills, no fear, tankers are not welcome here!"

As usual, the credit for the successful event must be laid at Bron's feet. Her mother said as much: that none of them would even know about the oil-tanker issue if Bron hadn't been delivering her weekly lectures at their breakfast table. In a way the whole day was an Otulah-Tierney-family festival in Bron's honor, since she'd just received her acceptance to the Stanford journalism program, her top choice.

But for me, the aspect of the day that made it feel most like the future was the briefest of moments, Kurl—thirty seconds, forty-five at most. Do you know what I'm referring to? You held my hand. We were marching along in the crowd, in public, in broad daylight, and you reached out and took my hand and held it. The best part was that it didn't feel strange or unnatural at all. It felt right.

Bron ruined it, bless her over-politicized little heart. She poked her head between us from behind and said, "Okay, see? When you two can do that at school, in the hall, without any recriminations: *That's* when we'll know we've achieved equality, and not until then."

Yours,
Jo

PS: In reference to your last letter: I formally forgive you. I forgave you the first time you apologized. Anger is a relatively small thing, Kurl. We are large, remember? We contain multitudes.

Dear Kurl,

I heard the news because in the middle of Math class Ms. Basu started to cry. She must have been sneaking a look at her phone under her desk while we were in groups grading each other's homework. I saw her suddenly cover her mouth and choke back a sob.

I went up to her and crouched beside her desk and asked her what had happened. Usually Ms. Basu isn't very chummy with students, but she must have been too distraught not to tell me. She took her hand away from her mouth and whispered, "Prince died." Then she said, "Excuse me," and she stood up and rushed out of the room.

I didn't really believe it at first. I walked back to my desk, entirely calm. But two seconds later this girl named Dia said it out loud, to everyone: "Prince is dead."

With the teacher gone, everyone was free to scroll around on their phones to find out more, and everyone shared all the details: the emergency landing, the canceled concert. The supposed case of influenza. They speculated: Avian flu? Or overdose? We'd all been hearing the drug rumors over the last couple of years.

No one in the classroom other than Ms. Basu got very upset at the news even though Prince is supposedly the pride and joy of Minneapolis. I thought of Lyle and the other Decent Fellows, imagining their shock and dismay. I thought of Bron and Shayna, of course, and you—but then I think of you every three or four minutes, Kurl, regardless of the circumstances, and I knew you were too recently introduced to Prince to feel much more than surprise at his death.

Lonely, though. I felt suddenly excruciatingly lonely, and I missed my mother. Who may or may not have even been a fan of Prince.

Anyhow. When Ms. Basu didn't come back, I packed up my stuff, wandered into the hall, and eventually found Bron and Shayna in the stairwell. Both of them were in tears. We hugged all around and talked about how glad we were to have visited Paisley Park last year—how unbelievable it was, retrospectively, that we'd been just in time, that it had been our last chance.

Then Bron happened to glance over at Shayna's phone. "Why is Axel texting you?"

Shayna hid her screen from Bron, but she'd clearly gotten good news: Her tears were gone and she was trying, without great success, to hide a smile.

"What?" Bron said.

Shayna hesitated. "He wants me to participate in this Prince tribute night he's going to do."

"He's already thinking about a tribute? That's just . . . opportunistic," Bron said. "That's downright sleazy."

"You're just jealous," Shayna said. She held a hand up to stop Bron from saying more. "You know what? I don't have time for this." And she headed down the stairs.

"Where are you going? First you blow off my tanker protest, and now you're ditching me again? Today? I need you, Shay."

"It wasn't *your* protest," Shayna said, over her shoulder, and I could tell from her tone this was part of a longer, ongoing argument. "And this isn't *your* day, either. Prince is dead; it affects all of us equally, all right?"

Bron and I followed her down one flight of stairs, but then Bron suddenly sank down cross-legged on the landing in front of the window.

"Are you okay?" I sat down next to her, but I was thinking about you, missing you. Maybe whatever class you were in, you hadn't yet heard.

"Axel is such a sleazeball. He talks like he's got all these connections in the music industry, like he's some kind of major talent scout or something. He's basically convinced Shayna to drop out of school. Meanwhile he's *nobody*. He's this coked-out loser. I can't stand him. I told her I'm not going to the Ace with her anymore."

"Isn't he giving her gigs, though?" I said.

"Sure, but he only pays her in booze and weed. Last time, I was like, 'Dude, she can actually get all the weed she wants from her own father,' so he goes, 'How about some MDMA, then? We should go dancing sometime; you girls would look so hot rolling on molly.'"

"Ew." I scanned the crowd streaming down the stairs past us, hoping to see you.

"It's a little more than 'ew,' Jonathan."

I looked at her. "I know. I'm sorry."

"Don't say anything to Lyle, but I'm starting to get really worried about her."

Is my sister in mortal peril? Bron takes everything so seriously that it's hard to tell, sometimes, which of her bandwagons to jump on. On the other hand, I've been so preoccupied in recent weeks with you, Kurl, that it's possible I've overlooked the extent to which Shayna is getting caught up in something dangerous.

Anyhow. Bron says she wants to do something for Prince tonight. A wake of some kind. She has invited us all for a sleepover.

I hope you can come, Kurl. I want to see you.

Yours,
Jo

Dear Little Jo,

I guess now you know why I was so distracted while you were giving me the grand tour of Bron's house. You showed me that freestanding bathtub in the master bathroom—I don't think I'd ever been inside a master bathroom before or even known there was such a thing—and you said, "It's as if a giant bird came in through the skylight and laid an egg in the center of the marble floor, and they simply hollowed it out and attached a gold-plated faucet to one end." I mean I did hear what you were saying. It's just that I couldn't really pay attention, because all I could think about was the hot tub.

You, Bron, and Shayna were already all in there by the time I got up the courage. Izzy and Ezra were slouching around in the den, and to kill even more time I asked them if they were sad about Prince.

Izzy said, "That purple guy?" and Ezra said, "Oh, gross."

No surprise really that if Bron's parents worship Prince as much as she says they do and all the Otulah-Tierney kids grew up listening to his music, at least a couple of her siblings would rebel against the family tastes.

When I can't put it off any longer I go out on the patio in just my boxers with a towel around my shoulders. I sit on the edge of the hot tub and stick my feet in.

"Adonis approacheth," Bron says, and Shayna goes, "Oh, this is going to be good." They do this a lot lately, those two. It's like finding out about you and me gave them free rein to treat me like a sex object.

I'm so nervous I can barely get the words out. I say, "I want to show you guys something." And I strip the towel off my shoulders, swing myself down into the middle of the tub, and stand waist-deep, facing you so that Shayna and Bron can get a good look at my back.

So what happens when Adonis takes off his clothes and reveals that he's deformed, ugly, scarred?

What happens is that they go very, very quiet. I was expecting gasping or retching, or I don't know, *some* reaction. Something. Bron at least would ask what happened to me, or something, right? I'm standing there in front of them listening for something, anything, and it's so silent behind me that I suddenly wonder if they've jumped out of the tub and run away and I haven't noticed.

And meanwhile there you are in front of me, Jo, with wide eyes and your hand on your throat and tears coming up in your eyes. I mean I did expect that.

Total silence. Finally I sort of awkwardly swish over to the seat next to you. I hook my legs over your lap. Sitting sideways so that my back is still mostly visible to Bron and Shayna. I mean maybe I should have let them off the hook then. Sunk lower into the water or something. But their silence made me paranoid that I was showing them and they somehow weren't seeing. That I would have to keep showing them again and again, forever, and we'd all be stuck in this eternal loop of horror and pity and shock.

You wrap your arms around my kneecaps, and I thread my

arm underneath so I can hold on to your ribs and feel your heartbeat and try to pace my own with it to calm myself down.

Then I start talking, and I tell them the whole story: This is why I quit the football team back in September. I'd gotten stomped in the back, the wind knocked out of me. Coach Samuels was worried I might have broken a rib.

I kept saying, "No, no, I'm fine," but during the very next down he noticed me wince or something, and pulled me out again. And when I refused to strip down for the medic, they got suspicious.

Samuels is ordering me to show the guy my injuries, and I'm backing away, basically playing keep-away around the locker room with him like a total lunatic. Finally he says I have to show him my back, or I can't play.

I start more or less begging him: "I'll sit this one out, Coach; I'll go to the doctor tomorrow. I won't come back until it's totally healed up," but he smells bullshit because he says, "Now. You let us treat you right this second, or you're out for good."

Finally I say straight out, "Listen, you don't really know what you're asking. This goes beyond this game and this one hit, all right? You have all these legal obligations to report stuff."

And he goes, "That's right, son. Now show us your goddamn back."

So that was it.

"So you walked away." Finally. Finally someone in this hot tub besides me is saying something. Shayna. Her voice is normal.

I untangle myself from you and turn to let the hot water cover my shoulders. "So I quit the team, yeah."

"It wasn't just scars, though, was it?" Bron says. "Or else you could have lied. You could have said someone did it when

253

you were little. A bad babysitter. Or even your dad, years earlier, before he died."

"No, a lot of it was fresh, that day. Uncle Vik lost a bid on a roof." Bron's brains are terrifying sometimes, aren't they? I mean she figures things out faster than anyone I know.

"Why hasn't Coach Samuels followed up?" she says.

"I gave him nothing to go on," I say. "He's stopped me in the halls a few times, asked me how things are going. But what am I going to tell him?"

"The truth!" Bron says. "You have to report this, Kurl. You need help."

"There you go again," Shayna says to her, "making shit your business that's not your business."

"My friend is in trouble," Bron protests. "When my friend is in trouble, I consider that my business"

"Well, that's a guaranteed excellent way to lose your friend!" Shayna heaves herself out of the hot tub, splashing me in the eyes and leaving a wake that lifts us practically off the seat. Without bothering with her towel, she stalks across the deck and into the den, ramming the patio door behind her so hard it rocks back on its rails.

"I'm sorry. It's—Kurl, we're not talking about Shayna; we're talking about you, here." Bron is crying now. "I'm sorry. It's just, with everything that's happened, I don't know what to do."

I reach over and hug her. Hold her for a minute until she sniffles and pushes me away.

"Well, this is textbook," she says. "Kurl, you finally disclose, and then you end up trying to comfort the person you disclosed to. This is so not cool. I'm sorry."

"I've had a little longer to get used to it," I say.

"Bron's right, though. We should report it," you say.

Bron shakes her head. "It's actually his choice, Jojo, not ours. It has to be his choice." Then she climbs out of the tub, saying she's going to go find Shayna.

It amazes me that everyone was so normal, actually. I mean obviously we're all upset about Prince in one way or another. The whole reason we're here at Bron's house is because Prince died today and this is supposed to be some kind of wake. And the girls are obviously in the middle of a fight about something else too. But still I was amazed that I could reveal this secret and the whole world wouldn't fall off its axis.

sincerely,
AK

Dear Kurl,

"So what was *your* problem tonight?" you asked me, after everyone had said good night. We'd stripped the coverlet off Zorah Otulah-Tierney's bed and piled all the extra pillows in the corner of the bedroom so it would feel less perverse to fool around in there.

"What do you mean?" I said.

"You were quiet."

So you *had* noticed. I'd thought you were too busy having fun with the Otulah-Tierney clan. You'd held your own surprisingly well against the twins through several rounds of *Overwatch* on the PS3.

"At first I thought I was embarrassing you, showing off my scars like that. Then I thought maybe you were pissed that I never told you why I quit the team. That you didn't like finding out about all that at the same time as the others."

I didn't say anything.

"I mean I'm sorry I never told you."

"It wasn't that," I said.

"Then what?"

I couldn't say it. Saying it, it seemed to me, would make it more possible.

"Your heart is beating so fast," you said, and laid your ear against my chest.

I ran my palm over your shorn scalp. Your broad, strong skull. "Come on, Hopkirk. Spill it."

"If you don't have secrets," I began, and my voice cracked. I heaved a breath and swallowed a throatful of tears. "If you reveal everything, and free yourself altogether of shame, then what? What can I give you that you can't get from anyone else?"

You lifted your head to peer at my face. Frowned.

Tears ran past my ears onto Zorah's pillow. "That group hug in the hot tub? You *attract* people, Kurl. As many as you let in, they'll come right in and adore you. There will be dozens. Hundreds. As many as you want."

You made a scoffing noise in your throat and started to lick the tears off my cheeks. Swift little touches, like a cat lapping milk. After a minute you stopped and switched to kisses, kissing my jaw and my ears, and then my mouth, lightly. Then without warning you hooked your thumb between my teeth, tugged my mouth open and plunged your tongue as deep as it would go. You groaned, and the sound moved up from your chest all the way down my throat and straight into my groin.

You pulled back. "You felt that, right?"

I was breathless, full of heat. It was so fast! I could barely nod at you.

"That's only you, Jo. That's all you. Only you do that to me."

"You did it."

"Nope."

I laughed. We were both wrong, of course: It was both of us at once, striking that humming, hungry chord together.

Yours,
Jo

Dear Kurl,

All our talk. All the beautiful sentiments we've expressed to each other about our limbs twining together like vines and our minds sharing the same food and our hearts drinking from the same cup.

All our talk is empty, isn't it? Or it's superficial, at least—it describes something we feel at certain sparkling moments, something we feel all over the surface of ourselves but not deep down, not truly all the way through.

I know now that there are depths of you to which I can't travel. There are areas I've never seen and am not permitted to go. You've cordoned them off, strung barbed wire around the perimeter, laid land mines. I get too close and you're instantly up the tower with a bullhorn, hollering warnings. Watch your step. Danger. Back off.

It was only our third time inside my tent together. It brings back all my anger and frustration to realize that it's only been three times, total, in all these months.

Lyle was out of town, and Shayna was singing at the Ace, and you and I were in my tent. It was late, Kurl; you'd come way later than you said you would. I waited forever. But I didn't mind because now that you were here, the tent had lost its musty canvas chill. It was warm, and it smelled like you. Like us. I was already naked and it felt hot and tender, and we'd only begun. We had the whole rest of the night, or so I thought.

And then I caught a glimpse of the raw stripe across your hip, the beads of drying blood. Did you think leaving your T-shirt on would be enough to hide it? Did you think it was too dark in the tent for me to see? Did you think I wouldn't feel you wince when I gripped your hip bone?

I sat up. You tried to pull me back down, but I shook you off. "You were late because of your uncle?" I said.

You sat up, too, and folded the sheet over your lap. You didn't answer.

"Did you have to wait until he was finished? Until he passed out, or something?"

"Yes," you said. Your mouth came to mine and your hand found my thigh, trying to end the conversation.

"Why?" I said. "Why didn't you just grab the keys, get in the car, and leave?"

Silence.

It made sense to me, suddenly, why you'd jogged over here instead of driving, arriving sweaty, saying you need to shower, asking to borrow a T-shirt of Lyle's even though his largest one is still too tight on you. You'd been in that state, hadn't you?—the state of needing to keep moving so you wouldn't feel like you were dying. Unable to rest or be still.

I pinched the hem of your shirt and lifted it. More stripes reached around your ribs. More raw skin.

You swatted my hand away. "Leave it."

I grabbed the hem again and yanked on it, hard, until the shirt ripped at the shoulder.

"What's wrong with you?" you said.

"With me? What's wrong with *me*?" I filled up with anger then. My whole body swelled with outrage. I said, "You're *hurt*, Kurl; why are you pretending everything's fine?"

"I'm not pretending," you said. "I just don't want to talk about it, okay?"

"It's *not* okay." I hunted around for my shorts and pulled them on. I was so angry that my hands were shaking. "You never want to talk about anything, Kurl. You're like an ostrich with its head stuck in the sand."

You laughed. "Really? I'm like an ostrich?"

"It's not funny." I crawled out of the tent and switched on the overhead light. Everything in my room looked pathetic to my eyes, naïve and juvenile. The bookshelf with its volumes of poetry, the row of comic books on the bottom shelf. The leather suitcase spilling out my vintage ties and handkerchiefs. *Leaves of Grass* lying on my desk, opened to a passage I'd planned on reading to you. Silly, romantic, superficial stuff.

And meanwhile you were hurt, Kurl. You kept being hurt, and hurt, and hurt, and there was nothing I could do to help you or to stop it. Nothing was helping.

You came out of the tent, blinking in the light.

"You don't want to talk about it? Let's talk about something else, then," I said. "Like your essay."

"What essay?"

"Your autobiographical essay. For college."

"What does that have to do w—?"

I cut you off. "Why haven't you written it yet? Why do you keep stalling, and refusing to talk about it, and telling me you have it under control?"

"Because I *do* have it under control."

I'd caught the sharpness in your voice and felt a nudge of satisfaction at eliciting a reaction from you, finally. I wanted to see you get as furious and desperate as I felt. So I pressed harder: "You're lying, Kurl; I can tell. Go ahead and stick your head in the sand, but I'm not going to."

"What are you talking about?"

"You're not planning on writing that essay at all."

A slow, angry flush came over your face. I could see the tightness in your jaw, that lockdown look coming into your eyes, but I ignored it.

"Tell me the truth. You're not even planning to try, are you?"

Silence.

"I knew it." I plucked *Leaves of Grass* off my desk and waved it at you. "Ms. Khang chose you for this. She wants you to have a future. Why are you throwing it away?"

"You and this fucking book." You snatched it out of my hand. "I don't have to take this shit from you." You hurled the book across the room so hard that when it hit the wall it thudded to the floor in two pieces, its spine split.

"Nice," I said.

You moved fast, scooping your sweats and soiled T-shirt from the floor, getting ready to leave, but I beat you to the door and raised both hands and pushed you back. "You're just scared," I said.

"Get the fuck out of my way," you said.

"You're a *coward*, Kurl."

Your fist crashed into the door beside my head. The splintering crack burst through my skull like a gunshot.

"You little asshole." You wrenched your fist back and cocked it again. It hovered in front of my face just long enough for me

261

to see how your arm shook and how blood sprang up across your knuckles.

Then you dropped your arm and flung yourself backward, so fast that you stumbled and landed hard on your ass. Your shoulder plowed into a tent pole, and you scrambled, crabwise, along the edge of the sagging canvas until you were backed up against the bookshelf. "Oh, fuck, I'm sorry," you breathed. "Oh, fuck."

I slid down to the floor and wrapped my arms around my knees. I was dizzy and cold. My heart was pounding, but it didn't seem to be circulating any blood around my body.

There was a long silence. You were still clutching your jogging clothes, and you used your sweatpants to mop up the blood on the back of your hand. You'd gouged your knuckles quite badly, and you looked at the injury with great absorption, holding your hand there, fingers trembling slightly, in front of your face.

"You should leave," I said.

You nodded but didn't immediately move. "There's no point to the essay," you said, quietly. "I can't go to Duluth."

"What?"

"College. I'm not going."

"Why not?" I said.

"I'm not leaving my mother in that house with him." You were still staring at the blood on your hand.

"That's insane."

"It's not insane. It's a fact. He works it out on me until he's spent."

"You can't—that's not..." But I couldn't think of anything to complete the sentence.

Another long silence. You looked up and gazed dully over my head, staring at the hole you'd punched in the door.

"Kurl," I said. "This is your *life* we're talking about."

A bitter, hopeless smile came over your face. You swept your hands in a gesture that took in the splintered door, the collapsed tent, the wrecked book, and your own damaged torso. "*This* is my life."

You left, then. Heaved yourself to your feet, walked all the way around the other side of the tent to avoid approaching me head on. I moved aside to let you out. I listened to your footsteps on the stairs, the shuffling sounds as you put on your sweatpants and shoes. Then the front door clicked quietly shut like a coffin lid.

This morning I found your socks still folded together on my desk. I sat here at my desk staring at your socks and remembering how, when you arrived late last night and headed straight into the shower, I'd picked up your sweat-damp socks off the floor and lifted them to my nose before putting them aside.

I remembered how you'd once caught me doing the same thing with another pair of your socks, and how you'd laughed and called me *pervy*.

"It's the socks' fault, not mine," I'd said. "They just keep floating up here to my face and forcing me to sniff them."

Silly. A silly conversation, just for the joy of it. Sparkly, superficial, like everything we've said to each other.

As I sit here this morning, writing all of this out, I know that I said none of the things I actually believe are true. I should have said that you're heroic, trying to keep your mom safe in the face of your uncle's abuse. I should have said that you deserve to be safe, too, Kurl, and that it breaks my heart into a million pieces to see you trapped like this. Instead, in my fury and helplessness, I managed to imply that somehow it's your fault for not writing the essay, for not taking the college lifeline. It's not your fault, Kurl. I know that. I'm sorry I called you a coward.

The worst part of all is that it wasn't just last night, was it? This fight has been brewing for ages between us. It's been weeks and maybe months already, Kurl, that I've been learning to watch for the coded signs of your temper. I've been teaching myself to recognize where the trees have been felled, where the soil is torn up, where the trenches are dug. Without realizing it, I've already been turning back before I get close to your danger zone. Your no-man's-land.

Yours,
Jo

Dear Little Jo,

I've written lots of letters this week and ripped them all up. What's the point though? You're right. You're absolutely correct to say that I'm dangerous, that I'm a minefield, that there is a no-man's-land around me. A place where you better not go. I mean look what I did to your bedroom.

You said that I'm throwing my future away. This future that Khang has chosen me for and that you keep imagining would be so great for me. But I hardly see it it as throwing it away, because there isn't any future for me. There never was, Jo. All those times you talked about the future after high school, all those amazing plans and opportunities. I knew it didn't apply to me. For me there's only Uncle Viktor.

Whenever I hear Uncle Viktor drunk and starting to yell and stomping around the house after my mother, I don't stay out of the way or leave the house. I go downstairs and get in his face and say things I know will set him off. Sometimes I take short-cuts even. I give his shoulder a little shove, or mess up his hair, or laugh in his face. I mean it doesn't take much.

I take off my shirt and kneel on the floor when he tells me to. Or if he comes at me with his fists instead of his belt, I back myself into a wall so he can get a better shot even if his aim is bad.

I can feel the anger pour out of him while he's doing it. Every blow he lands drains it out of him, and within a few minutes he's blubbering and swaying and begging for my forgiveness, for my mom's forgiveness, holding on to her while she leads him like a little kid to the sofa and pats his hands and says she'll make him another drink in just a minute, just rest a minute, just get your breath, Viktor, until seconds later he's passed out.

The anger pours out of Uncle Viktor onto my skin, into my skin. It seeps through my scratches and bruises and pools up at the center of my body, deep inside, and stays vaulted in there like toxic waste. And like any toxic waste dump, I guess eventually it springs a leak.

You're right, Jo, that you can't be anywhere near me when this leak happens. I mean look what I did.

I'm sorry I let things go so far with you. I don't just mean our fight, although of course I'm sorry about that too, about destroying your property and threatening you like that.

But I also mean the whole thing. Me and you. I should never have exposed you to me this much. I guess I thought maybe I was improving, that you were maybe improving me, or that I was improving under your influence or something. I should never have let it get so far though.

I'm so sorry, Jo. Especially because you're the kind of person who should never, ever get exposed to that kind of ugliness. I mean you are so generous and kind. And I don't know. Tender. I know you hate it when I say things like that about you but it's the truth. I don't know how else to describe this pure way you have of being in the world, of being with other people.

Anyway it's over now obviously. I'm sorry I waited until you had to see the ugliest part of me, the toxic, ruined center. At least breaking up means I can promise you won't ever be blasted by it again.

sincerely,
AK

Dear Kurl,

The butcherboys managed to sneak up behind me at my locker this morning. I honestly don't know how I let it happen. After all, I've been carrying all my books to and from school to avoid the locker altogether. I've learned that it's better never to show up at any specific place at any specific time of day; I've been cultivating randomness of movement and habit for ages now. But this morning, the one thing missing from my eight-hundred-pound backpack was the course-selection worksheet we were supposed to fill out in Careers class.

As soon as I sensed Maya's presence behind me—it was something in the air, like the advance front of a hostile weather system giving me a half second's warning—I slammed the locker door, because one of the ongoing experiments for the butcherboys this year has been How Much of Jonathan Hopkirk Will Fit Inside a Locker? This time, however, they had another agenda: Dowell performed a simultaneous hip- and shoulder-check that crushed my nose, hip bone, and balls against the metal door.

Laughter. The henchmen were out in full numbers, and everyone passing in the hall slowed down and lingered to see where things would go. I know better than to look out at the crowd, though. I hate to put anyone in that position. Just imagine the horror: someone with whom you'd worked on a group project in class just the previous day, someone with whom you'd flipped a coin for the last veggie dog in the cafeteria, and there he is being physically, psychologically, and socially abused right before your eyes. What's a bystander to do? It's hardly fair. I heard some girl's voice saying they'd better stop or she'd report it. But I've heard bystanders say such things before, watching the butcherboys at work. Nobody ever follows through.

Kurl, I can't stand myself when I talk like this. I should tear this letter to shreds. I hate its tone: so knowing, so smug in my ability to ironize, to hover above the whole squalid, humiliating scene and narrate it in an entertaining way.

And anyhow, why should I be attempting to entertain you? You probably won't even read this letter, now that you've made it clear you want nothing further to do with me. For the record, I accept your apology, but in no manner nor degree do I accept your breakup. I cannot actually think about you breaking up with me, not right now, hiding out in a bathroom stall trying to regain my composure enough to survive the rest of the school day, and for that matter not anywhere, not ever. I refuse your breakup, Kurl. I simply refuse it.

Yours,
Jo

Dear Little Jo,

I got home from school today and everything I own was sitting out on the front lawn. I knew right away my uncle had found out. I mean it's not necessarily a direct leap but I just knew. I think it was the way my babcia's quilt was spread over some of the stuff. I went over and lifted up the corner. Books, boxes of old school assignments, the old desktop from my room. My mom had probably put the quilt there to protect my stuff in case it started raining. But it was like the quilt was signaling something to me, like it was a message from Viktor to me: *I know all about you.*

And the very first thought in my head, looking at my pathetic pile of crap sitting there like some sad suburban garage sale and knowing exactly what it meant, was *finally.* I mean I guess I've been waiting for this for a while.

That's pretty much all I had time to think—*finally*—because one second later Uncle Vik and my mom are standing in the doorway together like they've both been watching from the living room window waiting for me to walk up the sidewalk. Uncle Vik comes out onto the driveway, and surprise: He's sober for a change. Completely calm and relaxed. He says that he never wants to see my face again. That this isn't my home anymore, from this day forth. He uses those exact words: "From this day forth, this is not your home." Like he's trying to be official about it or something. Like it's binding now.

I can see my mom has definitely been crying, but she isn't at the moment. She's just standing quietly beside Viktor looking at her arms, which are folded across herself as if she's worried I might do something to her. Uncle Vik hands me a piece of paper. Because of all the formality in his speech I'm half expecting it to be a restraining order or something. But it's just a letter. One of my letters to you, one I hadn't finished writing and had left in my desk drawer.

I'm embarrassed to admit this, but it was a poem I was working on. A love poem to you actually. I guess it's sort of funny, now that I'm thinking back on the whole thing. It's funny because I'd addressed your full name on the back of the page like Khang taught us to do for the box at school. *Jonathan Hopkirk*. I mean if I hadn't addressed it like that, they might have assumed "Jo" was some girl. But it was a fairly erotic sort of poem, and I might have mentioned some gender-specific body parts.

I can't go back and check, because Uncle Vik took the poem out of my hand again. He gave me just long enough to recognize it as mine and then snatched it back quickly, like it was evidence he had to protect. Which is also pretty funny, I mean in a twisted, vomit-inducing sort of way, to imagine Viktor Kurlansky reading something like that. It's funny to think that of everything, it's the fact that I was writing a poem in the first place that probably horrified him the most.

I called Bron. I mean at least she knows the truth about me and you, and about me and Uncle Viktor, so I didn't have to explain everything from scratch. She brought the Escalade and helped load all my stuff into the back. Viktor stood there not helping, and Bron somehow miraculously didn't try to talk to him.

My mom went back in the house, but she came outside halfway through and put this box on the back seat. It had some textbooks but also all your letters, Jo. I'd hidden them in a shoebox in the bottom of that other box and kept the whole thing in the bottom of my closet. By bringing that box out separately, my mom was telling me she'd found your letters and read enough of them to know exactly what they meant. Also that she hadn't shown them to my uncle, but that she knew everything Viktor knew, plus more. And most of all that she agreed with his decision to disown me from the family.

By the way I am really sorry about your letters. About letting them be discovered. I mean I thought they were hidden safely enough. To be honest I didn't think my mom cared enough to snoop through my boxes, let alone read anything. But she'd probably spent all day packing up my stuff so nothing would break when he tossed it onto the lawn. Maybe she had some last-minute curiosity, or something.

It stung a bit when Uncle Vik looked at me like something stuck to the tire of his truck. I'm aware this makes me extremely pathetic, but it's the truth. I'm used to getting rage from him. To seeing him red-faced and out-of-his-mind angry. It might not be kindness but it's something, some passion. Like he cares enough to get that angry with me, at least. But today I could see in his eyes that he'd realized I was never worth his time in the first place. He'd written me off.

It stung a bit, but I have to say it stung more with my mom.

272

She didn't meet my eyes once, not even when she put that box on the back seat. And all she said was, "It's better this way."

I said, "Mom."

But she only repeated that one statement: "It's better this way."

The second we pulled out of the driveway, Bron started bawling so hard she could barely even get the Escalade out of reverse. I had to make her stop at the end of the street so she could pull herself together. I checked inside the shoebox, and guess what the top letter was? It was that one you mailed directly to my house that time, just before Christmas. I never received that letter, Jo, so I assumed it got lost in the mail, but the envelope was open, so Mom obviously read it. For all I know she found my hiding place way back then and has been reading every single letter you've written.

So I'm at Bron's house. For now. Her parents are gone until Wednesday next week. Her brothers are throwing a big Friday the 13th party tonight, and a bunch of Lincoln people are coming too.

I've had a couple of beers with Bron already. She has now decided that getting kicked out of the house is the best thing that ever happened to me. "This is going to be your freedom party," she says. "The first-day-of-the-rest-of-your-life party. You're out, Kurl, in every sense of the word. Call Jo; get him over here! You're free. You can both be free!"

But I'm not calling you, Jo, obviously. It's not just because we've broken up. It's that I can't see it like Bron sees it. I don't feel anything like freedom. When she said "You're out, Kurl," I felt sick. I actually left the den and went to the bathroom because I thought I might vomit. She meant *out* as in openly gay, no more secrets, live your best life et cetera. But I just heard *out* as in out in the cold. Homeless.

Ironic isn't it? I'm finally out of that hellhole and now I'm homesick for it.

sincerely,
AK

Friday, May 13, 7 p.m.

Dear Kurl,

As I told you, I can't write about this sort of thing anymore. I can no longer narrate my own humiliation as though I'm the lovable antihero of some TV series. So why am I propped here on my elbow making attempt after pathetic attempt, and crossing everything out and crumpling up the pages and throwing them under the sofa? Why do I feel such an urgent need to record what happened to me after school?

I was riding Nelly home, and Liam VanSyke's car came up and tried to sideswipe me. To be clear, Liam did it, using his car as his instrument of destruction (no point blaming the car itself). The back window was open, and Dowell was hanging out with both arms extended, and I could hear Maya from the front passenger seat saying, "Closer."

Dowell got hold of my hair and spat on my cheek.

"Pull him right into the car," Maya ordered. But Liam swerved, and Dowell lost his grip. I nearly went down against the curb but managed to veer up onto the sidewalk in front of China King.

"You little rat!" Maya screamed. "You're dead! You're dead!" Liam pulled the car into the driveway next to the restaurant, and all three of them jumped out. I remembered that the chain-link fence was peeled back at the far end of the parking lot, so I

275

headed toward the gap. But I should have thought of the fact that if anyone knew all the secret ways into Cherry Valley, it would be these three. They're probably the ones who cut the fence in the first place.

They were right behind me, running along the lip of the ravine behind my bike. And they were *furious*. I deduced from the appellation "little rat" that one of the locker-incident bystanders—possibly the girl whose voice I'd heard telling them to stop—had actually followed through and told a teacher about what she'd witnessed. Maya was keeping up with Dowell and Liam—she is *fast* for someone so short—and calling me a variety of colorful names. No worries about going too far in choice of homophobic terminology, here in the wilderness. No worries about going too far with physical retribution, either. The only cogent thought that penetrated my fog of panic at being trapped like that was, You have wheels; they don't. And so I turned my bike and headed straight down the ravine wall.

There was a bit of loose dirt and leaf stuff at the top, so my wheels slid a few feet before they started to roll. And then I just shot straight down. I must have swerved around trees. I must have been searching ahead for an open route. I must have stood on my pedals and taken the jolts with my knees. I must have done these things, or I would have fallen long before I did, finally, fall. I am no mountain biker, and as you know Nelly is no trail bike. But for a few dozen seconds I must have been doing all the things mountain bikers do.

Inevitably, a tree intercepted me. I think it was just a small one, a storm-blown sapling arched diagonally across my way. But it caught my right handlebar and turned me perpendicular to the slope, and I flipped over and slid with Nelly for what felt like the same distance I'd coasted. I could still hear them above me, whooping at one another. I thought they must be coming down. Maybe there was a path I hadn't seen, or even stairs somewhere nearby. I'd landed across Nelly chest-first, and I could hardly breathe, but I pulled the bike upright and jumped onto the seat and steered downhill again.

Luckily I was nearly at the bottom already. I came out suddenly at the creek and biked along the bank where the retaining wall is flat—you know that side with the chicken-wire blocks filled with gravel? I don't know how you ever managed to fish Nelly out, Kurl. The wall on that side is high and flat, and the other side is sheer muck. Now that I've seen that creek again, recalling how you did that for me makes my chest start to ache even more savagely.

It's an utter mystery to me how I was able to bike so fast along that wall and not fall into the creek. Sheer adrenaline, perhaps? It felt good, Kurl. It felt like there was no room for mistakes. Looking back, of course, the whole thing was a mistake. I should have simply abandoned Nelly in the parking lot and headed into the China King. For that matter I could have wheeled Nelly into the restaurant with me. They wouldn't have kicked me out if I told them the truth. One day I will stand at the top of that gully and look over its precipice and feel nauseated at the thought of the stunt I pulled this afternoon. But at that particular moment, racing alongside the creek, it felt good. I could just keep going, I thought. This creek will lead me right out of town.

Somehow, eventually, I made it home. One whole side of my ribs had turned fantastically purple. I got a few handfuls of ice from the freezer and put them in a plastic bag and wrapped it in a dish towel and lay back on the couch with the bag on my chest.

It's an awkward writing position, but I wanted to get this down. For some reason having everything on paper seems more important than ever. Maybe it's due to the fact that you tried to break up with me in that last letter. I told you that I refuse your breakup, but in the meantime—until we have an opportunity to work things out face-to-face—I feel a vital need to document everything, to keep the record straight.

Yours,
Jo

Dear Kurl,

I must have fallen asleep on the couch last night just after tuck-ing that last letter in my pocket. When I woke up, my chest was throbbing harder than before. Lyle walked into the living room holding a glass of whiskey, and when he switched the light on and saw me lying there, he sloshed some of it out of the glass. "Jesus Christ, Jonathan!" he said.

"Sorry. I fell asleep," I said. I got up on one elbow. "What happened to your face?" There was a bruise on Lyle's cheek, right next to his nose, with a bloody scratch in the middle of it. When he sat down in the chair opposite me, I saw that the knuckles of the hand he was holding the glass with were all red and scratched, too. I sat up. "Did you get in a fistfight?"

"A brief one, yes," Lyle said. "What? Is that funny or something?"

I pulled my mouth out of its smile. "No. It's just...sort of shocking. Who did you fight with?"

"The owner of the Ace," he said.

"Axel?"

Lyle made a noise in his throat. "Don't tell me *you've* been going there, too?"

"No, I just know who he is," I said, and my heart started to pound at the possibility of betraying Shayna by accident. Just

279

because Lyle knew my sister had been there didn't mean he knew everything.

But he did know everything, apparently. "Did you know that asswipe has been letting your sister perform?" Lyle said. "Putting her onstage! Giving her drinks, and God knows what else!"

"How did you find out?"

"Bronwyn called me," he said. "She said she thought I should maybe go and 'check in on her, sometime.' Like it was no big deal. Like maybe one day I'd be like, 'You know what, I think I'll just go swing by the Ace today for a casual beer or two.'"

"So did you bring Shayna home?" I said.

"I should call the police, is what I should do." Lyle took an enormous swig of his drink. His hand was shaking. "That son of a bitch."

"Lyle," I said. I didn't think I'd ever seen my father so upset.

"That slimy, shit-sucking son of a bitch!"

"Lyle!"

He looked at me. "What? I'm sorry."

"Is Shayna here? Did you bring her home?"

"She wanted to go to Bronwyn's house; there's some kind of party there tonight." He sighed. "She was pretty upset with me."

"I can imagine," I said.

Lyle drained his whiskey and then just sat there, staring at the carpet and rattling his ice round and round in his glass.

I went into the kitchen and drank some water. My ribs were a volcano of pain. It didn't seem like the right time to tell my father about my afternoon adventure, though.

I lifted my shirt and marveled at the way the bruising had ripened to an Italian-eggplant purple. Then I fished around in the vitamin drawer until I found the bottle of Percocets from when Lyle threw his back out last winter. *Take 1–2 tablets by mouth every 4–6 hours as needed*, it said. I swallowed two pills and put the bottle in my pocket.

"I think maybe I should go back and get her," Lyle said, when I returned to the living room.

"Crash Bron's party, you mean? That doesn't sound like the best plan to me," I said. "Here"—I held out the baggie I'd filled with fresh ice—"put this on your face."

"Thanks," he said. "It's just...I said some things to Shayna in the car. I told her some things about your mother."

"What things?"

"Well, she heard some things, when I was arguing with Axel, so I had to say something. I had to tell her the truth." Lyle had lifted the ice pack to his damaged cheek for only the briefest of moments; now it sat forgotten on the arm of his chair.

I could tell that he'd already decided to tell me whatever he'd told my sister, and I had the sudden impulse to yell, "No, wait!" When I asked myself what I wanted him to wait for, the answer was for my ribs to stop hurting. Please, Lyle, would you mind just holding off with your big confession until these pills kick in? Naturally I didn't say anything, but I felt all the muscles in my body tighten a little, all at the same time, as if I were bracing for impact.

"Jonathan." Lyle looked me in the face a moment, but then his eyes skated sideways to the cushion next to me. "The truth is, Raphael had a drug problem. A very serious one." He shot me a quick glance and looked away again. "And Axel Duncan was her dealer. He took a lot of her money—our money. He took...Well, he took everything. He took everything from her."

Lyle stood up abruptly and stalked toward the hall. "I have to go get Shayna."

"Dad!" It was the same part of me that had wanted to yell, "No, wait!" a moment ago.

It stopped him. He turned around.

I wanted to ask him more about Raphael, but instead I said, "How about if I go to the party instead? You drive me there, and I'll make sure Shayna is okay."

Lyle rubbed a hand over his face and winced when his palm hit the bruised part.

"Okay?" I said.

"Okay," he said, and sighed. "Okay, that's a good idea. Are you sure?"

"Sure," I said.

Yours,
Jo

Dear Little Jo,

You would think I'd have learned from Uncle Viktor that drinking doesn't make anything better. You'd think that particular lesson would be deep in my bones by now, or at least scarred into my skin. Just because you're wasted enough to forget what's wrong doesn't make you any less upset.

We were half in the bag last night, Bron and me, by the time Shayna showed up. I mean we'd been drinking since way before the party started, and it was now, what—10 p.m.? 11?—when she came stomping into the house shouting for Bron.

"You bitch. You bitch," she kept saying. Yelling over the music. "I can't believe you'd actually tell Lyle, you stupid bitch!" Shayna was slurring—pretty drunk herself, probably. She wore a lacy top that left her stomach bare and a pair of those super-short cutoffs, the kind where the front-pocket linings actually stick out lower than the fringe. Thick black eyeliner. Huge silver hoops in her ears.

And Bron was trying to act all reasonable and calm. You know how she puts on that whole I'm-the-bigger-person-here act. "I did it for you, Shay. It was an intervention. You'll thank me, I promise." Et cetera. Which just made Shayna crazier.

The angry base of disjointed friendship is what Walt calls it somewhere. I had no idea what they were arguing about. To

283

tell you the truth I didn't much care. I just sat back on the sofa. I lifted my half-empty beer bottle and looked at the two of them through the glass. It was one of those expensive beers the Otulah-Tierneys drink, a green bottle with the brand name etched on the glass instead of a label. I watched their fight through the glass. Bron and Shayna were stretched and blurry and smaller than in real life.

I guess I must have been pretty drunk because I thought their voices were quieter too, through the glass. I kept experimenting—holding the bottle up to my face, to one side and then the other, to see whether the volume changed along with the image.

So I more or less missed the entire argument, but Shayna started getting more and more upset. Whatever anger she'd started with sort of cartwheeled right over into sadness. She started sobbing, and soon she couldn't get any more words through the tears. Bron tried to hug her but Shayna shoved her away.

"You're not my friend. You're not my friend," she kept saying, gasping and stuttering through all the crying.

Other people at the party started to notice and hang around and ask if everything was okay. Finally Bron punched me and told me to please get off my ass and take Shayna upstairs, to see if I could calm her down.

I had to pretty much carry Shayna upstairs. She wasn't fighting me so much as just crying so hard she couldn't move. Some freshmen were making out in Bron's bed. They threw their clothes on when I came swaying in with Shayna, saying, "Sorry, man, sorry, it's all yours." It was the kind of thing Shayna would normally find hilarious, but I don't think she even noticed them.

She did calm down though. She lay on Bron's bed taking long, shuddery breaths. Hiccuping. I lay there beside her and stroked her hair off her face, which was soaking wet with greasy black tears and probably snot. I just kept petting her hair like she was a cat.

I was drifting in and out a bit. Once I looked at her and my hand was just lying there heavy on her ear. Her eyes were open, bloodshot and miserable in their black raccoon-circles, staring at me. The next time I woke up, both my hands were squashed under my cheek, and Shayna's eyes were closed.

And the next time I woke up she was on top of me. Kissing me. Half her clothes off, then all of them. Then my shirt.

Why didn't I stop her? Why didn't I stop myself? I don't know. I wish I could say I was too drunk. That I didn't know what was going on. But the truth is, I knew. I knew. So why didn't I stop?

She unzipped my jeans or I did it myself. Pushed them down. There was a condom, and I rolled it on.

I don't know. Maybe I thought it would be easier this way. That everything would be easier.

She sat up on me and slid down and up again. Rocked forward and back. I don't know why I didn't stop it. But I have to say that it *was* easy. It was easy and fast.

Just like this, I was thinking, the whole time. Easy. Everything will be so much easier this way.

sincerely,
AK

285

Dear Kurl,

You're the expert in pain. We've never really talked about it, but you must be intimately acquainted with every detail of how pain operates inside the human body.

How many times must you have stumbled to the bathroom and run the water cold and cupped it for long, long minutes to your face, or put your back to the cold shower and bowed your head and waited for numbness? Waited, waited to feel something less, something else.

And there's no thought possible during that waiting, is there? The pain and the waiting for something other than the pain is all there's room for. Nothing else.

I don't need to tell you about pain, do I, Kurl?

I opened Bron's bedroom door and saw you. You and Shayna. The two of you. My sister's naked back arching. Her legs strad- dling you.

I didn't even look at your face. I didn't need to see your face to recognize your bare thighs, the sole of your bare foot with its ruddy toe pads and the wide, pale stretch of your instep.

I closed the door before I exhaled. Or I may not have exhaled at all. A lost breath.

The pain was still centered in my ribs, stabbing through my chest. But now it radiated everywhere, the pain. It torqued my ribs on both sides from spine to sternum. It seized my hips and knees, so that I missed four or five steps on the stairs back down to the main floor.

I spilled Lyle's pills everywhere in the hall. A few people started picking them out of the carpet, but I hollered at them until they backed away and let me grope around and shove the tablets back into the bottle.

One of Bron's brothers' friends poured me a few shots in the kitchen, and some time passed that way. After a while I went to the bathroom and vomited, and I saw some of Lyle's pills floating in the vomit in the toilet bowl.

So this time, when I went back to the kitchen, I crushed up a few more pills with the handle of a knife and bent over and licked them off the counter. I wanted to snort them—in that moment I very seriously wanted to be the kid at the party doing oxy on the kitchen counter—but I was too frightened by the specter of nosebleed, of overdose, of coma, or death.

Oddly enough, I wasn't thinking about Raphael at all when I crushed the pills. I wasn't thinking about Lyle's revelation. I'd forgotten it entirely, in fact. I wasn't thinking about anything except the pain, ending the pain.

Izzy and Ezra's friends took a few of the pills for themselves and gave me a few more shots.

I started joking around a bit. I folded paper towels into various birds. Someone pointed out that my scarf had puke on it, so I took it off and fed it into the garbage disposal, which got jammed and made a loud whining noise. One of the twins got upset about that and told me it cost $1,700 to repair that machine. For some reason this was the funniest thing I'd ever heard: Bron's younger brother knowing the precise cost of repairing a garbage disposal unit.

Someone put on Barry White, so I climbed up on the kitchen island next to the sink to do a strip tease. I took off my belt first and did a few lariat moves with it, then got to work on my shirt buttons, which proved quite difficult because my fingers had begun to feel like rubber bands.

There was lots of laughter and jeering at my performance, but when I started to feed my belt into the garbage disposal alongside the scarf, the twins—Izzy and Ezra both, this time—decided enough was enough. They each grabbed one of my arms and hauled me down to the floor. They threw my shirt and belt at me and told me to get the hell out of their kitchen.

Out by the pool was Dowell. He and the other butcherboys weren't in the hot tub, just sprawling on the deck chairs watching the girls splash around. Maya was wearing a red bikini.

Why were the butcherboys at Bron's party? It didn't make sense, but then suddenly it made perfect sense to me. Perfect that they should be there, right in the middle of all this pain.

I dropped my shirt and belt on the end of Dowell's lounge chair and sat down directly in his lap. I wrapped my arms around his neck. I don't know exactly what I said to him—"I miss you," or something—but he got to his feet so fast that his beer bottle shattered on the concrete.

The butcherboys started shoving me around, but I kept managing to shimmy up against Dowell anyhow. I guess he was so used to me trying to put distance between us that he didn't know how to defend himself when I was determined to close the distance instead.

Maya was hopping around, all excited, back on her theme from earlier, in Cherry Valley: how I'd ratted them out and how they were going to kick my ass. "Hit him, already!" she yelled.

She picked up my belt and shoved it into Dowell's hands. "Here! Hit him, you moron."

Dowell obediently swatted me with the belt once, twice.

I kept talking, I don't know what—"What's the matter, Christopher; we used to be such good friends"—something like that—and one of the butcherboys, Liam, I think, held me by the arms while Dowell started smacking me harder with the belt.

I marveled each time it made contact with my back, my shoulders, my neck, how little it hurt. Lyle's pills were marvelous. The adrenaline and fear coursing through me felt fresher and less poisonous than the pain I'd been feeling earlier, upstairs.

Then the belt struck Liam's fingers. He swore and dropped me, and my chest bounced off the edge of the deck chair right where my ribs hurt worst, and I heard myself let out a scream.

By now a whole circle of people had gathered around, and Dowell kept swinging with the belt but missing as often as he hit, saying, "You sick little perv; you dirty little faggot," stuff like that, really gasping now, too, all out of breath with the effort and his fury.

I turned to look at him and the belt caught me across the cheekbone and eyelid. I heard the scream again—mine, my scream. I couldn't see, and I put up my hand to check because I thought he'd put my eye out.

But there was less pain, Kurl. That was all I'd been waiting for, all I'd been working toward, since I saw you upstairs with my sister.

Yours,
Jo

Dear Little Jo,

Shayna and I came downstairs to the empty den. We didn't say much. I'd asked her a couple of times, as we put our clothes back on, if she was okay.

She'd finally said, "Don't be an idiot. Nothing is *okay*."

There wasn't much to say after that. In the den a thread of smoke ran diagonally from a hole in the couch cushion to the open patio doors. A cigarette butt. I plucked it out of the hole and dropped it into an abandoned beer. I wondered how much time had passed, because the crowd had really thinned out.

Then I heard you scream, Jo.

I mean maybe any teenaged boy's voice would break on a scream like that, but I knew it was you, and Shayna knew it too. She was out the doors ahead of me, shoving through the crowd by the pool.

I didn't see the butcherboys. I don't think I even saw you, not really, not until afterward.

I saw only one thing: the belt. The belt striking bare shoulders, the belt coming down and biting into bare flesh. That belt was the only thing in the universe.

The report they asked me to sign stated that it was *a short fistfight*. I guess Shayna must have told the cops that, or maybe Bron. I remember those specific words from the report because of how much they looked like a lie. *Fight* was the wrong word. *Short* was wrong too. It went on forever. Like pulling a trigger again and again and waiting for the chamber to be empty and the chamber never emptying.

I swung and hit and held on and hit more until my fists were pulped. Until my palms throbbed and my knuckles were numb. Then I got hold of the belt and swung it and struck with it until I felt the muscles burn in my elbow and shoulder. But even then, nothing had emptied out of me. Nothing lessened or eased even by the smallest amount.

So what finally stopped me? Nothing. I could have kept going forever. I could have killed him. And I'm not saying that I eventually noticed I was overdoing it and chose to stop. I'm saying that I could easily have killed Christopher Dowell and not even known the difference.

The thing about writing is that it depends on facts. It depends on knowing certain things: the meanings of words, for one. Like *temper*. As in, *Adam Kurlansky has quite a temper*. As in, *Adam Kurlansky lost his temper*.

So which is it? Do I have a temper or did I lose it? Which is better? Is a temper a fever, as in running a *temper*ature? Or is it a kind of madness, as in a dis*temper*ed dog that attacks a baby and needs to be put down?

In my case I guess it's distemper. This rage. It's like a sick old dog that someone left on my front doorstep, this hideous creature I never wanted to be in charge of. It stinks, this dog. It's ugly and vicious. I leave it locked in the mudroom, and I keep guests in the other part of the house so they won't hear the whining or smell the piss.

But it is always there, this rage. It won't die even though I

291

starve it. It's always there, just waiting for someone to open the door. It doesn't care who happens to open the door either. It's just waiting for someone to make a wrong turn in the house and reach out and turn the knob. It's waiting for its chance to lunge and bite down and not let go no matter what.

sincerely,
AK

Dear Kurl,

All I really had in mind was keeping the pain at bay as long as possible, and the hot tub seemed like a pretty good bet. No one was in the tub anymore—they were all gathered around you and Dowell, or what was left of Dowell. Apparently I am the one who insisted Bron call the police—Shayna says I started yelling at her to call the police as soon as I saw you pick up my belt. I honestly have no memory of that, though.

I just remember realizing, halfway into the hot tub, that I was still wearing my trousers and that the hot water and chlorine would almost certainly ruin the wool. And then my sock slipped on the wet vinyl and I went in up to my neck and felt the hot water against my back like knives slicing into every single one of the welts at once.

By the time you guys figured out where I'd slunk off to, the cops were on their way and everyone had fled the party. You came over and tried to lift me out of the water by the armpits, but I slipped away from you. I ducked my head under the water and came up gasping at the pain in my eye.

And that's how the police found us: me stretched out in the hot tub with my wool trousers turning to felt around my legs, you crouched at the tub's edge with your hands submerged in the foam, Bron and Shayna arguing in furious hushed voices a few feet away, and Dowell slumped all alone nearby, hands over his face.

The paramedics took care of Dowell first, tipping him over like a side of beef and levering him expertly onto a stretcher. Professionals.

Then one of the paramedics told me to get out of the hot tub. I tried my best to comply, but I was so dizzy that two of them had to help me. They propped me on the deck with a blanket wrapped around my shoulders and helped me to drink a glass of water.

"They've been at him all year," Shayna told the cops. "You can ask anyone."

"There was a big incident earlier today at school," Bron said. "Look at the bruises on his chest. He's a target, pure and simple."

"Look at his back. Just look at it!" Shayna started crying. The cops were trying to talk to you, Kurl, but Shayna wouldn't let anyone get a word in. "Adam really cares about my brother. Enough was enough. Something had to be done."

"Adam is your boyfriend?" the one officer asked her, and Shayna didn't answer.

I saw your head turn to look at my sister.

"Adam," said the other cop, the female one. "Are you her boyfriend? Is that why you got involved?"

"Is this a bullying scenario?" the male cop asked. "Your girlfriend's little brother is gay, and he's getting picked on?" He was writing it all down on his pad of paper.

You didn't say anything, and neither did Shayna. But Bron was nodding, now. "Can you blame Adam? It's really hard to watch. Jonathan is a really sweet kid; he doesn't deserve this abuse. Gay bashing. All this homophobia."

The cop wrote everything down. They hunted around the

house for more witnesses, but everyone was gone, including, of course, the butcherboys.

They consulted with the ambulance crew about Dowell and me and decided that I shouldn't be forced to ride in the same ambulance as my assailant, so they called a second one for me. They needed to run an X-ray on my chest, they said.

As we waited for the second ambulance to arrive, I volunteered the information about the painkillers and alcohol in my system. It took me a few tries to get the words clear enough for them to understand me. I was dizzy and getting sleepy in the blanket, and I was suddenly worried I might die. It felt like I might be dying.

Meanwhile I could hear that the police kept threatening to take you into the station, Kurl, to get a proper statement if you wouldn't tell them, in your own words, what had happened.

But you wouldn't say anything beyond your name. You just kept saying you were sorry, and your eyes were empty black hollows in your face. Your knuckles were bruised and scraped raw, so it was obvious that you'd done a lot of punching.

And Bron—and eventually Shayna joined in, too—both of them kept saying that you had merely been defending me, that you'd had to intervene to defend me from the bullies. Me, meaning your girlfriend's little brother. The little brother of your girlfriend, Shayna.

Yours,
Jo

Dear Little Jo,

The most important thing isn't even that I'm sorry. I mean I *am* sorry. I've never been sorrier for anything in my life. I know it must feel like betrayal. It is betrayal. Not just with anyone but with your sister. The worst kind of betrayal probably. I'm so sorry.

But that's not the most important thing. What's most important is that you're done with me, Jo. It's absolutely crucial. It's not just that it's easier for both of us. It's safer too. It will be safer for you. Because there is one fact in all of this you can depend on. One fact that I have now proved to myself and everyone else without a doubt: I am totally out of control. It could have been anyone I was hitting on that pool deck. It could have been you, Jo. I mean I couldn't even tell the difference.

sincerely,
AK

Dear Kurl,

The emergency room was teeming with emergencies. There was a wheezing toddler blue around the lips. There was a drunk man with a nail through the palm of his hand. There was an old woman lying across three seats crying and moaning and clutching her side while a younger woman spoke to her angrily.

Shayna and I sat side by side in egg-shaped orange plastic chairs. She'd somehow found my shirt on the pool deck, so I was wearing that, but they'd peeled off my wet pants en route so I had just the ambulance blanket wrapped around me from the waist down. They'd talked about leaving me on the gurney, but then they needed the gurney for a man whose appendix had exploded.

The chairs were bolted to the ground but they swiveled, which I thought was a curious design idea for an emergency room. Why did they think patients would want to swivel back and forth in their chairs? Was it supposed to encourage self-soothing? Was I supposed to swing myself gently side to side and imagine I was rocking in my mother's arms? The hard plastic slope of my egg knocked against Shayna's each time I turned it in her direction.

"What's the point of an ambulance if they just abandon us here?" Shayna said. "They may as well have left us at a bus stop."

"Why do you think these chairs swivel?" I asked her.

"Your ribs will be healed if they wait much longer," she said.

"Maybe they're designed to calibrate your inner ear," I said, swiveling. "Or lull your pain receptors."

Shayna got up and went to the Plexiglas check-in booth. She bent to speak into the intake nurse's microphone. STOP! said the sign taped to the window next to her head. DO YOU HAVE A COUGH WITH FEVER?

I was enjoying the foggy, floaty feeling of the drugs in my bloodstream. It was like lying on an air mattress inside my own skin. Time passed unevenly, in little spurts with long lapses in between. The paramedics had found Lyle's prescription bottle in my trouser pocket, and apparently the dosage wasn't high enough to kill me, even if I had ingested more than those three or four pills I'd managed to lick off Bron's kitchen counter.

Shayna came back and sank into her egg chair.

"You know what all the doctors are probably doing?" I said. "They're probably all working on Dowell."

"Fuck Dowell," Shayna said. "I should go unplug him."

"You think he's on life support?"

"Fuck if I know," she said. Then, after a minute: "He's not on life support. I'm sure he's fine, Jojo. Bruises. At most a concussion."

After another minute she said, "It turns out Mom was a hooker."

I paused my swiveling, knocking my chair into hers. "Don't say that."

"She was. She went to be a prostitute in LA."

"Did Axel tell you that?" I said. "Because if he did, he's full of crap. It doesn't even make sense."

"He didn't say it to me; he said it to Lyle."

"What did he say, exactly, though? What were his exact words?"

"He said, 'She turned her own tricks, man. You can't put that on me.' And it does *too* make sense," Shayna added. "She was a heroin addict. She needed money."

I resumed twisting my chair.

"Jojo," she said, "I'm really sorry about what I said to the cops."

"It's okay."

"I'm really sorry. I just thought Kurl would—"

I cut her off. "It's *okay*." I couldn't stand the way your name sounded in Shayna's mouth. It jumped out from the rest of her words and hit me like a punch to the face.

"I thought he'd get in less trouble, you know? If we said—"

"I get it," I said.

"I'm sorry for lying, though," she said.

I shrugged. "Or it was the truth."

I felt her look at me. "No."

"Maybe it was."

"No. Did he say something to you? Kurl and I are not—*no*."

The swiveling had the opposite of its intended lulling effect. I had to vomit. I clutched my ambulance blanket around my waist and made a dash for the restroom but only got as far as the garbage cans.

"Nice save," a man said. He was wearing scrubs and had paper slippers over his shoes. He handed me a tissue to wipe my face.

I rinsed out my mouth in the restroom sink and then locked myself inside one of the stalls and sat on the closed lid of the toilet with my forehead resting against the metal wall. I thought of Shayna, who had just apologized to me for lying while simultaneously lying to me some more. Who did not know I knew she was lying. Who did not know that I'd walked in on her having sex with you, Kurl.

I thought of you hunched by Bron's hot tub with your hands in the foam. Your eyes like black holes. Nausea ripped through me again, bile rising in my mouth.

There was a knock on the stall door, and Lyle's voice said my name. When I came out he threw his arms around me, then dropped them and apologized when I squeaked at his touch on my shoulders.

Lyle was pale and teary-eyed with worry. "Are you all right? Are you all right?" he kept saying, and of course, seeing him upset made me start to cry as well.

He'd brought pajamas, socks, and shoes for me, and he helped me get dressed, there in the restroom, while I cried.

I was exhausted. I think I kept crying continuously from that point on, mostly from exhaustion and maybe a sort of relief, too, as though now that my father was on the scene I could safely fall apart. So I cried a bit on and off all through the X-ray process and afterward, waiting for a doctor to come and look at the X-ray and tell us that I'd fractured two of my ribs.

We'd already learned all about the fractures from the X-ray technician, who was a short woman with a very tight pink set of scrubs and cornrow braids. She pointed out the harder-to-spot break, a hairline fracture in the bone under my right nipple, and she told us that they might tape the ribs but it wouldn't help one whittle. *Whittle* is the word she used.

The doctor didn't tape my ribs, though. She felt around until the pain cut through the painkillers and I yelped. "Once we make sure they're aligned, they'll figure out the rest," she said. "Bones know what they're doing."

For some reason Shayna giggled at this, and the doctor seemed pleased. She seemed to want to egg her on. "You put two bones in a room together," she said, "and in a couple of weeks they'll be one bone." Shayna laughed so hard I suspected she was edging into hysteria.

On the drive home I rode in the back seat, half-asleep, queasy. Shayna had lit Lyle's hash pipe but was refusing to pass it to him.

He tried to joke with her: "Don't stinge me," he said. *Stinge* is the verb form of *stingy* invented by the Decent Fellows to describe the act of not rolling a joint fat enough, or underpacking one's pipe or vape, in a selfish effort to avoid sharing one's green.

Shayna didn't answer him, just unrolled her window to exhale so he wouldn't even get any of her secondhand smoke.

"It's my green," Lyle pointed out, but she remained unmoved.

They'd given me new painkillers, proper ones, but I wasn't allowed to take the first one until the morning. I had to sit in the back seat, lean forward and hold myself perfectly still so that nothing on my body would make unnecessary contact with anything in the car. It was exhausting, and after a minute I closed my eyes and rested my temple against the car window. I thought of your back, Kurl, how many times you must have leaned forward in a chair, and I fought the nausea that rose anew.

Shayna had turned the music up loud, and when Lyle tried to turn it down a few notches, she twisted the knob even higher.

"How did she die?" I asked.

"What?" Lyle said, over his shoulder.

I leaned farther forward and spoke louder: "How did she die?"

"Who?" Lyle said.

"Raphael," I said.

"Mom," Shayna corrected me. She switched off the music. "Yeah. How *did* Mom die, Lyle?"

"It wasn't a bicycle accident, was it?" I said.

"I don't know," Lyle said.

"What?" Shayna said.

"I don't know how she died."

"Stop lying to us!" Shayna yelled.

Lyle pulled over. He unclipped his seat belt and turned in his seat so that he could look at both of us. "They found her in her room, in this motel in LA she'd been staying in. The guy...The man she was with had checked out the week before. He'd used a fake name anyway."

"Mom was murdered?" Shayna's face was white.

"*No*, Shay. No, the man was long gone when she died. She was..." Lyle stopped, took a breath.

"*What*, Lyle?" Shayna said. "Just fucking say it, will you?"

"He's trying," I pointed out.

"They did an autopsy, including a tox screen. She was on everything: booze, heroin, meth."

"An overdose?" Shayna said.

"She also had pneumonia," Lyle said, "so it could have been that."

"So she was sick," Shayna said.

"She was very sick, yes," Lyle said.

"And you just let her die."

"I didn't—*no*, Shayna. I couldn't—"

Shayna cut him off. "Drive the car."

"Look, I'm sorry I never told—"

"Drive the car," Shayna yelled, "or I'm getting out right here!" When Lyle pulled back onto the road, she punched the knob to turn the music back on.

At home I went straight up to my tent.

"Do you need an assist?" Lyle called after me up the stairs, but I told him I was fine.

"Drink some water," he said. "I'll swing by on my lunch to check on you."

My clock said it was 8:40 Saturday morning. Lyle had a full day of guitar students lined up at the music school.

I was asleep almost before I could close the flap on the tent.

Sleeping all day. This must be one of the ways people hide from pain.

Yours,
Jo

Dear Kurl,

I finally woke up at 7 p.m. Merle Haggard was on the turntable, and I could smell Lyle's spaghetti sauce on the stove. I stood under the shower a long time, letting the water sting my shoulders and back. I had the creepy feeling that the music and the food scents were terrible deceptions designed to disguise the fact that our house was cracked through the foundation and would, at any moment, collapse on our heads. As soon as I descended the stairs, I would see floodwaters engulfing the front hallway. The funnel cloud was just on the horizon, already veering toward us to peel off our roof and toss our furniture into the air like lawn clippings.

Shayna brushed past me when I emerged in a towel from the bathroom. She was dressed to go out: short skirt, crop top, eyeliner.

"How's the hangover?" I asked.

She slammed the bathroom door behind her.

I stood there facing the shut door, and all at once I wanted to smash it in. I wanted to smash the door, and then keep right on going and smash my sister, too. I wanted to smash Shayna to pieces for all the times she'd shut the door on me, shut me out, shut me up. For doing whatever she wanted, without ever asking me what I thought. For taking whatever she wanted, without asking. For taking you.

"How was it, having sex with Kurl?" I asked.

There was no answer.

"I'm just curious," I said. I raised my voice in case she wasn't listening. "Was sex with Kurl amazing?"

Silence. It felt good, shocking her. Shayna didn't know until just this moment that I'd seen her with you. It felt powerful, wielding that knowledge like a sledgehammer against her.

"Did you plan it for a long time? Or was it a sudden break-through? 'Oh, all I've really wanted all this time is to get with Kurl. Now's my chance!'" I used a nasty soprano voice to imitate Shayna's voice.

"What are you talking about?" Lyle's voice behind me made me jump. I had assumed he'd be downstairs in the kitchen, super-vising his spaghetti sauce, not up in his bedroom. He had tired pouches under his eyes. "Shay?" he called. "What is your brother talking about?"

"Fuck off, Lyle," came Shayna's voice. "It's none of your business."

Lyle asked me, "What happened between Shayna and Kurl?"

And just like that, my powerful sledgehammer feeling evap-orated. I felt weak and sick.

"What can I say?" Shayna flung open the bathroom door and came out. She stood in front of Lyle and me. "I guess I'm a selfish, fucked-up, piece-of-shit slut, just like her."

"Like whom?" Lyle said.

"Like *Mom*."

Lyle gripped her arm. "Watch your mouth!"

"What are you going to do," she said, "throw me out on my ass like her?"

He grabbed her other arm and shook her hard, until her head snapped back, then forward. "Shut your goddamn mouth," he roared.

She wrenched out of his grasp. "Don't worry; I'll be fine. Maybe I'll move to LA!"

Then she was down the stairs and out the front door.

I turned my back on Lyle, stalked into my room, and slammed the door.

"Jonathan?" he said.

"Leave me alone, Lyle," I told him.

Then I sat down here at my desk and started writing it out, all of it—every terrible thing that happened from the moment I first showed up at Bron's party until exactly this minute. I've been sitting here writing for hours, Kurl. My head is aching, and my injuries are throbbing, and I honestly can't bear to write another word. But I'm terrified to stop writing, too, because I have no idea what else to do. What do I do next? What do I do now?

Yours,

Jo

Dear Little Jo,

So I just got off the phone with my brother Mark. I'm sort of in shock about it. I mean there I was talking to my brother for almost half an hour. Hearing his voice say things I never in a million years thought I would hear. Not from Mark. And me saying things I never thought I would say, not to Mark.

And then at the last second before hanging up he tells me you've been passed out on his sofa the whole time he was talking to me. It's surreal.

Mark says, "He's still here, as a matter of fact."

It's so surreal that I can't really picture it. I can hardly picture Mark's apartment to begin with—I've only been there once, and it was only for about five minutes when Sylvan had to drop something off. I mean he's never invited me.

Picturing you in there with him, sleeping on his sofa—I think I'd have to see it with my own eyes to really believe it.

But Mark said he doesn't think it's a good idea for me to come over, not yet. He said he thinks you're likely not ready. He said, "likely not ready," and I lost my breath for a second, hearing, *likely not ever.*

I'm not fooling myself, Jo. I mean I know it's better this way. I know how thoroughly I destroyed it. Us.

I'm just, I don't know. I'm sort of giddy and stunned at the conversation. It's not even anything we said specifically. More that the conversation happened period.

Mark starts the call something like this: "So a friend of yours came into the Border last night. Jonathan Hopkirk?"

This is already plenty enough information to strike me mute on the other end. Here I am, just over twenty-four hours after Bron's party. I haven't been arrested. I haven't had to go to the station to give a statement. Bron is saying she thinks it'll be okay unless Dowell's parents decide to file charges against me or something. But I'm still absolutely certain that someone, somewhere, is going to call Mom and Uncle Viktor. I mean I may be eighteen, but theirs is still my home address. I've been waiting for Sylvan to show up in the roofing van, or Uncle Viktor himself, maybe, knocking on Bron's door.

Maybe I'm hoping it'll happen. Maybe I'm waiting for it and I'm actually hoping it'll happen. Because someone has got to get a grip on me. I have no grip on myself, so someone—Uncle Viktor is the likeliest choice, the usual one—has to do it.

So Mark's call comes through to the Otulah-Tierneys' landline, and I'm thinking, Okay, I guess Mark will be the one. I guess for some reason the police have called my brother Mark.

This will be harder, I'm thinking: all of that disgust and disappointment coming from Mark. It'll be harder than Sylvan or Mom or Uncle Vik. The hardest. And after Mark's done picking me up and taking me to the station and watching me get charged or whatever, he'll hand me back over to Uncle Viktor anyway. But I'm ready for it. I mean I'm braced for it.

And then, instead of any of that, what Mark says on the phone is your name. *Jonathan Hopkirk*. He says, "A friend of yours came into the Border last night." And I'm struck mute by it. I can't say anything.

How could you have been at the Texas Border, Jo? They'd taken you to the hospital in an ambulance less than twenty-four hours earlier. It made no sense.

"I have to say he was pretty fucked up," Mark tells me.

Jo, I may as well try to tell Mark's story the way he told it. I mean it wasn't dialogue. I wasn't saying anything, the whole time he was talking.

So Mark says, more or less in these exact words: "Jonathan went right up onstage, right up to the microphone between songs. And it's not like it was open mic night or anything either. The band didn't know what to do with him.

"He starts playing the mandolin, strumming away as if nothing unusual is going on. He leans into the mic and starts singing this bluegrass tune, 'Mother's Not Dead.' Do you know that one?

"*Mother's not dead, she's only sleeping.* It's a classic, right? Bill Monroe played it all the time. You know how my office is way down the hall, opposite end of the building from the stage? Well, I was sitting at my desk and I heard him loud and clear. *She's waiting for Jesus to come.* This high, sort of spooky-sounding voice. Well, I'm sure you've heard Jonathan sing before, right?"

I managed to say "Yeah," or something like that—I mean I could barely choke out a single word. You onstage at the Texas Border! Talk about homophobia. Talk about gay bashing. That crowd would have eaten you alive.

Jo is not dead, I'm telling myself. If he were dead Mark would have already told me he was dead. Wouldn't he? Or will that be the punch line of the whole story? Is this going to be Mark's way of punishing me—making me listen to this whole story, the punch line of which is that Jo is dead, or in a coma or barely escaped with his life and found bleeding in an alley somewhere?

I didn't want to hear the rest of the story but I was listening so hard to it that I couldn't breathe.

Mark says, "I can hear some of our finer patrons are yelling at whoever this is to get the hell off the stage, so I go see what's going on. Derek, the regular drummer, is looking irritated, shaking his head—he can be a real dick about any changes in the set list, that guy—but the guitar player has started picking out chords, playing along with Jonathan.

"Yeah, I recognized him right away when I saw him, even though his face was a total mess—same kid I met at the house that time when Mom and Uncle Vik were gone, right? The mandolin player. I didn't know he could sing like that though. I had shivers, seriously.

"So when the song's over, Jonathan just stands there looking bleary, swaying a bit. At this point I'm not sure he's unsteady because he's drunk or because he's been beaten up so bad. Both, as it turns out. Next thing Jonathan does, is he swings the mandolin by the neck and chucks it, overhand, into the crowd. It bounces off the pool-table light, its brass shade, and smashes all over the floor. Pieces of mandolin everywhere.

"Then Derek, that asshole, steps forward and shoves Jonathan right off the front of the stage. Not more than four, four and a half feet down, but still. Like I said, he can be a real dick. I push my way up there as fast as I can, but Jonathan is just sitting there on the floor with his knees up and his head in his arms. He's not hurt, at least not more than he was when he walked in. Crying pretty hard, though."

Jonathan. Mark kept calling you *Jonathan.* He kept saying your name. It sounded respectful, not mocking, and he had said you weren't hurt. I started to breathe a bit better.

Bron was hovering around me by this point, going, "What? What's happened?" Because I guess I was pretty pale.

I told her everything was fine and took the cordless phone down to the den. The place looked amazing. Bron's sister, Zorah, had showed up and called a cleaning service, and they'd taken all the empties away, mopped up all the spills. They even shampooed the furniture. While Mark was talking I lifted the couch cushions to check, though, and the hole from that burning cigarette was still there. They'd just turned the cushions upside down.

Mark told me he took you to his office—half carried you, he said—and asked you what you were doing at the Border.

You were there to see him, actually, you told him. Mark says, "Jonathan immediately starts pacing around the room, apologizing over and over. He's looking really upset and agitated. I ask him what's wrong—because drunk or not drunk, he really seems way more upset than the circumstances call for—and he says, 'I confess, we have a bit of a situation on our hands, Mark.'

"'Is it about Adam?' I ask him, and he goes, 'It's about your brother, yes. Your little brother. I did something really bad to Adam, and now he's in trouble with the law.'

"So I ask him what he did. I'm thinking, I don't know, maybe drugs or something—maybe you both got busted for something, and he threw you under the bus or something. But Jonathan says, 'I seduced him. He didn't want me at all; he was in love with my sister, Shayna, and I confused him and tricked him into thinking maybe he was gay. And now he's going to have a criminal record and he'll never get into college.'

"I have to tell you," Mark says, "I couldn't really make much sense of the story; none of it was adding up for me at all, and meanwhile Jonathan has started crying harder. He's pacing and crying and picking random things up off my desk and putting them down again, and I can barely understand anything he's saying because he's crying so hard.

"He keeps saying college is your only way out. 'College is Kurl's only way out, and now I've taken that away from him.'

"'Out of what?' I keep asking. 'His only way out of what?' And Jonathan finally says, 'Out of Uncle Viktor. Away from Uncle Viktor.'"

Then Mark stopped talking. He said he had another call, asked me to hold on a second. He got back on the line and said he had to go to work. The day manager was sick, and they were supposed to clean the keg lines today. He was about to wake you up, Jo, and call you a taxi. "I'll call you again in an hour from the bar, okay?" he said.

"Wait," I said.

"I promise, I'll call you back within one hour," he said. "And Adam?"

"What?"

"It's going to be okay. All of it. It's going to work out okay."

Sincerely,
AK

Dear Little Jo,

Mark called again an hour later exactly like he'd promised. I didn't want him to know I'd waited the whole hour on the sofa in Bron's den, just sitting there holding the phone in my lap. When it rang I practically dropped it. I was that wound up.

"I'd come pick you up," he said, "but it's crazy over here; I can't leave the bar."

I told him it was all right.

He said he had just called Mom and found out I'd been booted out of the house.

"Did she tell you why?" I said. My heart started beating like crazy.

"More or less," Mark said. "Listen, though. About Jonathan. Can we talk about him first?"

"Sure," I said.

Mark said, "When I woke him up this morning, I asked him what the hell was really going on. You know, what had him so upset last night. He told me about that party the other night— just the night before last, right?—when you beat on that kid. What does he call them? The butcherboys. He told me he'd walked in on you and his sister having sex. Shayna—her name's Shayna, right? And he told me a bunch of stuff he'd discovered about his mother, about how she died."

I didn't say anything.

"I'm not trying to grill you here," Mark said, "but that is some heavy shit. That last part, about his mom. Did you know about all that?"

"No," I said. "Well, some of it. Not all."

Did I know? I didn't know, Jo. For one thing I didn't know you'd seen Shayna and me at the party. I wasn't planning on lying about it—I mean I'd written to you about it already; the letter is sitting in my backpack in a stack with a bunch of other undelivered letters—but in that moment I realized that, of course, you haven't read that letter yet. And so maybe you've been thinking that on top of everything else, I'm going to lie about it to you. As if you need more betrayal.

"Anyhow," Mark said. "About you getting kicked out of the house? Mom said she believes you're a homosexual. Her word. She said Uncle Vik found a love letter, or something."

I said, "He did."

"A letter to a boy named Jonathan."

"Yes," I said. I swear at that point I wasn't even nervous about telling Mark, about confirming it for him. Because all I could think was, What is it you discovered about your mom, Jo? What is it about her death?

How it must have felt for you to hear something like that, whatever it was. How what I did with Shayna, and then what we said afterward to the cops about Shayna being my girlfriend, must have made it so much worse for you. How being with Shayna may have seemed easier to me for a messed-up minute or two at that party, but it must have made everything so, so much more horrible and sickening and complicated and lonely for you.

314

I didn't say any of this to Mark. It was just like the first call: all that stunned silence on my end of the phone. Maybe worse this time. I was so stunned by the fact that it was my brother Mark on the phone saying any of this in the first place. I mean I had to say something, but all I could finally manage to say to him was, "Are you mad?"

"At you?"

"Yeah."

"No, Adam," he said, "I'm not mad at you. I feel horrible about all this. Uncle Viktor beating on you, all this time? Jonathan told me about it this morning, that Uncle Vik beats you, so I asked Ma about it. She didn't exactly deny it. I mean, Christ, Adam! Why didn't you ever say anything?"

I said to Mark, "Me being gay, I mean. Are you mad about me being gay?"

"Well, I'm not an idiot." He sounded kind of impatient now. "You've had, what? One girlfriend? For, like, five minutes?"

"That doesn't mean—"

"I'm saying I knew, all right? Since you were in junior high at least. You were what, thirteen? You had that magazine in your room."

"What magazine?" I said. I couldn't believe what I was hearing. My brother had me confused with someone else.

"Some gay magazine. You know, boy bands or something. *Tiger Beat* or something."

"*Tiger Beat* isn't a gay magazine." Despite everything I laughed.

"It is if a dude's looking at it in bed."

"That's—that's insane." I was laughing.

Mark started chuckling a bit too. "Oh, come on. All the

315

queers on tour read that magazine. It was all they could get over there."

"There are queers in the army?" I said. I couldn't believe I was having this conversation with my brother. I just couldn't believe it.

Everything, everything out in the open. And suddenly I was really worried he would hang up, and it never would have happened in the first place. I got really panicky all of a sudden that I was imagining the entire phone call.

Mark said, "Where the hell have you been, Adam? This is the twenty-first century. The whole world is crawling with queers."

I was crying. I mean the laughing had shifted directly into crying. I couldn't speak at all. I held my hand over the phone.

"I have to go," he said. "The beer truck just pulled up."

"Okay," I said. I had to try really hard not to let him hear I was crying. I don't know why I cared, after everything else.

"You'll be staying with me for a bit," he said. "Drop by the Border for the apartment key later today, okay?"

"Okay," I said.

"It's all going to work out okay," he said. "I promise."

Sincerely,
AK

Dear Kurl,

Bron just dropped by. I'm feeling slightly sheepish, in retrospect, about the fact that we wouldn't let her into the house. My excuse is that I was in no shape to answer the door. I'd taken a cab back from your brother Mark's apartment this morning and crawled directly into my tent.

Lyle barged into my room and lifted the tent flaps to examine me, demanding to know where I'd been all night, complaining about how frantic with worry he'd been, accusing me of stealing his booze and deliberately engaging in irresponsible and dangerous behavior by mixing my medication with alcohol after the doctor had explicitly warned me about drug interactions. He confiscated the prescription bottle and told me that from now on, he would be serving as my pharmacist, and that I was officially grounded.

I didn't say a word, just stared him down until my eyelids were so heavy I couldn't not close them. I believe I may have fallen asleep while Lyle was still mid-lecture.

He was right about all of it, of course. I'd polished off most of a pint bottle of Lyle's bourbon on my trek to the Texas Border. It hadn't been a particularly well-formulated plan—neither the drinking nor the onstage performance at Mark's bar. I'd had only one cogent thought, the same thought that had been spooling

317

through my head continuously since Bron's party: less pain, less pain.

Anyhow. I heard the doorbell ring, and then Shayna came into my room, leaned over my desk to the open window, and yelled a bunch of obscenities down at Bron.

"Come on, you guys," Bron called back. "Just come for a drive with us."

Us. She'd said *us*. I scrambled out of my tent as fast as my sore ribs would let me and looked out the window, but the Escalade wasn't there.

Bron had moved from the front step to the center of the lawn so that she could see into my window. "Jonathan, Kurl is so ashamed that he made me park at the end of the street, so you wouldn't have to look at him," she told me. "But he wants to see you."

I wasn't buying this for a second. Who wants to see someone but stays in the car?

"You've done enough damage," Shayna yelled, over my shoulder. "You need to leave us alone."

"Fine. I'm leaving your mail here in the box," Bron told me. "Do you have anything to send back with me?"

"No," I said.

"Hold on. Aren't all of these letters for Kurl?" Shayna said. They were scattered over the surface of my desk.

"No," I said, but she could see they were all addressed to you.

She scooped up the envelopes and held them behind her back. "I feel bad enough already," she said. "Don't make me feel worse by breaking up over me."

"It's not over you," I said. I wanted her hands off my letters and her out of my room.

Shayna leaned over the desk again. With one sharp movement she flung my stack of letters out the window.

"Hey!" I said. A shiver of relief came over me, though, as I watched Bron gathering them up where they'd scattered in the grass. I hadn't known what to do with all those unsent letters, and I'd been watching them pile up with an increasing sense of dread. Bron stood on tiptoes to retrieve an envelope from the hedge.

"Sorry about this," I called down. "Thanks."

"Yeah, thanks for fucking up my whole life," Shayna called, beside me.

Bron walked away, down the street, and as soon as she disappeared I went downstairs and pulled your pile of letters out of the mailbox. The return address on the envelopes says *Mark Kurlansky*, but it's definitely your handwriting.

To be honest, Kurl, I haven't decided whether I'm actually going to read all these letters or not. The last one I read was your breaking-up-with-me letter, in which you referred to yourself as toxic waste and told me I would be better off without you. It made quite an impression on me, that letter. I'm not sure I'm ready to subject myself to more of the same.

Yours,
Jo

Monday, May 16

Dear Little Jo,

You're not at school today. Not surprising I guess. I had no idea about your ribs being broken when you fell off your bike in the ravine that afternoon before the party. About you being already injured before the butcherboys got to you a second time. A third time, if you count getting crushed into your locker. All in one day.

I mean I still feel bad about Dowell, about hurting him so badly. This morning someone told Bron that I broke Dowell's nose and his wrist. And that he needed stitches in his tongue where he bit it. Those would be the official medical-treatment items, but based on my firsthand knowledge of punch-to-bruise ratios I bet Dowell is barely recognizable under all the swelling.

He's not at school today either. If he was—when he is, in a few days or a week, maybe, tops, I think I'm going to have to say something to him. I wanted to go see him right away, at the hospital or at his house, but Bron said I should proceed with caution. Her words. She said his parents may still be on the fence about pressing charges, even if their son is a notorious bully, and if I went around there and started professing my guilt and regret, it could give them the opening they're waiting for.

I don't know. I still feel awful about it, but maybe I feel a tiny bit less awful knowing the butcherboys were after you not just at the party, but that whole day.

I wish I could see you, Jo. Just for a minute, just to see you looking different than last time I saw you. Did you know that you were smiling? You were floating there in the hot tub, showing me how your trousers were getting ruined by the water. I mean I didn't understand what you were saying at the time. Your words were all garbled together. Your eye was swelling shut where the belt had smacked it.

I was just coming around, coming back to myself. And I thought at first maybe I'd done that to you, that swollen eye. I mean for a few minutes there I honestly wasn't sure. It's not perfect. I'm aware it wasn't perfect, me gapping out like that in the middle of a massive temper blowup. It still freaks me out pretty badly, remembering it.

And you were floating in the water, trying to lift your knees to show me your trousers. Grinning at me like some kind of nightmare.

Jo. I wish I could see you. I wish at least I'd had the guts to get out of the car with Bron so I could have seen your face in your window.

sincerely,
AK

Dear Little Jo,

I told Mark about the party, about beating on Dowell like that. When I said I barely knew what I was doing, that I barely saw who I was hitting, I thought Mark would be really shocked. I thought he'd think I was mentally unbalanced or something. I mean I've been worried about that quite a lot actually.

But Mark told me it happened all the time in Afghanistan. In a firefight someone would fire his weapon and later not remember doing it. They'd have to file reports after any conflict, and they often couldn't agree at all what had happened, or in what order.

He said once this guy in his unit named Ostend got his thigh grazed by a bullet. He went down but then popped back up and kept running like nothing had happened. And when they got to safety, Ostend was bleeding all over the floor and didn't even notice. He was swaying from the blood loss, Mark said. Mark and another guy had to pin him down and bind up his leg for him, and it was like the leg wasn't even attached to the rest of his body: Ostend kept looking down saying, "What the hell are you guys doing to my leg?" As though his brain couldn't hold on to the knowledge that he'd been hit. He just kept blocking it out and blocking it out, like it didn't exist.

Mark said all this has something to do with trauma. The flow of information gets interrupted somehow in your brain.

"Did it ever happen to you?" I asked him.

"Not over there," he said, "but when I arrived home at the airport, I didn't recognize Mom."

I laughed, until I realized he was serious. "What do you mean you didn't recognize her?"

"Sylvan and Mom came to meet me at the airport," Mark said. "A flight attendant was wheeling me across the tarmac, and Mom came running at me, running in for a hug. I sort of hugged her back out of politeness. I was thinking, 'Wow, some weird lady is getting all emotional about a veteran coming home.' Then she stepped back, and I looked her straight in the face, and I still didn't recognize her. She could have been anybody.

" 'It's Mom,' Sylvan told me. 'Your mother, Irena.'

" 'Hi, Irena,' I said to her, as if she was my sister, or something, not my mother."

"Did it hurt her feelings?" I asked.

"I think it scared the crap out of her," Mark said. "It's funny now, but it wasn't funny at the time. It scared the crap out of me too, to tell you the truth, when I realized later what I'd done."

Sincerely,
AK

Dear Kurl,

Shayna left today—up to Moorhead to stay with Gloria until further notice. Her room, full of the things she left behind, looks like a shipwreck. Apparently she phoned Gloria late last night, and then woke Lyle up and said Gloria wanted to speak with him, and by morning all the details had been worked out. Lyle is not particularly happy about the arrangement, but he says it's the lesser of evils. Her school semester is a lost cause at this point, anyway. Better Gloria's influence than Axel's, he says.

Yours truly,
Jo

Dear Little Jo,

A girl came up to me at the bus stop after school. She had more freckles than I've ever seen on a human face. Bright orange curly hair. "Abigail Cuttler," she says, and sticks out her hand for me to shake.

My bus arrived, and she asked if I minded waiting for the next one so we could chat a bit about you. "My correspondent, Jonathan Hopkirk," she called you.

So we stood in the bus shelter and she talked for a while, nervously and fast. She kept swallowing between sentences and her mouth kept making little sticky sounds like she didn't have enough saliva. The whole thing was a confession, Jo. Apparently you haven't written to her since the week before Bron's party. "Three full weeks ago," in Abigail's words. And apparently she thinks it's entirely her fault. Turns out she's the one who saw the butcherboys slam you up against the lockers that day and went to the office and reported it. She didn't just report that incident, she said. I guess you'd written her about some of the other times those guys harassed you.

"I only wanted to be a good citizen," Abigail said, "and not a harmful bystander. I felt like a harmful bystander reading his letters already, and then when I actually saw it happening with my own eyes..."

And she stops talking finally and starts to cry a little, or starts to try not to cry, so I dig around in my backpack for a tissue to give her. What Abigail thinks is that you're pissed at her. She thinks she destroyed your confidence in her. Her words: *destroyed his confidence.* I mean she is taking this really hard, and really personally.

Jo, you and I both know who destroyed your confidence in whom, and we know it wasn't Abigail Cuttler. So I try to explain some of this to her. I say it was my fault, not hers. I say it turned out I couldn't be anywhere close to the person you wanted me to be. The person you needed. I say I couldn't change who I am.

Abigail acts completely confused by this. Her eyes get really round and she blinks a lot, which looks kind of extra-dramatic since her eyelashes are invisible. "Jonathan writes about you all the time," she says. "I've never gotten any indication from him that he wants you to change who you are."

I mean she obviously doesn't know anything about Bron's party, or about any of the unforgivable stuff I did after she reported the butcherboys.

"You'll have to take my word for it," I tell her.

"He called you a marvel," Abigail says. "He said he was trying every day to deserve you."

She's still blinking really fast as she talks. Somehow it convinces me that she's remembering the exact wording of the letter she's quoting.

"He said he was watching you create a new world in front of his eyes."

I mean it sounds like one of your letters, Jo. I almost recognize it. And I can feel my face getting hot. Listening to your words recited by this girl I don't even know.

"He was keenly aware that you were a gift to him, a temporary blessing he had to make himself worthy to receive."

I want her to stop talking, but I'm having trouble getting the words out. "That was before," I finally say. "It's ruined now. I ruined it."

She stops blinking and stares at me. "No," she says. "You couldn't have ruined it. No."

"I'm sorry," I say, and I feel like I'm letting Abigail Cuttler down. Suddenly this almost feels worse than all the other horrible things I've done in the last few weeks. And now it's me trying not to cry. I mean I can't even look at her.

She doesn't say anything. After a minute she just exits the bus shelter and walks away across the street.

Jo, will you please write to Abigail again? It doesn't bother me that you wrote to her about me. In fact I'm really glad you did, because now she's someone you can write to who will understand what you're talking about.

You need someone, Jo.

sincerely,
AK

Dear Kurl,

The dilemma I'm struggling with is that when I don't write to you, Kurl—when I fight the impulse to write and force myself to do other things instead, like read or watch TV or ride Nelly randomly around town—I start feeling increasingly ghostly and unreal, as though I'm only half awake and may or may not have been dreaming the whole day. For example, I have been spending quite a bit of time over these last two weeks not fully believing Lyle's revelations about my mother. I keep wondering whether I misheard—I was on Percocet, after all—or experienced a series of auditory hallucinations. Or maybe he lied about it all, for reasons that are currently unfathomable but will become clear at some point in the near future.

So I keep asking him questions, even though I know it pains him to have to answer. "When did Mom get addicted to heroin?" I asked him, as he dressed for work this morning.

I watched him wince a little, and then square his shoulders in a conscious decision to be honest and face this head-on. "She broke her leg," he said. "One summer, when you'd just turned three. We played at a festival, and she slipped on some rocks at the river."

"Shayna remembers that," I told him. "We found a photo at Gloria's house of Raphael in traction."

"Yeah, well, it was a bad break," Lyle said. "They gave her a ton of painkillers after her surgery, and she was still in a lot of pain after the prescriptions ran out."

"So it was Axel to the rescue?" I guessed.

Another wince. Another shoulder-squaring. "Not right away. She shopped around, took whatever pills she could get on the street. I didn't have the whole picture, of course. But yes, that was the year she starting playing at the Ace, so it wasn't long."

Be real and be true. Remember I told you that that was Lyle's motto? The truth is, I don't think Lyle ever said those words, exactly. I think I may have invented them myself, and ascribed them retroactively to my father, deep in the fog of my Lyle-as-Hero fantasy. My beautiful, laughable fable of a life.

Yours truly,

Jo

Dear Kurl,

I'm writing you again after a ninety-minute internal struggle not to write. Giving in makes me feel weak and pathetic on top of lonely and depressed. Bron came over after school this afternoon. She's been stopping by to drop off your letters, and I've spoken to her out my bedroom window. But this time our front door was unlocked, so she came right up to my room without ringing the doorbell.

"You know, before she started cutting class all the time, Shayna used to look for you at school every day," she said. "She worried about you all the time. She'd drag me over to wherever she thought you might be skulking around at lunchtime, just to get you in her sights and reassure herself that you were still alive."

"What a burden I was," I said. "She must be so fancy-free in Moorhead."

I'd taken my tent down last week and left it by the curb on garbage day, so now there's just a mattress on the floor. I've taken most of my posters down, too. I could see by Bron's expression that my Inner Sanctum appears forlorn. Derelict. Woebegone.

She sat in the desk chair in front of the window and snooped through my bookshelf for a few minutes. Then she said, "Listen, Jonathan, I need to apologize to you. That's why I came over. For telling the cops that Kurl and Shayna were a couple, you know? I'm really sorry about that."

It hurt. Your name hurt. Why did I ever call you by the same name everyone else uses? I should have made something up for you, something private, like you did with "Jo." Then I'd never have to hear it in other people's mouths.

I'd been playing a Prince record, and when it ended I went to put on another one. I pulled *Dirty Mind* out of its sleeve, but then realized I had no desire to play it. I put it back onto the pile, and then I picked up the whole pile. I asked Bron to help me bring all the records downstairs, back to Lyle's milk-crate shelving. When she left, I made her take my turntable with her, suggested she donate it to Isaiah and Ezra or something.

"I'm only taking this to keep it safe for you, so you don't throw it out your window or something," she said.

But I know with absolute certainty I won't be asking for it back.

Yours truly,
Jo

PS: I wrote to Abigail, by the way. I assured her I'd forgotten all about someone reporting the butcherboys after the locker incident, that I wasn't the slightest bit upset with her for intervening. I didn't tell her this: If anything, I'm grateful to her, and you should be grateful to her, too, Kurl. It's thanks to her that the school has a record of Dowell's assault against me that day. If his parents have looked into filing a complaint against you, I'm sure they've come directly up against that. Any official investigation would result in a bullying charge on his academic record.

Tuesday, May 31

Dear Little Jo,

It was good to see you at school today. You looked so different in jeans and that hoodie. I mean I've never seen you in ordinary teenager clothing before. It looked like you were wearing a costume. I'm aware how ironic it is to say that. Back when we first met—or when I first saw you in the hall at school anyway— I thought you were wearing a costume. Remember? And now you're wearing ordinary clothes, and to me it looks like you're wearing a costume again.

I also noticed how you turned around fast and walked the other way when I came around the corner in the hall. It's okay, Jo. I mean I get it. I swear I won't try to talk to you if you don't want me to, which you clearly don't. I'm done causing you pain, Jo. That's a promise.

So today after school I was watching TV while Mark got ready to leave for work. There wasn't much in the fridge so I made him an omelet, and I was worrying about it getting cold on the stove while Mark showered because he doesn't own a microwave.

Mark comes into the room and hands me a letter and goes, "Open it."

Of course I'd spotted the stack of mail in the hall as usual when I let myself in after school. But I'd only glanced through the envelopes for your handwriting, and this one was typed. I mean why would anything other than a letter from you have come for me at Mark's apartment? Nobody except you and Bron even knows I'm living here.

So I recognize the return address on the envelope right away, and I fold the whole thing in half to stuff it in my back pocket.

"Open it now," Mark says.

"I'll look at it later," I say. Trying for casual. Trying for no big deal.

Mark sits next to me on the couch. He picks up the remote control and switches off the TV.

"I made you a mushroom omelet," I say, "but it's getting kind of cold." I'm trying for a distraction now.

Mark gets up and goes to the kitchen with the remote control in his hand so I can't turn the TV back on. He comes back with the omelet. He sits down in his chair and eats it but doesn't stop eyeing me the whole time. Then he puts the plate on the coffee table and says, "I want you to open that letter and read it to me."

By now I'm thinking, who cares about the stupid letter anyhow? It's worse to build up suspense. I mean I didn't even finish applying to U of M. I didn't send in half the documents they wanted. It's not like they're going to want me based on my transcript all by itself. No way Khang's recommendation letter could have been that good.

So I pull the envelope out of my pocket and toss it over to Mark. "Read it yourself, asshole," I say.

The envelope falls on the floor halfway between us. The whole thing is getting more idiotic by the second. It's like a farce.

"I don't read other people's mail," Mark says. And he smiles at me in that stupid, smug way he has sometimes, so I know he's referring to our letters, Jo, yours and mine. He's referring to Uncle Vik reading my letter to you. My love poem.

It's like a massive hole opens up inside me. A hole made of homesickness, so that I am actually feeling physically sick with how badly I want to go home.

And you, Jo. I'm sick with missing you, with wanting you.

A hole opens up, and I fall right down into the hole. My face gets red-hot. I feel the tears coming up in a rush. I turn away from Mark and press my hand over my eyes, but I'm basically bawling like a baby right in front of my smug asshole of an older brother.

And then something even worse happens. Mark comes over and puts his hand on my shoulder, and I am suddenly certain that he's about to hit me. I mean I can feel him winding up. I can feel the punch coming at the side of my head.

So I throw myself off the couch, onto the floor. I'm on the rug on all fours. I'm crawling away from him, cowering, crying and whimpering in a voice that doesn't sound like my voice at all. Saying, "I'm sorry. Don't. Don't hurt me. Don't, don't, don't. I'm sorry, I'm sorry, I'm sorry."

This is me being completely delusional. Because Mark isn't coming after me at all. Mark has never in his life lifted a finger against me or against anyone as far as I know. He would never do something like that. He's just sitting there on the sofa staring at me with a shocked expression on his face. He's gone kind of gray. Stunned.

It takes me a full two, maybe three minutes to get ahold of myself. Then I sort of just sit there on the floor with my back to the wall, wiping away tears and shaking all over. Looking at Mark while he looks back at me.

I watch his face change from shocked to sad to furious to sad again. Neither of us says anything for a long time.

Then Mark picks up the letter and comes over and holds it out to me. When I reach out to take it from him, he holds on to it for a second. He says, "He is not going to hurt you again, Adam. All right?"

"What about Mom though?" I say, before I can stop myself.

Mark jerks his head a bit. "He's not going to hurt her either," he says. "I promise you. We're making certain, Sylvan and me." He says they're dealing with Uncle Viktor, that down the road we'll likely be having a conversation about legal options but for now the objective is day-to-day safety. Stability. He says there's lots of time and no need for me to think about any of it until I'm ready. "We got you, Adam," he says. "All right?"

"All right," I say.

He hands me the letter. "Now open your goddamn college mail."

So I rip open the envelope, and it's an invitation to visit the campus to speak to the admissions committee. It gives some dates and times and a number to RSVP.

Mark makes me call the number right away. He says to tell them I'll be there next Wednesday. Then he calls Sylvan and tells him to book off work; we're going on a road trip to Duluth, the three of us.

It's probably nothing. I mean they'll probably just ask me why I didn't bother sending in the Autobiographical Creative Essay part of the application. It's probably too late to submit one even if I bring it to them next week.

sincerely,
AK

Dear Kurl,

I'd told Bron to take you to the memorial, not me. I'd been really clear with her about not wanting to participate. Nonetheless she showed up at my house at seven last night and marched up the stairs and burst into my room in a shimmery purple dress and said she wasn't taking no for an answer. I looked out my window to make sure you weren't sitting out there in the Escalade—I wouldn't have put it past Bron to engineer a trick like that—and felt the usual mixture of relief and disappointment at your absence. Mostly relief, this time.

"You have Prince in your blood," Bron said. "It has to be you. My other friends don't even get it. They'd be going for all the wrong reasons."

On our way out the door, she grabbed Lyle's mando from its peg. She put it on the back seat of the car. "We are not discussing this," she said. "This is not negotiable."

We parked at the Chanhassen Walgreens and walked the half mile or so to the gates of Paisley Park, which to our surprise were standing wide open. The Facebook event page had been very specific: They were not going to let us in; we would be holding the whole memorial right there in front of the gates. Instead there were already about fifty people inside, in the parking lot, and it was all set up like an impromptu festival: string lights, banners, flags, lawn chairs, coolers.

Rich and Trudie and Scarlett were there, and a number of other musicians I recognized. More and more people arrived, I suppose as news spread online that they'd opened the gates for us. Bron said probably people were hopeful of being let into the building. She said even if they did open the doors, she wouldn't enter.

There were masses of flowers, ribbons, and stuffed toys. Everyone was singing "Happy Birthday" to Prince over and over, even though his birthday technically isn't until Tuesday. There were lots of tears. Everyone wore purple, of course. I was glad Bron had made me wear a purple velvet bow tie and purple suspenders; anything else would have felt disrespectful.

I drank some champagne from a bottle being passed around. Bron flagged down some green, but she wouldn't share it with me.

"You need to stay sharp," she said to me. "This is crucial. This is important."

Less than twenty minutes after we arrived, she shoved the mando into my arms and dragged me over to Rich. She bent down and switched off some guy's boom box. "Play 'Alphabet Street,'" she ordered me, and then stood and waited, hands on her hips, ignoring the guy's girlfriend saying, "What is your problem? Turn that back on."

I started to play "Alphabet Street," and after a minute Rich took it up on the guitar. As soon as people nearby recognized the tune, they started to sing. Another guitar joined in, and before the song was over, an upright bass had appeared out of nowhere.

So it became an acoustic jam. There was a trombone, a harmonica. Scarlett had her tambourine, so that was the next song: "Tamborine."

"Sing it, Jojo!" Bron yelled, so I went ahead and sang it—I

just let all those high notes loose on that crowd, and I suppose people liked it, because there was loud cheering afterward.

At one point while we played, Bron gave one of her revival-tent speeches: "Prince changed us; he altered our DNA. Prince flows in our veins. Prince changed life on Planet Earth." The gospel according to Bronwyn Otulah-Tierney. People loved it, though. There was so much weeping!

Later, Trudie came over to me and took a photograph out of an envelope in her purse and handed it to me. She said she'd brought it in hopes of seeing me today.

It took me a few seconds of staring at the image to recognize Raphael standing there on the sidewalk between Rich and Cody. There was hardly any of her left. Her white legs stuck out of her skirt like broomsticks. The black dye had grown partway out of her hair, and the lighter-brown part lay like dead grass against her scalp. Her face under her makeup was a skull.

"We tried to bring her home," Trudie said.

"She's so skinny," I observed.

"She was very fucked up, honey." Trudie put her arm around me and looked at the picture with me. "We went to LA four times over eighteen months. Lyle went alone, the first time, but she wouldn't see him. So the second time he bought a plane ticket for me to go with him. Rapha and I were pretty good friends, once."

I saw Bron and Rich heading our way, and I tried to give the photo back to Trudie, but she said I should keep it. I didn't really want it, but I slid it into my back pocket so Bron wouldn't see it. I didn't want anyone else to see that horrible picture, ever.

"Lyle kept begging us, and buying us the tickets," Trudie said, "and so we kept trying. It took us longer to find her every time we went down."

I'd started crying, and I turned my back to Bron and Rich to hide my tears from them. I kept my voice low: "Why are you telling me all this?"

"Because you need to forgive your dad, honey."

I looked at Trudie. "For what?"

"He's really hurting right now. He knows Shayna blames him for your mom's death, and he's worried that you do, too, and just aren't saying."

"I don't blame Lyle," I told her. But even as I said the words, I realized that I am quite angry with my father. Savagely angry, in fact.

On the way home I told Bron about it—not about Trudie's photograph, but about being angry with Lyle.

"You didn't realize you're angry at Lyle?"

"Why *would* I be angry?" I said.

"Because he tried to control the story," Bron said, "obviously. He lied to you guys for basically your whole lives."

"To protect us, though," I said.

She shrugged. "And look how that's worked out."

Yours truly,
Jo

PS: Mark must be amused at all these old-fashioned letters arriving in his mail. Did Bron tell you she's started writing letters to Shayna in Moorhead? She's sent three or four already and swears she's going to keep doing it even if Shayna never replies. The US Postal Service is abuzz with the missives of sad, solitary, estranged teenagers.

Dear Little Jo,

I'm in. I got in. I mean I still don't know whether to thank you or to kick your ass for going behind my back like that. And for not telling me even when you knew I was going up there for an interview.

It was only driving home from Duluth today with Sylvan and Mark that I put it all together, how you must have done it. I'd already figured out *what* you did. You packaged up all the letters I sent you—every one of those private, soul-baring letters, from day one to the end—and sent them in to the Admissions Committee as my Autobiographical Creative Essay submission. I mean I still can't believe you did that.

The thing is you must have done it not before but after I wrecked everything between us. After everything with me and Shayna, and the butcherboys, and your mom, and then with Mark at the Texas Border—after all that. Because when you sent in my letters you must have already known about Uncle Viktor kicking me out of the house. You listed Mark's apartment as my mailing address, and so that's where their reply letter arrived. I mean I'm still trying to get my head around all of this, Jo.

So Sylvan and Mark and I drive up to Duluth together this morning, and we get an official tour of the whole place. I go into the interview without the slightest idea what to expect. I mean I am deathly nervous, but the three committee people— two women and one man, whose names I forgot two seconds after they introduced themselves—are nice right off the bat. Not in a fake way either. They're each looking me in the eye, saying they're so glad I came and they've been so looking forward to "putting a face to the voice." Those are their words, *putting a face to the voice.* Which of course makes no sense to me at that point, but only later in the interview.

We sit down, and one of the women tells me they aren't looking for particular, correct answers to any of their questions. They just want to get a kind of live confirmation of who I am.

"As you know, the Bridge to Education program is designed for a very specific kind of student," she says. "We're looking for a special blend of resiliency, adaptability, and tenacity. We call it *fire in the belly.*" This woman who is saying all this has got the biggest front teeth I've ever seen in real life. There's a gap between them that somehow is making everything she says seem not ridiculous and corny like it's sounding now, as I'm writing it out, but sincere and heartfelt. I don't know how that works, exactly—how a gap between someone's front teeth can make her seem sincere—but it's working on me in the interview.

They ask me about my goals. Where in the world would I like to travel and why? If I were going to make a documentary film, what subject would I choose?

It's surprisingly easy to answer these questions. I mean I just make things up. I don't even remember exactly what I told them. Things just came into my head and I said them, and they were somehow true.

And then the second woman says she's surprised I'm not talking more about becoming a writer. She says how enchanted they all were by my letters. How moved. "It was such a bold decision to send in your correspondence with Jo as your ACE piece, Adam," she says. "I mean, for me, that's the fire in the belly, right there. That decision in itself."

"Not to minimize the literary quality of the letters themselves," the man says. "The way the voice emerges slowly, over the span of months. Coming out of its shell."

"Like a butterfly from a chrysalis," the second woman says.

I mean writing this down now, it sounds like utter bullshit. But somehow I swear it didn't sound that way in the interview room.

I was in a bit of shock I guess. I had been sort of panicking all week about not having written the ACE thing. I'd wanted to write something to bring with me, but I hadn't been able to think of anything. In the end I'd brought my Walt Whitman essay with me, which I knew wasn't personal or creative enough but I figured would be better than nothing.

But halfway through the interview they still haven't asked for it. Instead they're all complimenting me on my skills as a writer and a storyteller, and saying how brave and open-hearted it was of me to share my story with them. And they've said your name: *Jo*. Not just your name, Jonathan, but my personal name for you, the one that only I use for you. I mean it's taking me forever to figure it out, but eventually I realize that you must have done it. I realize that it was you, Jo. All of it. You did it.

Sitting there in the middle of the interview, I shove the thought away as soon as it occurs to me. It's too risky. I mean I can't risk cracking wide open again like I did the other day with Mark. That black hole of missing home and missing you, all that homesickness blended viciously together? Not in front of these people.

But anyway the interview was pretty much over at that point. They asked me to wait outside the room. Mark and Sylvan were right there, all over me: What happened, what did you say to them, did they tell you one way or the other?

But it was less than a minute before the door opened again, and all three of them came out wearing these gigantic smiles. I would get an official phone call within twenty-four hours and written notice within five business days, but they were confident everything would work out, and they were delighted to offer me a spot in the program.

"Full ride?" Sylvan asked, and the man laughed and said, "Full ride. Tuition, residence, meal plan, laptop, textbook stipend. He just pays for his beer."

"Once he's of age, of course," the first woman added, and everybody laughed.

I have to say the best part of the entire day was seeing that both my brothers were really happy. They were happy for me. That was already a big enough deal. I mean I always thought Sylvan wanted me to work with him and Uncle Vik. On the way home we stopped at Wings 'n Things and got a pitcher of iced tea. Sylvan made a toast to me, and he said, "A scholar in the Kurlansky family." So I guessed he was happy not just *for* me but also *because of* me.

And I knew Mark had already told him about me and you, about me being gay. Mark told me weeks ago that they'd had that conversation. And so I knew the information about who I am was in the background of everything for Sylvan, but somehow it wasn't diluting his happiness about me at all.

I'm trying not to think about college, Jo. Now that it's all over and I'm writing this letter here on Mark's sofa. He's got this clock in the kitchen that makes a hollow ticking sound even though it's a regular electrical clock. It sounds loudest when Mark's working late, like tonight. Did you notice it when you slept here? You slept on the couch I'm sleeping on.

Jo. I'm trying not to think about college, and I'm trying not to think about you. I'm trying pretty much every second here not to fall into that hole again. I just keep trying until I'm so sore and exhausted from all the trying that I fall asleep. It's taking a long time tonight though. What does Walt call them? *Sullen and suffering hours.* This goddamn clock.

I guess I am writing this letter in order to thank you though. After I showed you the worst of me, treated you in the worst way possible. Like always, you still kept in mind the future—*my* future even. There is no way in which you could have sent in my letters to benefit yourself.

It was for me, after everything I did. After everything, you were still generous. Vastly, extravagantly generous.

What is it Walt says? You said it to me when we first started writing, when you were introducing yourself. *Spending for vast returns.* Bestowing yourself. Not asking the sky to come down to your goodwill, but instead *scattering it freely forever.*

Jo, I shouldn't even be surprised you were generous where it wasn't deserved. It's just who you are. But thank you anyhow. Thank you. Thank you.

sincerely,
AK

Dear Kurl,

Yesterday at school, when I walked past Maya and Dowell and a couple of the other henchmen sitting outside on the stacking chairs by the gym door, Maya said, "Oh, hey, it's Kurlansky's buttplug."

The others laughed. At first I kept walking, but then I looked back to see whether Dowell was laughing along with them. He wasn't—he glanced away from me, across the parking lot at the empty school buses.

I turned around and walked back to Maya.

"What happened to your buttplug costume?" she said.

Kurl, I will confess that I was terrified. I had no desire to face any more physical pain. But the stakes seem to have shifted, somehow, since the last time one of the butcherboys made a crack at me or tripped me or jabbed me with a sharpened pencil. It's not been that long, just a few weeks, since the party at Bron's. Dowell is still in his arm cast, though he always wears his hoodie sleeve with the cuff slit open and pulled down over it. Partly my newfound courage must have come from the news that he'll be switching schools after this year. Bron told me she heard that his parents are sending him to a boarding school in Connecticut, that he has an aunt there with gobs of money who offered to "step in."

So what does this news mean for me? A foreseeable end to the threat, I suppose, or a fundamental shift in the nature of the threat, at least. The butcherboys without Dowell—without the enforcer, the muscle behind the operation—are purely a psychological menace. I suppose I decided, right at that moment, that I was finished allowing my psyche to be menaced. And as this was Maya's first overture since the party at Bron's house, her first attempt at post-cataclysm humiliation, I felt it was an important juncture.

Anyhow. I was terrified, but I still walked right up to her. And when she asked about the buttplug costume, I said, "Listen, I really need to know what more you want from me, Maya."

"What the hell are you talking about?" Maya said. She hopped down from the stack of chairs, and Liam and the other butcherboys followed. Dowell stayed where he was, though.

"I would just really like this to be over," I said. "Maybe you could tell me what you want from me, in order for us to be finished."

Maya laughed so that the others would laugh, which they did, except for Dowell. "Oh my God," Maya said. "Do you think you can *take* us now, or something?"

"Of course not," I said.

"So what are you going to do, sic Kurlansky on us like he's your dog? Do you have him on speed dial or something?"

Laughter, but Dowell wasn't laughing.

I said, "Maya, you've been siccing your friends like dogs on me for nearly two years straight. I've gotten hurt. Christopher's gotten hurt. I'm not that interested in keeping it going, and honestly, I don't think Christopher is, either."

"Shut up, Jonathan," Dowell said, but he wasn't getting down off the chairs. Also, he'd used my name. Not *a* name—not a derogatory name—but *my* name.

Maya looked up at him. "What are you, friends now? Wait. Are you *fucking* him now?"

Laughter, laughter. "Shut up, Maya," Dowell said.

"Maybe he's *your* buttplug. Is he your buttplug now, Chris?"

"Shut the fuck up, Maya!" And now Dowell got down off the chairs. He stood there a moment looking from me to the others as if he was trying to decide whom to punch first.

The others had stopped laughing, distracted by anticipation. Then Dowell shifted his weight, shuffled a step back, and drifted casually away along the wall.

"Where are you going?" Maya said.

Dowell didn't turn around. He used his cast to shove off from the wall and struck off across the parking lot. He lifted his good hand to shoulder height. His middle finger poked up out of his hoodie sleeve.

"See? Nobody is interested," I said. "I'm actually not that interesting of a person, to tell you the truth."

Liam laughed at this—accidentally laughed at what *I'd* said—and Maya had to shoot him a look so he'd stop.

It occurred to me that it must be something of a slog, heading up the butcherboys. Maya's a hateful, vicious little reptile, but she's also surprisingly intelligent. In Geography last year she gave a presentation on water conservation, and her slide show impressed me with the depth of its analysis and the elegance of its design.

"My clothes were interesting, maybe," I told her, "but that's over now, too. I'm just a boring, scrawny little gay kid. Nobody's interested."

It was unprecedented, Kurl. I couldn't read Maya's expression. If I had to guess, I would have said *wary*. It was as though she was suddenly waiting for my next move, rather than making the next move herself. It was nothing I'd experienced before.

Even as I turned around and walked away I was bracing

myself for attack. I was certain she'd see her mistake, feel the ground she'd lost, and attempt to recuperate it by ordering Liam to give me a punch to the back of the head or at least a good hard shove to send me sprawling. "*Now* you're interesting," she'd say, or something. Anything, to get the butcherboys laughing at the correct person again.

Miraculously, though, at precisely that moment Mr. Kwan rounded the far corner of the building and came strolling toward us, straight for the gym door. By the time he was past, I'd put enough distance between the butcherboys and me that I knew I was off the hook, at least for the time being.

Kurl, I need to give credit where credit is due: It's you I have to thank for my newfound perspective, for my sudden awareness of the relative triviality and irrelevance of the butcherboys as predators and me as prey. You told me right from the start that I was drawing fire for my aura, for the bubble I was in. And I kept making a case for deliberately living in a bubble over the gruesome realities of high school. Well, the evidence is in: You were right and I was wrong. There is no advantage to remaining inside a bubble when all it does is leave you floating around delusional, isolated, the object of everyone's sharpest weapons. I like to think I've finally, officially burst out of my bubble once and for all.

Yours truly,
Jo

Dear Little Jo,

Mark says people are always asking him these questions. How was it? Did you kill anyone? Are you like one of those crazy Vietnam vets? Did you read about fill-in-the-blank that happened over there? What do you think about Abu Ghraib? How come you only did one tour? Aren't you glad you didn't end up in fill-in-the-blank?

Mark says these are all the wrong questions, but he doesn't think there are any right ones either. He said he knew these two marines who died in Bagram because the magic mushrooms that one of the guys' girlfriends sent him accidentally had a poisonous mushroom mixed in.

"Nobody wants to hear that story," Mark said. "They never reported the cause of death either. Nobody wanted to know it was something like that."

In a lot of ways, he told me, it was worse than somebody getting bumped in the line of duty. "There we were in all this danger all the time," he said, "and these losers go and die in this ordinary way, just like someone could have died back home."

Mark's been talking to me a lot about PTSD. About how my trauma from being Uncle Viktor's punching bag for so long likely triggered my blowup at Bron's party, especially the part where I felt totally out of control and didn't even know who I was hitting. But my brother says PTSD also likely contributed to the other blowups, like when I wrecked your bedroom or called you horrible names or attacked Dowell that time in the library. He says it's probably what causes all my nightmares too. I mean I sleep on his sofa, so he hears it when I wake up yelling.

Mark talked to his VA social worker and got me on a waiting list for some counseling. He says counseling really helped him figure out how to trust himself again.

I told Mark about this old book I found in the library once called *Nature's Killers*. It was from 1904. I'd memorized a bunch of the names in this book that people had given to various poisonous mushrooms: armed stinkhorn, jelly babies, bog beacon, scaly tooth, cramp balls, poison pax. There are lots of mushrooms in Minnesota you can die from. Even the smallest amount can paralyze you or give you severe liver damage.

It made Mark laugh, hearing the names. "We should discover a new mushroom," he said, "so we can call it something insane like that."

He got quiet for a minute. Then he said, "I'm serious. We should go on a canoe trip this summer, or something. Off in the woods."

"Okay," I said.

"Adam," my brother said, "let's not be the type of people who are afraid to live because we might die."

sincerely,
AK

Dear Kurl,

I'm glad it worked out with the Bridge to Education people. I'm glad you're not angry with me for sending in your letters to the admissions committee.

You referred to the *sullen and suffering hours*, so you must be reading Walt's "Calamus" poems. I've been reading those same poems, actually, over these last few weeks.

Did you know that Walt was in love for years with a man who didn't love him back? After "Song of Myself" comes heartbreak. He feels it with his entire body, that yearning and loneliness, just like he feels everything with his entire body.

In these later poems Walt is starting to figure out that his standards for love are way too high. His vision of it was too good to be true. He realizes that he doesn't even want love, if love is going to be this watered-down thing, this ordinary thing full of compromises and lies. That's why these poems are so bitter: He's realizing that he'd rather be alone than paired up partway.

So he says, *Therefore release me now, before troubling yourself any further—let go your hand from my shoulders, Put me down and be on your way.*

I'm glad you got into U of M, Kurl, and I'm glad it's all the way up in Duluth. It's exactly the way forward from this, from us. It's exactly right.

It's exactly as Walt says. Let go your hand from my shoulders. Put me down, Kurl, and be on your way.

Yours truly,
Jo

Saturday, June 11

Dear Little Jo,

Please don't send this back to me. Don't give it to Bron to give back to me either. You can throw it out if you want, but don't give it back. I saw it in the window of Mr. Ragman's store on Lake Street and I couldn't not buy it for you.

I tried walking past. I mean I felt light-headed at the thought of buying it and you not wanting it. And I know it's not like your old scarf either. It's actually flashier. More fringe and shinier silk. Iridescent, Mr. Ragman called it. Grass green. Spring green. Like the flag of your disposition. I just couldn't not buy it for you, Jo. Don't send it back.

And since I'm making requests I have no right to make, I also want you to stop throwing away your things now. Lyle's paisley scarf in Bron's garbage disposal at the party. Your mandolin splintered on the floor of the Texas Border. Your tent out at the curb, your turntable, your LITTLE WIZARD lantern, which Bron delivered back to me at your request.

I mean you've even quit wearing a lot of your vintage clothes. I saw you sitting in English on Monday. Was that your last English class of the year? Probably. I looked in the window of Khang's room just for a minute. You were wearing a T-shirt and those jeans again, and you'd cut your hair so short that I almost didn't recognize you.

So I read the "Calamus" poems again after I got your last letter. And I do see it, how you can read it as *Put me down* and *be on your way*. How Walt wants to live in the real world, not inside some beautiful fable that nobody else has read. I see it.

But Walt doesn't leave it there, does he? He doesn't rip up *Leaves of Grass*, does he? He doesn't go out and destroy everything he loves and stop writing and start wearing T-shirts and jeans to school. Does he? You know what I mean. He doesn't stop writing.

I'm not asking you to live in a bubble, Jo. But there has to be a way to live in the real world without giving up all the things you love. All the things that make you *you*. I mean I can't stand to see you acting like you can't have these things. It's worse than missing you, worse than not being able to talk to you or touch you.

You can tell me to let go of your shoulders, Jo. You can tell me to put you down and go on my way. But I can't do it. I'm sorry; I know it doesn't make it any easier for you. I just can't.

sincerely,
AK

Dear Kurl,

I've promised myself this is my last letter to you, Kurl, because I'm keenly aware of the hypocrisy of me saying, *Let go your hand from my shoulders* and then tapping you on the shoulder with another letter.

Yesterday Lyle and I drove up to Moorhead to visit Shayna. I'm still finding it hard to know what to say to my father. In the car he played Tony Rice and I drowned it out with Prince turned up loud in my earbuds.

Life in Moorhead seems, surprisingly, to agree with my sister. She looked older than I remembered her, even though it's only been three weeks. Her hair looked shinier—she'd dyed it a brown-black shade instead of blue-black—and she was wearing new clothes.

She wouldn't come out of Gloria's guest room to see Lyle, though. She let me in and then locked the door behind me. I sat next to her on the bed while Lyle conversed with her through the door for a few minutes—long paragraphs of apology and rec-onciliation from Lyle, eye rolls and monosyllabic responses from Shayna—until Gloria called to him that the coffee was ready, and he retreated to the kitchen.

Shayna said she and Gloria get along pretty well. "Gloria makes me go with her every day to this place called the Harbor where she volunteers. All these down-and-out people, basically. After school all these kids come to get free snacks. Mostly I just play guitar for them. There're a couple guitars the kids like to mess around on. This one kid is actually getting pretty good."

I showed her my picture of Raphael, the one Trudie had given me. Shayna didn't look all that shocked or impressed, though. She told me that Gloria has some similar pictures. "She and Grandpa Hanssen went to LA a couple times to buy her dinner and stuff. Once they tried to check her into the hospital, but she jumped out of the car."

I'd assumed Shayna must still be furious with Bron, since she hasn't been answering any of Bron's correspondence. I told her about the Prince memorial and tried to portray Bron as humbled and contrite about her role in the Axel/Lyle blowout.

But Shayna says it's more that she needs to make a clean break. "Bron is separate from me," she told me. "I barely knew that, I think. I need to have a life. Not the life *he'd* want for me— Lyle—but not Bron's, either, you know?"

We didn't talk about you, Kurl. About what happened between you and my sister. I suppose I hoped Shayna would bring it up—deliver a formal apology for her part in it, report on the deep psychological analysis she'd been performing on herself to figure out her motivations, reassure me that she never meant to hurt me, her beloved brother. But she behaved as if nothing had happened, and I found it was actually a relief not to have to talk about you, not to hear your name spoken aloud. And anyway I would have had to tell Shayna that all was forgiven. I would have had to admit to her that I no longer have any claim over you, nor did I, technically, even at the time of Bron's party.

We said goodbye, my sister and me. We hugged in front of

the guest-room door and then she unlocked it for me and swung it open, and we both froze where we stood. From the kitchen came Lyle's sobbing, and his strangled words: "I can't lose her. I just can't. I don't think I'd survive it."

And Gloria's reply, loud and clear: "Listen, you need to understand something. Shayna is nothing like her mother. *Nothing*. Something was damaged in Raphael, her whole life. Some deep-down damage."

Gloria was weeping, too. We heard the sound of her blowing her nose. I started down the hall but Shayna held me back by the arm and put a finger over her lips.

"I blame myself," Gloria said. "Rapha's daddy...well, Lyle, you know he was not a good man. He wasn't good to her. I blame myself."

"Oh, no, come on," Lyle said. "That's not—"

Gloria plowed on: "Shayna, though. Shayna's different. She's...fine, Lyle. She's *whole*. She's fierce as all hell."

Lyle gave a laugh-sob.

"She's angry at you right now because she wants her mama, that's all," Gloria said. "But she is going to be *fine*. Trust me on this one."

They were quiet a minute. I crept down the hall toward the kitchen while Shayna leaned in the guest-room doorway.

Lyle took a shuddering breath. "I loved her so much," he said.

"I know you did," Gloria said. "I did, too."

Another quiet minute. Then: "I know you're there, Jonathan," Lyle called. "I can hear you sniffling."

Behind me the guest-room door clicked shut.

More bitter than I can bear. I was remembering, just now,

357

those suffering words from Walt. *You burn and sting me.* Is that how Raphael feels to Lyle and Gloria as well as to me? The lost Raphael, the ghost of Raphael? Or is it different for those who remember her, who knew her before she was a ghost?

Goodbye, Kurl,

Jo

Dear Little Jo,

The summer before my father died there was a family picnic down at the river. Sylvan had his own car by then, and one of Sylvan's friends was there with his truck, and Uncle Viktor in the company van. I remember that for some reason they parked all the vehicles in the gravel lot with the noses together, like bison.

My dad cooked sausages and steaks on the barbecue. I remember swimming with the sun getting low and the green water sparkling in its shallows. Later the supper smells died under the woodsmoke. Sylvan's friend played Zeppelin on his car stereo, and Dad and Uncle Vik stacked the fire against the cold.

Mark rolled a cigarette and passed it to Sylvan. Dad reached for a puff, but Sylvan laughed and said, "It's a joint, Dad."

Our towels dried on the bushes. Uncle Vik pinched a mosquito on his arm and licked the blood off his fingers. He was just Uncle Vik to me then, nothing but a shadow in the background of my father.

Night, fire, music. The dirt cold under my butt, my face warm against Dad's knee, my head joggling as he kept the beat with his toes. I remember his bare shins were crisp and hot under my hand from the close-by flames.

And I was happy, so happy.

I mean I was young—way younger than my brothers. All I

knew was that there were these men around me—all these strong Kurlansky men surrounding me, who would always be there, I thought. Who would keep me safe. Who would show me the way.

sincerely,
AK

Wednesday, June 22

Dear Kurl,

All right, then: one last letter, as I feel your invitation deserves a considered response. Lyle was waiting for me when I got home from work, and he told me about your visit. Did he mention to you that I've been doing some work for the music school? I'm mostly helping organize the summer camp schedules, processing cancellations and late registrations from the wait list. Anyhow, Lyle said that you had come by with Mark and written him a check for the amount you thought it would cost to repair my bedroom door. The three of you talked for quite a while, apparently. You and your brother filled Lyle in about your uncle's abusive behavior, your current living situation, and your plans for next year.

And then you told him about U of M's Summer Poetry Seminar. That you'd gotten the Bridge to Education people to agree to admit me even though I'm only sixteen, so long as I get Lyle's consent.

I guess I asked for it, by sending in your application. It's ironic, isn't it? The e-mail message you printed out for Lyle says, *We have, of course, read about your friend Jonathan, and have great respect for his abiding and well-informed love for the poet Walt Whitman. We agree that he would make a valuable contribution.*

Of course they know about me. I'm all over your letters,

Kurl. I knew that, and I cringed a bit when I reread them before sending them in on your behalf. Somehow I thought of myself as a character in *your* story, though—or I assumed that's how the admissions committee would see me.

And then you went ahead and asked them to consider me as an actual, flesh-and-blood person. Ironic, and now I have a very clear idea of how it must have felt for you. Shameful. Exposed. I apologize again, retrospectively, for the violation, even if the outcome was a happy one.

Thank you for the offer, Kurl. Truly, it means a lot to me. I can see how you tried to do the same thing you thanked me for doing—for being generous, for considering your future despite everything.

I do appreciate it, but I can't say yes. I can't ride out of my life on the tail of your life. It would be a fantasy, nothing more—two months of wandering around a sunny, idyllic college campus, letting myself swallow the illusion that my biggest problem in life is iambic pentameter.

And then I'd have to let go of it and come home, and here would be high school and Maya and the butcherboys and not Shayna and not Bron and not you. To be honest, I'd rather skip the fantasy and stay in the reality than have to adjust to the reality all over again.

I'm sorry you went to all that trouble, Kurl.

Yours truly,
Jo

Dear Little Jo,

So I went directly over to your house last night, after I got your letter saying thanks but no thanks to my offer about the Summer Poetry Seminar.

You opened the door and said, "Oh, hi, Kurl." There was your crooked hair, your fine nose, your hand coming up to your throat.

"You've grown," I said. Of all the things to say. It brought heat into my face.

There were tears already in your eyes. "Damn," you said, wiping them away. "Ignore the crying, okay? I'm serious. Just edit it right out."

"Okay," I said. I had thought maybe you'd slam the door in my face. But asking me to edit out your tears meant edit them out of something bigger, something that was still going to happen, like maybe a whole conversation. So I stepped forward and you stepped back and let me come in.

You led me into the living room and we sat down. Lyle's records in their crates, the monstrous stereo components, the 1970s orange lampshade with the fringe, the musical instruments hanging from their pegs, the purple glass bong. Everything looked different. I thought of your mother. I thought of Shayna, her daughter, living up in Moorhead now.

You were wearing my scarf. Your scarf, the new green one I sent you. You saw me notice it and you unwound it from your neck, fast, and crammed it down between the sofa cushions like it was a dirty picture or a love letter.

Jo, your flushed cheeks. Your raw eyes. Your chapped mouth. I remembered the roughness of your lips, the feel of them, and my blood rushed. Urging, urging. I had to look away to concentrate on what I wanted to say.

"You're ignoring the crying, right? It doesn't mean anything."

"I know," I said, and I remembered what I'd come over for: "I want you to do the seminar without me," I said. "You can have my dorm room to yourself. I'm going to stay at Mark's for a few extra weeks, and then I'll get a room somewhere near campus when the football stuff starts in August."

"What football stuff?"

A grin took over my face before I could stop it. "They want me to try out for the varsity team at U of M."

"No way," you said. "Kurl, that's incredible. That's amazing."

"Yeah."

"College football star." Your voice cracked a bit, and you made a half wave in front of your face to remind me to ignore the crying.

"Listen. I'll rent a room somewhere else. They said there're tons of sublets available in the summer; it won't even cost that much. Okay? You won't even have to see me."

You were shaking your head.

"Come on. This is something *good* for you." I got up and sat next to you on the sofa. "If you say no to this, you're just being stubborn. It's stupid. It's just stubbornness."

You turned on me. Your face had changed. "Why do you

think you can have it both ways? You can't do that, Kurl; that's not how it works." You'd stopped crying just like that. Angry replacing sad.

"What are you talking about?" I said.

"It was you who said it was better this way," you said.

"What way?"

"Alone. Apart."

"No. No, I didn't."

"You said it was easier. You said breaking up was for the best."

"I did not," I said. "You're misquoting me."

You narrowed your eyes. Sat back and folded your arms. "It was right in the last letter I sent to the Bridge to Education people. The last two letters, in fact. Word for word."

"Then you're taking them out of context!" Now I was getting angry too. The idea that you'd been refusing to see me, had kept vowing to stop writing—that all this time you'd thought it was *me* wanting to be apart? That *I* was the one behind all these wasted, heartsore, miserable days and weeks?

The anger stirred in my gut, shoved at my back, stung behind my eyes. And it—the anger—made me suddenly remember that I *had* said it to you—that we'd be better off apart. And I remembered *why* I'd written it, why I'd believed it. It was because of exactly this, this anger.

"Oh, no," I whispered. I leaned forward and put my head in my hands. "You're right. I forgot I said it. No, no."

You were quiet, and after a minute I turned to look at you. Your wide, raw eyes. The ridge of your collarbone and the soft hollow where it meets your neck. Jo.

I said, "It's not, though. It's not better apart. I was wrong." I didn't think of sliding closer to you on the sofa, of putting my mouth into the hollow at your neck, but I was there and my mouth was there.

You went rigid, gasping.

I pressed my mouth against your throat. I heaved a breath into your ear. I lay heavy against you, pinning your folded arms between us. My body felt like sand pouring out over your body.

You turned your head, and I felt your teeth scrape against my cheekbone, and I lifted my mouth to yours. *Urge and urge and urge.* It wasn't kissing so much as looking for air.

You said, "No, no. Stop it." Shoving me away, twisting.

"I don't want to," I said, though I sat back. "I don't want to stop. I love you. You know I love you."

You turned and climbed up over the cushions, kneeing me hard in the jaw on your way, and wedged yourself down behind the sofa.

I looked over the edge but your face was hidden. Your arm was curled up over your bent head as if to shield you from falling debris.

"Hey," I said. "Come out."

"I don't want to live inside a beautiful fable," you said, the words muffled.

"What do you mean?"

"What we had. Us. You said we invented a universe, remember? This whole delicate, fictional universe that only you and I knew about. And maybe the ghost of Walt Whitman was in there too."

"Okay," I said. From where I was sitting twisted around backward on the sofa, I could see the neighbors across the street unloading groceries from the trunk of their car. The mother handed grocery bags to the little boy, and the little boy switched each bag to his other hand, loading himself down and reaching for more, obviously trying to see how much he'd be able to carry at once.

"Well, look what happened to it," you said. "It was shredded." The word *shredded* broke on a sob. "I don't want to live in a beautiful fable if it's just going to get shredded like that."

"Me neither," I said. "But it's not a fable anymore if other people live inside it too. Then it becomes real. Mark and Sylvan, Bron, Lyle"—I was about to list Shayna, but I thought better of it—"all the U of M people...I mean, hell, my mom and Uncle Vik may not like it but they *know* about us, at least; they know it's real."

The mother across the road slammed the trunk. She tried to take some of the grocery bags back from the little boy, but he staggered away from her and up the driveway, set on doing it all by himself.

"It's not a fable anymore," I told you. "We are two people in the real world. What does Walt call it? *Dauntless.*"

"I'm not dauntless though," you said.

"You are." I reached down and found your hand, threaded my fingers through yours. *"Unscrew the locks from the doors!* Remember?" I said. *"Unscrew the doors themselves from their jambs!"*

"I can't."

"Please, Jo." I pulled your hand up to my lips, licked your palm and pressed it against my lips.

"No," you said, and tried to pull away.

I held on. I needed to hear you make a sound other than *No*, so I bit into your palm.

A startled yelp, and then a muffled laugh. You tipped your head back, finally, and stared up at me. Blinking, your pupils constricting in the daylight, your lashes still glimmering with tears.

Your eyes had such hurt in them though. And fear—I could see that you were afraid. "I can't do it, Kurl," you whispered. "I'm sorry, but I just can't."

So I let go of your hand.

I stood up and took the poem out of my pocket, the one Uncle Viktor confiscated when he kicked me out of the house. I'd remembered some parts of it, and I'd composed the rest from scratch. I dropped it down for you behind the sofa.

And I said goodbye.

Sincerely,
AK

GREEN
by Adam Kurlansky
(for Jo)

From the start you saw the truth of me,
Grown slowly up out of the dark,
A pale green thing reaching for the sun.

Like a mirror you showed me to myself,
All bluster and scars.
I was uneasy with the reflection
And moved away but you pulled me back
And back again.

Before you I never noticed daybreak,
Crimson then yellow then white.
I never saw how the clouds rush the sky.
I never knew how soft the skin is behind a knee,
How skin can smell like milk, like grass, like the sea.

I never noticed how an ant will climb to the tip
Of a blade of grass for no reason,
How many things happen for no reason,
And how no reason can mean joy.

Now I notice it all:
I notice all this heaviness,
How blood moves unevenly through a body,
Flames in some places, freezes in others,
And how a heart can hurt inside a chest.

Dear Kurl,

I called Mark this morning to find you, and he said you were somewhere you called your Outer Sanctum. "What is that," he joked, "some kind of gay-football-player-slash-poet hangout?"

"It's down by the train tracks," I told him.

I apologize if it was meant to be a secret, Kurl. I reasoned that, first, Mark is the person with whom you used to explore all those wild places of the city, so he'd be intrigued to know you still return to them, and second, someone should know where you are when you go off-road like that. We all need someone watching out for us, Kurl. Even you.

I rode Nelly down the new section of the bike path you mentioned. My ribs were only a tiny bit sore going uphill, and riding over the parts where the tree roots had already pushed the asphalt out of shape. I found the spot with the spray-painted word BREATHE, just like you said.

You were lying on a blanket in the sunshine. "Sit down," you said.

Right away you took off your flannel shirt for me to wear against the mosquitoes. "It's fine," you said, draping it over my shoulders, doing up the top button, adjusting and tucking in the edges of my green silk scarf to seal the gaps. "They don't like the way I taste."

Kurl, the reason I'd sought you out was that I wanted to talk. I wanted to explain how utterly breakable I've been feeling since my sister left, since I found out about my mom. How I have felt brittle and porous as an old clay pot, leaky with tears.

And I wanted to tell you that Abigail Cuttler phoned me the other day, and that we talked for ages. And for some reason, instead of the expected things, I started to talk to her about Prince, about Prince dying like that right at the height of his career. Abigail was attempting to ask me how things were going at home and whether I was sleeping okay, and all I did for the half hour on the phone was sit there on my bed weeping about Prince, and blabbering about the time Lyle and I arranged "Little Red Corvette" for mando and banjo and performed it with Shayna at Rich and Trudie's anniversary party.

I was sure Abigail would tell me that I was trying to deflect from the real issues by focusing on Prince, that I was in denial or I was repressing my true emotions.

But it turned out she wasn't fazed in the slightest by all the Prince talk. "You're grieving," she said, "plain and simple."

It turns out Abigail's mother is a psychotherapist, and so Abigail has learned all kinds of different theories about grief. Grief doesn't attach very well to "proper" objects, she said. If someone close to you dies, for instance, you might find yourself grieving not that person but someone who died ages ago, or not a dead person at all but an ex-spouse or estranged friend. "Or all of the above," Abigail said. "You might be grieving everybody."

I told her how I tend to cry at inappropriate times. She said, "Maybe part of you has always been grieving, in a low-grade way.

Maybe it's been happening in the background, all along." We didn't have time to get into it, but I strongly suspect she was talking about Raphael Vogel. About my mom. I've been writing to her quite a bit about Raphael, recently.

Anyhow. I was planning on telling you all this, Kurl, in an attempt to give you some context for why I hid from you when you came over, why I flat-out refused your offer to rent an apartment off-campus so I could attend the Summer Poetry Seminar without you.

It was the idea of you leaving, Kurl. I hadn't spoken to you face-to-face in weeks, yet somehow, without being aware of it, I'd managed to convince myself that you weren't going anywhere. And then there you were in my living room, talking to me, touching me—and telling me you were going away to college, not in the fall but for the summer, too. For more than the summer. For good.

I was planning on explaining all this to you, how the realization that you were actually leaving had shattered me and saddened me too much to bear. It was too much for me even to get out from behind the sofa.

I didn't end up explaining anything, though. Instead I just kept my eyes down, sitting beside you, and picked at the new shoots of grass at the blanket's edge. Despite the polite inches between us, it felt as though your body next to mine was throwing off a charge, as though you'd been absorbing solar energy and were now radiating it to me. I tried to gather my words, but they kept getting scattered into the vibrating air.

And then you wrapped a heavy, casual arm around my shoulders. Your other hand gathered the ends of my scarf together and tugged, scooping me toward you, turning me in so that my ear was pressed against your throat. I felt your pulse beating at my temple, heard you sigh from deep in your belly.

Held in that gentle lasso, that warm half hug, what was I supposed to say? Suddenly none of the explaining felt very urgent or crucial. You weren't asking me for anything, and I didn't need anything from you either, beyond that solid contact. There was suddenly nothing that needed to be said.

I realized that it was the first time since Bron's party that my mind had gone still. I could feel my blood moving around inside my body, my muscles resting, my skin warming against yours through our clothes. *Now, now, now*, said your heartbeat.

And then I saw it.

"Is that a Red Eft?" I said.

"Ha," you said.

"Look," I said. "Look, slowly. Look!"

You released me in slow motion and swiveled your torso to look in the grass where I was looking.

"No," you said.

"It is, right?"

"No. No way."

"It's red," I pointed out. "Is there another kind of red salamander?"

"They don't live this far south," you said. You moved your weight onto your hands, slid your knees around, and came up to all fours. You eased forward six inches, maybe twelve—and the little creature ducked its head under the thatch and was gone.

We were silent a moment. I didn't want to interrupt whatever you were thinking.

Finally you turned back to me with wide, spooked eyes. "You're a miracle," you said.

I laughed. "What did I have to do with it?"

"You conjured it," you said, "obviously."

"Obviously."

Then you took my face between your hands and kissed me.

"Kurl," I said, after a minute or two, "I don't want to live in your dorm room by myself. I want you to do the Poetry Seminar with me, if I'm going to do it at all."

You sat back on your heels. "Okay."

"You must have signed an acceptance form for U of M's offer, right?"

"I guess so," you said. Your face was perfectly still, and I realized you were poised between happiness and fear of what I was going to say next.

"On paper," I said. "You had to sign something on actual paper, and mail it in."

"Yeah," you said. "I mean, they wanted my signature."

"*I* want your signature," I said.

"On what?" you asked. "What for?"

"Everyone has left me"—I heard the sad little quaver come into my voice and felt my face heating up—"or lied to me."

You lifted your hand to my jaw, the pad of your thumb on my lips. "I'll sign anything you want. Ask me anything, Jo; you know the answer is yes."

So I unzipped my backpack and took out my taped-together *Leaves of Grass*. I slipped out the contract that I'd written and tucked into the back of the book. I unfolded the paper on the blanket.

"I signed my part already." I showed you.

You read it over slowly, out loud. My heart was beating so hard in my chest I could barely hear the words.

"I have amendments," you said, when you'd finished.

I handed you a pen and watched as you scratched out some parts and wrote something new. Then, carefully, you signed your name.

Yours,
Jo

I, ~~Adam Kurlansky,~~ Kurl hereby agree to register for and attend the Summer Poetry Seminar at the University of Minnesota Duluth. I further agree to share my allotted on-campus accommodations with ~~Jonathan Hopkirk.~~ Jo Together we commit ourselves to the pursuit of truth and happiness as exemplified in the work of poet Walt Whitman and summarized as follows:

Let us be poets of the body and the soul!

Let us loaf together on the grass!

Let us press together our bare-stript hearts!

Let us sound triumphal drums for our dead!

Let us listen to the beat and urge of the world!

Let us unscrew the locks from the doors!

Let us unscrew the doors themselves from their jambs!

Let us be together ever dauntless!

Signed,

Adam Kurlansky   Jonathan Hopkirk